CRIME CLASSICS

Blueprint for Murder

AN INSPECTOR JAMES MYSTERY

ROGER BAX

ABOUT THE AUTHOR

Roger Bax is a pseudonym of the classic crime writer Paul Winterton. Born in Leicester in 1908, Winterton was both an author and a journalist whose prolific output included over 40 novels, ranging through the genres of mystery, detection, thriller, espionage and romance.

His first book, *A Student in Russia*, appeared in 1931. The nom-de-plume Roger Bax saw its first outing with *Death Beneath Jerusalem* (1938), a crime fiction set in Palestine. Five more Bax crime novels were to follow it, including *Blueprint for Murder* in 1948; his later novels were published under the pseudonyms Andrew Garve and Paul Somers.

Winterton was a founder-member of the Crime Writers' Association in 1953. He died in 2001.

This edition published in the UK by Arcturus Publishing Limited
26/27 Bickels Yard, 151–153 Bermondsey Street, London SE1 3HA

This edition published in Australia and New Zealand by Hinkler Books Pty Ltd
45-55 Fairchild Street, Heatherton Victoria 3202 Australia

Design and layout copyright © 2011 Arcturus Publishing Limited
Text copyright © 1948 The Estate of Paul Winterton

Cover artwork by Duncan Smith
Typesetting by Couper Street Type Co.

AD001954EN

Printed in the UK

Cross stepped over the blackened body, reloaded his gun, and stood tense at the edge of the camp, wondering if the moment had come to run for it. Two or three other grey-green figures, fifty yards away, were mechanically going on with their butcher's work. The flames, rising higher than the tops of the silver birches, made all the open space as light as day. But here, in the shelter of the wood, he was in shadow. No one would notice if he slipped away. The time was very near when every man would be thinking only of himself.

The Russian guns were unmistakably closer, and seemed to be working round to the south. The camp ought to have been evacuated earlier, before the offensive, before the break-through. But that did not worry Cross till later. His sole interest now was that there should be the maximum of chaos and a disorganized German retreat. That would give him his best chance of going underground. He had to gamble on his judgment, and his judgment was that Germany was finished.

Suddenly, above the rumble of the guns, the crackle of the burning logs and the hideous sounds of men and women in agony, he heard a new note. The Russian Stormovik came in low, without opposition. A bomb fell plumb into one of the blazing heaps, scattering it. Cross dropped behind a fallen tree-trunk, while red-hot embers showered around him. The least injury now might be fatal to his plans. The bomber was circling, and as it came in again he saw the trail of its rockets. The Commandant's block blazed. There was a little flak, desultory and futile.

Cross was just deciding to make a move when there was a new

explosion, loud and near. Surely that whine had been a shell! He peered over his tree-trunk. A sleek black car was shooting away from the Commandant's block – making a getaway. Another shell burst near the car. Cross could hear a great deal of shouting, could see running figures. In a moment he knew why. A dark shape was suddenly silhouetted against the flames – a heavy tank. Cross could see the red star and the long barrel of the 88-mm gun. This was the end. The Russians could shoot up the whole camp now. The moment had come.

He turned and plunged into the birch-wood. It was hard going; at every step his boots sank deep into the sandy soil. There was enough light from the blazing camp to guide him to his cache. He quickly found the spot where he had buried his pack the night before, and heaved it out of the ground by the strap. It felt a fearful burden on his narrow shoulders, but there was nothing in it that he would not need. It would have been safer to take twice as much. His food, unsupplemented, would last him about a week. He had good maps, identity papers, field-glasses, and his gun. He took a quick glance at his luminous compass and set his face to the west. Away on the right there was a glimmer of moon over the Baltic. To the south, the enveloping Russians. Ahead, woods and lakes and rivers, birches and pine trees and sand. He plodded carefully forward, alert for any movement. The ghastly inferno of the camp was now only a glow in the sky behind him. The air was cool, touched with the light frost of early spring.

Towards dawn he lay down in thick undergrowth and slept for an hour. His sleep – as so often – was troubled, for scenes which appeared to leave no mark on his conscious mind came back with added vividness at night. Blood and fire and pain. He woke in terror at first light, unrefreshed, and pushed on after a hurried breakfast of bread and sausage and cold water. The guns were still drumming on his left. Of all the dangers perhaps the greatest was that he would be taken by the Russians. He must get right away from them, even at the risk of marching by day.

He walked by compass, on a prepared course which skirted all known centres of population. Once the sounds of battle had died away he lay asleep or hidden while it was light, for his grey-green uniform might attract unwelcome attention, particularly when he left the shelter of the woods and began to cross cultivated fields and pastures. It was hard work marching at night, for the ground was often rough and treacherous. Twigs and branches scratched his face and hands, ditches yawned before him, rabbit-holes invited careless feet. There were lakes to avoid, rivers to ford or swim. All the same, he covered a lot of ground. He saw practically no one. Avoiding all roads, except to cross them after careful reconnaissance, he saw no military traffic, no soldiers. In the daytime, from some hide-out, he would watch farmers working in the fields, seemingly unaware of the conflict raging not far away. Cross, indeed, found it difficult to believe, in his unbroken quiet and total isolation, that the German Army was being compressed and crushed between two greater ones, and that guns and tanks would soon be rolling over these fields, too.

Water was one of his earliest worries, for he could carry only a small quantity in his bottle, and marching was dry work. Some-times, of course, there was plenty of water, but he could rely on finding it only if he worked forward from stream to stream with the help of the map. He had some thirsty days, but he found that with care he could manage. Food was a greater problem. Whenever an opportunity came to supplement his meagre rations, he took it, but such opportunities were rare. He was no woodsman; he knew nothing of edible plants or fungi, or of trapping rabbits, and he was reluctant to approach inhabited places in search of food.

But as the days passed he was obliged to take greater risks as his
need increased. His appetite was heightened by fresh air and
exercise, and he was always hungry. One night he broke into a shed
near a farmhouse and filled his pack with potatoes, which next day
he roasted over a fire by a stream.

Though most nights passed without incident, others were
nerve-racking. Once he blundered suddenly on a military encamp-
ment and was challenged by a German sentry. He lay motionless
in the undergrowth for an hour before he dared to crawl away out
of danger.

The days were tedious. His only companion was anxiety. He
still had hundreds of miles to go, and as he reviewed his situation
his prospects looked poor. His boots were in a bad state and
would evidently not last out the journey. If it had been dangerous
for him to show himself in his uniform in the early days, it was
unthinkable now, for the grey-green was filthy and torn. Though
he still kept himself shaved, he knew that he looked more like a
deserter than an officer. Somehow he must get hold of some civilian
clothes before long. He had other troubles. The weather was not
always kindly, and constant sleeping in damp places had brought
rheumaticky pains to his shoulders and back.

Through the long idle hours his mind was occupied with sharply
contrasted hopes and fears. His life was a thing of extremes. Hell
was behind him, and heaven ahead. He was going to make up to
himself for the wasted years and allow nothing to stand in his way.
He was going to find luxury and ease when he reached safety.
He would soak himself in all the pagan pleasures of the world –
pleasures for which he had already paid. How he had paid! Hatred
and resentment burned fiercely within him. He had sold his soul
to the devil – at least he would get his money's worth of fun.

He crossed over into the Polish Corridor on a moonless night, the frontier being apparently unguarded. His maps were not so good now, but the country was more open. In East Prussia he had had to steer a careful course among the neat Teutonic villages, the many roads. Here, in Poland, there was more elbow-room. Concealed one day in a copse on the side of a hill, he saw for the first time the stream of refugees moving westwards ahead of the Russian advance – an endless line of women and children and old men, of waggons and handcarts and prams, of people loaded with bundles, of limping wounded. In civilian clothes he might at a pinch have joined them. His condition was beginning to get desperate. His store of food was almost gone, and the little he could collect in his daily march was not enough to maintain his strength. Around harvest-time, or even in high summer, there would have been no great problem, but at this season Nature was at her meanest. Food was all stored at the farms, and at the farms there were dogs and men.

He knew that he could get what he wanted through sudden violence, but he was anxious to do nothing which would leave any kind of trail. Yet hunger would not be denied. One night Cross stunned a sheep with a piece of rock and then beat out its brains. Clumsily, with the help of a jack-knife, he cut the wool and skin away and hacked out bits of bloody meat. Deep in a wood, when daylight came, he lit a fire and did his best to cook the mutton on a spit. He gorged himself with the half-raw flesh, slept heavily and at dusk carried a packful of reeking meat away with him, having first thrust the torn carcase into a ditch. He lived on the meat until it began to go bad. Once, for twenty-four hours, he ate nothing but mangold wurzel, picked up from an old dump. The day after that he was luckier. Emerging cautiously from a wood to look around after a morning's sleep, he saw in front of him a poultry farm, sloping down the length of a ten-acre field to a shack at the bottom. He knew the risk, but he accepted it. The nearest hen-house was less than fifty feet away, and he made a quick sortie. He collected nine eggs from four nest-boxes, and retreated unobserved into the wood.

If he could have walked openly by day it would have been easier to pick up food of sorts. But at night he could barely see what he was doing, and the need to keep marching was almost as great as the need for food. By day he watched with hatred the well-fed labourers who, in distant fields, carried on their daily work. For hours he would observe these men, wondering if the time had come to kill one of them and steal some clothes. One day, cautiously skirting a field, Cross took the hunk of bread and sausage which a labourer had left there for his lunch. But each small capture sufficed only for an hour or two. Cross knew that a crisis was approaching. He had become very thin. He could feel with his fingers the deep hollows beneath his cheekbones. His joints ached so much that it was becoming painful to walk.

One night he was caught in the open by heavy rain, and, not for the first time, was soaked through and through. Previously he had taken no harm, apart from a little more stiffness, but now he caught a bad chill. He felt his temperature rising; he had alarming pains in his body. He felt certain that unless he could get food and rest he would die; to struggle on was beyond his strength. That evening, when he cared no more what happened to him, a light in a farmhouse window beckoned him. He would have to trust to the friendliness of these Polish peasants. He dragged his body to the door and knocked with his water-bottle. He felt light-headed. A man appeared against the light, and Cross said in Polish, "Not German – English escaped prisoner." And that was the last he remembered for quite a time.

*

Returning to consciousness after the crisis, he became aware of a thin shaft of sunlight across a bare room and of clumsily tender hands arranging his blankets. They belonged to the farmer's daughter, Dziunia, a stocky peasant girl of twenty or so, with high Slav cheeks and yellow hair. Neglecting her other duties, she had devoted herself to this frail young man whom chance had brought to the farm. He made no prepossessing picture, with his sunken eyes and grey, bearded face, but to Dziunia he was a romantic stranger.

She chattered a good deal, and Cross soon found that he could converse with her scrappily in a mixture of German and Polish. Stanislav, the farmer, was hardly more conversational than his animals, but the grey eyes in his hard, round head were friendly as well as shrewd.

For several days, Dziunia said, they had thought he would die. He had been delirious, apparently, and had raved wildly. "It was a strange language," said the girl, "so we knew you were not German, in spite of your hateful uniform." Cross smiled and told them as much of his story as he thought they needed to know. After escaping, he said, he had killed a German officer and stolen his uniform and his belongings so that he could get through Prussia. Stanislav grunted approvingly – there was no doubt what he thought of the Germans. Cross knew that these Poles were risking death by sheltering him, but if they were uneasy they gave no sign.

The farmhouse was only a big log hut, devoid of comfort, but the food was all that a convalescent could want – milk and butter and eggs in abundance, and good home-baked bread. Cross knew that he had been incredibly lucky. He constantly expressed his gratitude in words, but there was no gratitude in his eyes. The more his strength returned, the more morose he became. There was nothing to read or to do, and these stupid peasants irritated him. He fretted to get away. Inactive, he became the prey of old and new fears. His thoughts went back to the night of his escape, and the sudden eruption of the Russian tank. The camp demolitions had not been completed, the prisoners had not all been dealt with. There were facts which might come out. . . . Somehow, he had to keep ahead of those facts.

Every day he asked Stanislav for news of the war. The farmer said it was impossible to believe the German papers, but the 'underground' was certain all would be over in a few weeks. The advances had gone on, east and west. One night, coming in from the farm when the wind was in the east, he declared that he had heard gunfire. Russian gunfire.

The possibility that the Russians might catch up with him made it imperative that Cross should continue his journey at once. It was nearly a month since the farmer had taken him in, and his recovery had been steady. He felt strong enough to face the last leg of the long march. Careful preparations were made. Stanislav provided him with some old clothes, badly fitting and patched, but perfect to disguise him as a farm-hand. More surprisingly, the farmer – having borrowed one of Cross's old boots – found him a pair of sound ones which fitted. Cross imagined that the 'underground' had helped. On the last evening Dziunia filled his pack with food till it bulged. It was decided that he should leave just after dark.

It was irksome, waiting for night to fall. Dziunia was gazing at him with sad cow's eyes, so that he wished he could get the hell out of it. He had carefully planned his route across the North German plain and hoped to run into Allied troops somewhere south of Hamburg. With civilian clothes and plenty to eat, what lay ahead should be comparatively simple.

Dziunia said: "You will soon be in England. You must write us a letter when you are safe and the war is over." Cross said, "Of course," and was silent. Stanislav was busy outside. Cross, drumming with his fingers on the chair-arm, heard the latch click and turned his head. The farmer stood in the doorway with the old grey-green uniform across his arm. He looked puzzled.

"I was going to burn this," said Stanislav slowly, "but I found *this*." He held out a paper, and Cross saw that it was his German identity card. What a fool he'd been – what a thoughtless, blundering fool! To forget a thing like that, just because he'd been ill! He got up slowly. Should he try to bluff? Could he get away with a new story? Suddenly he knew that he couldn't. His only hope of safety lay in undisturbed flight. He was surrounded by enemies, any of whom would be glad to hang him – the Russians, the Germans – yes, and now the Polish partisans.

The farmer blocked the doorway, stolidly accusing. As Cross reached for his revolver, Stanislav moved lumberingly across the room. But he was much too late. Cross fired once, expertly and without pity, shooting to kill.

The girl screamed and Cross turned on her. She flung herself on him, blind to consequences. Even the sight of the pointed gun did not stop her. He had to fire three times before she lay still.

He did not give the bodies another thought. He reloaded his revolver and prepared to leave. There was nothing he need do, except destroy the uniform and documents. He opened the stove and pushed the clothes deep down among the hot embers. He watched them burn, saw his photograph turn brown at the edges and curl and flame. Then he went out into the darkness, listened for a moment, and turned west once more. By morning he would be twenty miles away.

Life was easier now. As a labourer, Cross could move with considerable freedom even by day. The grey-green uniform had been a menace; the farm clothes were the ideal form of protective colouration in the fields. The large military pack might attract some comment, Cross thought, but he was unduly sensitive to danger and, in fact, it gave no trouble. He was travelling much faster than before. Whenever he found an unfrequented road or track going his way, he took it. He passed the time of day with many people, both before and after he crossed over into Germany. He was cheered by the reassuring weight of food on his back. For the first few days after leaving the Polish farm he tired quickly, but gradually his body became reaccustomed to the hard routine. The April weather was kind. Altogether, his prospects had vastly improved. The chief risk now was that, through misfortune or folly, he would find himself asked for papers. But who, in this crumbling State, would be likely to trouble the solitary straggler out of millions?

When he lay basking in the sun and peace of the deep country-side, it was difficult for him to tell how far the disintegration of the Reich had progressed. The villagers were going on with their work much as usual. But on the main roads, and in the small towns that he touched, the evidence was unmistakable. The German newspapers which he bought were trying to hide their panic under a din of threat and exhortation, but already it was difficult to tell from their reports where authority lay. The snatches of conversation he heard as he walked left him in no doubt that the ordinary German was waiting for the end and believed it to be near. Military traffic was still rumbling east, in a futile effort to plug the gigantic Russian breach, but the refugees from East Prussia and Poland, gathering snowball strength in every town, were convincing evidence of final disaster close at hand. By day and by night Cross witnessed scenes of utter chaos. The ring of fire and steel was closing and, in the narrowing gap between, frightened people were milling to and fro without clear purpose. The military had their hands full with their own problems, and it seemed unlikely that there was any longer an effective check on civilian movements. Cross felt that he had no more need to worry. Boldly marching through a small village named Grunfeld in the early evening, he passed a row of silent cottages from which every inhabitant had fled. The door of one was wide open, and all was confusion inside. It was obvious that the tenants had hastily packed all the possessions they could carry and had abandoned the rest. There was food in the larder – tinned meats and cheeses and wine – and Cross helped himself.

There were other signs of the approaching climax. Three times in a day great armadas of heavy bombers coming in from the north-west passed unmolested overhead. They bore American markings. Of the Luftwaffe there was almost no trace.

For two days Cross marched north of west, covering twenty-five miles a day on secondary roads. The weather was perfect, and so, he felt, was his timing. Very soon now he should reach the western battle zone. He wondered what it would be like, crossing a Front. Here, in the hinterland, it was almost like being a peacetime tourist.

Seventy-two hours later he heard the first rumblings of gunfire in the west. By imperceptible degrees, the noise of battle swelled. Waking after a short afternoon nap under an old strawstack, he found the air humming with planes, none of them German. There were silver specks reconnoitring high in the blue, and others studying the ground almost from tree-top level. Every now and again there would be a rattle of machine-guns, or the crump of a bomb not far away. He had no idea along what line the advance was taking place, or what the objectives were. He had an impression of a struggle so mobile and so confused that it was more like mopping-up than a battle. Once, crouching in a ditch, he watched four German tanks pass in silhouette across the brow of a hill. Once he saw men running across a distant field. The time had come, he decided, to go to ground. Crawling on hands and knees for the better part of a mile, he came suddenly upon a wide military road and settled himself in deep grass under a hawthorn bush to watch what happened. This, at any rate, was the main line of retreat for the sector. Trucks and ambulances, guns and tanks were streaming from the west. Many were in bad shape, and it seemed unlikely that they would fight again. A quarter of a mile away a tank was blazing, and as dusk fell Cross could see that fires were burning at intervals far along the road. Darkness had increased the congestion and brought the traffic almost to a halt. There were lights and shouts and curses and all the familiar chaos of defeat. Cross watched, indifferent to the fate of armies. He wanted the play to be over, and the curtain to fall, so that he could go home. He had had a bellyful of war.

All through the night the traffic jerked its way to the southeast. Planes dived so often to strafe the helpless target that Cross sought a safer hiding-place a mile back from the road. He slept a little, and when he awoke the road was quiet. It seemed to him that there was already gunfire behind him – that the battle had somehow passed him by. He moved back to the hawthorn bush. As far as he could see in both directions, the road was littered with wreckage, and the air was acrid with the smell of burning. Almost at his feet were three corpses beside an overturned car.

Suddenly he heard a plane and in a moment it had roared by, flying a hundred feet above the road. It circled and flew back. Presently there were fresh sounds of traffic. Cross peered from behind his concealing bush and saw three light tanks ambling up the road in line ahead. Once they stopped and two of them went off the road for a while, reconnoitring. Then they linked up again. Cross saw that they had British markings. He sat with his pack at his feet, a couple of yards above the road, waiting for them. He would call out in English when they were level. As they drew near two of them again plunged into the undergrowth and the third stopped almost opposite the bush. He stood up excitedly, his heart pounding. His pack rolled down into the road. The tank swung round, and as Cross shouted a machine-gun spat precautionary bullets into the hawthorn. Cross felt a blow on his head and pitched forward into the road beside his pack.

CHAPTER I

On a russet afternoon in October 1945 a car drew up with a scrunch on the gravel of Wheeler's boatyard, just below Teddington Lock on the River Thames, and three men got out. Their movements were rather slow, for it was hot, and they had just enjoyed an excellent luncheon at the 'Star and Garter' in celebration of their post-war reunion.

The elderly man, with the shining, sun-browned scalp and the bottle of port tightly clutched under his arm, was Charles Hollison, the paint manufacturer. The much younger man, in the uniform of a Lieutenant-Commander, R.N.V.R., was his only son Geoffrey. The man in the pin-stripe 'demob' suit, also young but without Geoffrey's breadth of shoulder, was Arthur Cross, Hollison's nephew.

It was a very special day for all three of them. For Charles Hollison because against all reasonable expectations both young men were home from the war, safe. For Geoffrey because he was fond of his father and because – having been at sea on and off for seven years – he longed to settle down and live a normal life again. For Arthur because he desperately needed money to save his neck – and Uncle Charles had lots of money.

Charles Hollison, a widower for twenty-five years, had given all his affection to these two young men. After Arthur's parents had died, he had become the boy's guardian and treated him as a second son. Geoffrey and Arthur had been educated at the same school; had graduated at the same Oxford college. Both had been given equal opportunities in the family business.

When Arthur, a rear-gunner in a 'Wellington', had been reported 'missing' on a Baltic raid in 1940, Hollison had felt a father's anxiety and grief. The miracle of Arthur's survival, so recently revealed, had lit up the old man's life. With Geoffrey back as well, unharmed in spite of all his adventures in the Pacific, Hollison felt ten years younger. Sometimes, during the war, his loneliness had been almost more than he could bear. Now all that was over. The boys were home.

"Come on, let's get aboard," Hollison called, leading the way down to the water's edge. The tide was low, and they had to drag the dinghy across a few yards of wet gravel to launch her. Arthur took the oars, Hollison sat in the stern, and Geoffrey – seeming to take up all the rest of the room – gazed across to where *Truant* was riding to her moorings.

"Nice picture!" said Geoffrey appreciatively. "This is *really* like old times. What a lovely boat she is!"

"She could do with a coat of paint," said Arthur, a little sourly, resting on his oars so that he could turn to look at her.

Hollison nodded. "Now the war's over, perhaps she'll get one. We'll have a look at the shade card, and find something really smart. Easy, Arthur; don't bump her."

Arthur put the dinghy alongside, and Geoffrey tied her up. Hollison, with an agility remarkable in a man of his years and bulk, climbed aboard and threw back the tarpaulin which covered the cockpit. He looked at Arthur with a twinkle in his eye. "Do you still remember where the glasses and corkscrew are kept?"

"It's about all I do remember," said Arthur, going below. He had never been as crazy about boats as the other two.

Geoffrey was already off on a tour of inspection. He had rarely felt so elated. Everything he saw delighted him. The river had never looked more peaceful. The willows at the water's edge, over on the far bank, were barely stirring; the droning of insects and the occasional quack of a duck or plop of a fish were the only sounds disturbing this drowsy afternoon. Even the tall chimney of the refuse destructor, sticking up behind the boatyard, did not quite ruin the beauty of the scene. Geoffrey sniffed with satisfaction the peculiar remembered smell of *Truant* in summer – a rich mixture of diesel oil and hot varnish, of paraffin and dry cordage and bilge water. He strolled up and down the forty-five feet of well-caulked and beautifully cambered deck; he leaned over the side, examining a small dent above one of the ports; he peeped under the canvas cover of the eight-foot tender stowed beside the davits on *Truant*'s cabin-top. Then he went through into the wheel-house and down into the tiny engine-room, and scrutinized the twin diesels with the zest of a schoolboy. He saw at once that they had been well cared for. He would have liked to have given them a run, but there was a call from the cockpit. His father had just poured out three glasses of tawny port.

"I saved this specially for you two," said Hollison. "It needed a lot of faith!"

"A lot of self-control as well, I should think," said Geoffrey. "Well . . ." He raised his glass, first to his father, then to his cousin. "Happy landfalls . . ." He sipped and smiled. "It was certainly a wonderful idea finishing our celebration here."

"I wanted to talk," said Hollison, "and there's nothing like a boat for privacy. By the way, has *Truant* passed your survey?"

Geoffrey gave the 'thumbs up' sign. "She's in much better shape than I expected. What do you think, Arthur?"

"She's fine," said Arthur. He was drinking his port rather fast.

"Mind you," said Geoffrey, "we'll have to get another sailing dinghy. I want to do some more ditch-crawling next summer. But *Truant*'s a ship – she can really go places. Are the engines as good as they seem?"

"They're as good as new," said Hollison. "I've had a chap in from Wheeler's to keep an eye on the boat, and we've run the engines every two or three months. With diesels there's been no real trouble about fuel. Lack of time has been my worry. As a matter of fact, I've kept her ready for sea, the way she was before Dunkirk. The water-tanks are full, there's plenty of oil, and even some rations in the lockers. Mostly bully and biscuits – pinched from the Navy, I'm afraid – and a few tins that I managed to wheedle out of Mrs. Armstrong. There's nothing to stop us going straight off to France tonight, if you feel like it. We'd be there tomorrow evening."

Geoffrey grinned. "Nothing to stop us except a couple of dozen formalities, and mines all over the Estuary, and no up-to-date charts. I bet those sandbanks have shifted a bit since we last ran aground! We ought to be able to do something fairly ambitious next season, though. I'd like to cruise to the Aalands. What do you say, Arthur?"

Arthur shook his head. "Not me. I've *had* the Baltic."

Geoffrey remembered. "Yes, of course. Too full of nasty experiences. I expect I should feel the same if I'd been shot down into it. It's amazing you escaped alive – I suppose the tail stuck out of the water for a while. You were darned lucky."

"Perhaps," said Arthur. "I sometimes wonder." He was staring down at the deck, the smoke from his cigarette curling up between his nicotine-stained fingers. He was silently congratulating himself on his lunch-time performance. The atmosphere had been just right, of course – a bit emotional; and they had naturally been impatient to hear his story. He had told it skilfully. There had been, he thought, just the right amount of corroborative detail to make it sound convincing, and no obvious gaps. The crash, the internment, the escape – he had dealt sketchily but adequately with all of them. He had described the hardships of his life in camp and of his journey across Europe with a restraint commanding admiration as well as sympathy. He had rehearsed the tale so often in his mind that now he could almost believe it himself. And anyway, it did contain more than a kernel of truth.

"Of course," said Geoffrey reflectively, "if you hadn't socked that guard after your capture and tried to make a getaway you'd have been taken to an Oflag and we'd have heard about you."

"I know," said Arthur. "It was a damn silly thing to do, but the idea of being in a P.O.W. camp all through the war was more than I could face. I nearly pulled it off, too. Of course, I knew I was taking a big chance. I thought they might shoot me. It didn't occur to me that they'd take it out of me by virtually writing me off. I imagine I just ceased to exist for them when they sent me to that ghastly dump in East Prussia. After that I was just one more anonymous slave."

Hollison nodded. "That's about it. No wonder we couldn't get any information. I went up to the Air Ministry, naturally, and they told me they'd made all the usual inquiries. They hadn't much hope, because of that last radio signal from your plane, but they were obviously doing all they could. Then when the report came through from the Red Cross that the Germans had no knowledge of any survivors, I had to make up my mind that you'd gone."

"As a matter of fact, Arthur, you had unusually bad luck from beginning to end," said Geoffrey, "apart from not being killed, of course. If you hadn't been hit in the head by that tank gunner, you'd have been home months ago. Losing your memory on top of everything else was really tough. I don't know why we don't finger-print chaps in our Forces, the way the Yanks do. It would save a lot of trouble."

"Wouldn't it?" said Arthur, without enthusiasm. The port did not seem to be cheering him up very much. His thin pale face had a little more colour in it, but he seemed unable to relax and his lips worried incessantly at the cigarettes which he chain-smoked. There were deep lines etched from above each eye slantwise to the temples. Geoffrey could not remember having noticed them before the war. In fact, Arthur was not looking at all fit in spite of his long convalescence.

The same thought had been in Hollison's mind from the moment of their reunion. He was deeply concerned about his nephew. A man couldn't possibly go through all the horror and strain that Arthur had been through and not feel serious after-effects. Hollison said: "Now you're back, Arthur, I think we ought to get a good man to overhaul you. You need looking after, building up—"

"Oh, I'm sick of doctors," said Arthur irritably. "I'm all right – I just want to be left alone. Let's forget it all, shall we? As far as I'm concerned, those six years never happened. Life begins again." He drained his port.

Hollison gave him an affectionate smile. "Perhaps you're right – anyway, we'll see. As long as you take things gently—"

A small pleasure steamer chugged by, and some children shouted and waved. Geoffrey waved back abstractedly. He was thinking how wars changed people. *Truant* rocked gently in the wash. When the river was still again, Hollison said, "You know, I think a speech is called for while there's still something in the bottle."

"Why not?" said Geoffrey encouragingly. "Go ahead!"

"Perhaps I'm a sentimental old man," said Hollison, "but I'll never have another opportunity to tell you both how . . . how proud I am of you. You both did your job . . . different ways, of course . . . different luck. I'm very proud – and very, very glad to have you both back. This is the greatest day of my life." He blew his nose violently, and with fingers that trembled slightly he pierced and lighted a cigar.

Geoffrey got up and quite unnecessarily gave an extra half-hitch to the dinghy's painter. Fancy the old man getting all emotional! He looked at Arthur and nodded towards his father. "To hear him talk you'd never think he'd been at Dunkirk with his toy boat, would you? How many fellows did you bring back, Father?"

"Seventy-three," said Hollison. "You know I could never resist a cross-Channel trip. And don't try to put me off – I haven't finished yet."

"Oh, come off it," Geoffrey protested. "You'll have me weeping over the side."

"Well, I'll pass on to business. I've been thinking a lot about your future – yours and Arthur's. You see, I'm not as young as I was. Sixty-six next birthday, you know. I've felt the strain this last year or two – rushed Government orders, chronic labour shortage, and all the rest of it. Mind you, I'm not grumbling, but now the war's over I think I'm entitled to a bit of a rest. I want some help, and I'd like both of you to come back into the business."

"Will it stand it?" asked Geoffrey.

"It needs you," said Hollison. "It's still a first-class concern, but it needs new blood. I've always said it's the Hollison blood in the paint that makes it better than anyone else's. Of course, I know it may seem a little dull after all your adventures, but it's a job you can be proud of. The name of Hollison has a fine ring in the trade. If we've fallen short of our own standards, it's been because of circumstances outside our control – chiefly substitute materials. The future's bright enough. Why, the whole world needs repainting!"

Geoffrey grinned broadly. "You sound quite lyrical. That ought to be the first line of a song, 'The whole world needs repainting—'"

"So it does," said Hollison stoutly, "and the fairies won't do it, either. It's going to take a lot of hard work. I've got some excellent technicians on the research side, and a first-class works manager. I need a couple of directors to take the bulk of the administrative responsibility off my hands. You both know the ropes. What about it?"

Geoffrey tapped his pipe out into the palm of his hand, and carefully threw the dottle overboard. "Count me in, by all means. I shan't be out of the Service for a few months yet – you know I was on radar work, fighter direction, and I've been pulled in to give a course of lectures at the Staff College during the winter. A quite exceptional compliment to the R.N.V.R. As a matter of fact, I'm rather looking forward to it. After that we'll get together. We'll paint the town red."

Hollison looked earnestly at his son. "You're quite sure? If there's anything else you want to do—"

"Well, of course," said Geoffrey, "I'd rather like to *travel* . . ." He saw the quick flicker of anxiety on his father's face and repented. "It's too bad to pull your leg, isn't it? The fact is, I'm so cheerful today I can hardly be serious about anything. Honestly, there's nothing else I want to do; my ideal job at the moment is just something quiet and steady like making paint."

"Splendid," said Hollison. "Now what about you, Arthur? I've missed you at the Works, you know. It seems an age since you were with us, but I've never forgotten how you were always turning up with new schemes. The 'ideas' man! We need a quick, fertile brain, particularly if we've got to go on squeezing permits out of civil servants."

"You flatter me," said Arthur. "I must say it's very tempting."

"There's no need for an immediate decision, of course," said Hollison, who had clearly made up his mind that he was going to have his own way. "Heaven knows I don't want to worry you about it. But it's a good chance, and there's plenty of money in it. But perhaps you've got other plans?"

Arthur smiled – a faint sardonic flicker of a smile – and shook his head. "None worth talking about," he said. He allowed honesty to get the better of him. "I feel a bit lost," he said. "I've forgotten what it feels like to do a day's hard work voluntarily. I'm flat broke, of course. Just how much money is there in this job?"

"I suggest two thousand a year," said Hollison, "for each of you."

Arthur sat silent. He was wondering, again, just how much money the old man had.

Geoffrey nudged him. "Come on, Arthur, it's a living wage!"

Hollison seemed a shade bewildered. "It's quite a lot of money, even for these days. But I'm determined that you shan't either of you be troubled with financial worries. This is the way I look at it. From the worldly point of view, both of you have virtually sacrificed six or seven years of your lives – years when normally you'd have been making your way and building up your fortunes. We've got to make up for that. I'm a rich man. I was before the war, and I've made a lot more during the war without particularly trying – in spite of E.P.T."

"I hope you're ashamed of yourself," said Geoffrey.

"Naturally – and that brings me to my last point. As you know, I've no one in the world except you two. All through the war I've been telling myself that if you survived I'd do everything I could to make it up to you when peace came."

He paused. Arthur, on edge, lit another cigarette and ground the old stub under his heel.

"Of course," Hollison went on, "I'm not suggesting that money will make you happy – and I'm not suggesting, either, that it would be a good thing for you to have a lot of money now – just to throw around. But I dare say both of you will be happy to feel that there's something substantial at the back of you. So, to cut a long story short, I thought of seeing old Hetherstone this week. You'd hardly recognize him now, Geoffrey, he's such a frail old chap. He'll bring my will up to date. Apart from a few small bequests, you, Geoffrey, and you, Arthur, will be the beneficiaries. I don't suppose that'll surprise you, but I thought you'd probably like to know. Though, mind you, I'm good for a great many years yet. Well, there it is." And Hollison leaned back against the bulkhead, as though conscious of a load off his chest and a long-planned duty performed.

A burden was rolling away from Arthur, too. Two thousand a year, with strings attached to it in the way of work, would not have helped him much. The uncertain prospect of being an ultimate beneficiary would not have been much good, either. But here was certainty – and the chance of quick returns. In a few days' time he, Arthur Cross, would be co-heir to a considerable fortune. And if Uncle Charles died the fortune would be available right away.

As Arthur gazed across the boat at Hollison's hairless scalp, he thought he had never seen a head that so obviously asked to be bashed in! One well-directed blow should do it nicely.

He felt much better now. His highest hopes had been realized. The thought of action, after all his anxiety and fear, strengthened him like a blood transfusion. He was going to get what he wanted, what he needed – a lot of cash, a plane to South America, and a new life. But from now on he must play his cards very carefully.

He said: "It's really frightfully good of you, Uncle Charles. I must say I don't know what I've done to deserve it. After all, Geoffrey's your son, but I – well, I know you've always treated us the same, but I really haven't any claim on you. Anyway, that's all in the future – far in the future, eh, Geoffrey? And I'll be glad to come back into the business. I'll do the best I can. If you find I've lost my grip, you can always fire me. I'll start as soon as you like."

"I'm delighted," said Hollison. "Then that's all fixed. Now where are you going to live, Arthur? There are several spare rooms at home, in addition to Geoffrey's, and you'll be very welcome. In fact, I should be glad of the extra company. Mrs. Armstrong is a good soul, bless her heart, but she's a bit austere. I'd like to see some life in the house – a girl or two – it's time you young fellows were thinking about settling down, you know."

"Give us a chance," said Arthur. "Geoffrey, you'd better invite some Wrens over, and throw a party."

"That's an excellent idea," said Hollison, beaming. "I can provide a bottle or two—"

"A port in every girl," murmured Geoffrey, "the nautical touch." He laughed boisterously. "Sorry!"

"So you ought to be," said Arthur. "Oh, about the house, Uncle. I'd be glad to come along for a while, if I may, but you know I've a flat at Twickenham, with all my books and furniture in it. I'd like to get it back if I can. I've still the old hankering for a dug-out of my own."

"Just as you like, my boy, but the house is always open to you. At least, I hope the three of us will be able to get together regularly."

"Of course," said Arthur.

"Well, that's that. Now I vote we go home and get some tea," said Hollison. "The sun's not as hot as it was." He sighed happily. "What a day it's been!"

Geoffrey washed up the wine-glasses in the neat little galley, and left things ship-shape in the cabin. They climbed back into the dinghy and this time Geoffrey took the oars. As they slid away from *Truant* on the tide, Geoffrey found himself admiring yet again the thrusting bow and graceful flare of the yacht.

"I suppose you know," said Arthur, "that you have an idiotic smile on your face."

"I dare say," said Geoffrey. "*Truant* is my pin-up girl."

"What a sailor!" said Arthur.

CHAPTER II

Cross began at once to plan the murder of his uncle. He was troubled by no pangs of conscience – his conscience had died slowly, painfully, in the concentration camp, like the nerve of a rotting tooth. He felt no affection or pity for Hollison, nor any dislike. There were quite a lot of ordinary human emotions which Cross no longer shared with other people. His strongest impulse now was fear. He had watched so many people die, and he had no desire to die himself. He was going to live, and enjoy all that the world had to offer.

He did not know, of course, just how much money he would get by his uncle's death, but he knew that Hollison had been very prosperous for many years and that he had lived modestly. There was certainly nothing luxurious about his house near Richmond; the domestic staff consisted only of the housekeeper and a girl who lived out; even *Truant* was hardly the luxury yacht that the old man could so easily have afforded. The fact was that Hollison had built up his business, knew the value of money, and didn't like wasting it. So this should be a really lucrative murder.

From the very beginning Cross set himself to prepare his blueprint methodically. He had to make quite sure that he had a fool-proof plan, and then stick to it exactly. It must cover all contingencies, like the solution of a chess problem. Day after day he turned ideas over in his mind as he sat in his office down at the Works. It might be that he was taking on staff, or interviewing a buyer, or dictating a letter, but all these things were done only with the surface of his mind. When, after a week or two, he obtained possession of his flat, he began to shut himself up for hours on end, smoking and thinking. It was there, on an evening late in October, that the main outlines of the problem were sketched.

It seemed to him, as he lay sprawled on a settee three floors up in Alum Court, that one outstanding danger threatened any scheme, and must somehow be overcome before he could proceed. In whatever circumstances Uncle Charles met his death, suspicion would inevitably fall on himself and Geoffrey as the beneficiaries. And on Cross first of all, because nephews were notoriously more prone to kill rich uncles than sons rich fathers. The suspicion might be only faint, but it would colour the investigation. If the police had an unsolved murder on their hands, they would dig and probe until they found something either to justify or to destroy their suspicion. The murder, therefore, must be committed in such a way that the police would have to rule him out from the beginning. He must have an unbreakable alibi. And if Geoffrey didn't have an alibi, so much the better. That was a possible refinement that could be considered later.

There was one expedient which Cross did not exclude without close examination. If the death could be made to appear accidental, an alibi would not be necessary. Cross pondered the possibilities of such a murder, and was not attracted by them. There were many methods, but none was reliable. Poison taken by mistake; a fall downstairs; a slip into the river from *Truant*'s wet deck. But to engineer such an accident would mean taking great risks. Poisons were difficult to get and tricky to handle; and there was always an expert witness to say that a particular injury could hardly have been caused by a fall. Cross considered many alternatives, and finally decided to reject this approach altogether.

So back to the alibi. In real life, as in crime stories, faked alibis always seemed to come to grief in the end. And an alibi that went wrong would be far worse than none at all. Those delicate manipulations of watches and clocks, for instance. . . . Cross decided at once that he would have nothing to do with that sort of thing.

What, he asked himself, were the qualities that made up a good faked alibi? First of all, of course, the time of death would have to be established within narrow limits – and arrangements would have to be made to see that it was so established. That should be fairly simple.

Then there must be good witnesses. They must be disinterested; they must be reasonably normal people, not eccentrics; they must be sober at the time, and in good mental health. And there must be at least two of them, for safety.

They must be able to swear that they were with the suspect throughout the period during which the murder could have been committed. . . . No, that was impossible with a phoney alibi, since the murder had to *be* committed, and there must, therefore, be a period, however brief, when they would have to admit that they were *not* with the suspect. Unless, of course, they could be persuaded by some device that the suspect had never left their presence. Cross's thoughts floated away into the realms of fantasy for a moment or two, and then jerked back to realities.

Put the thing another way! The period of the murder – the few minutes of crucial danger to the whole structure – must be covered by the absolute knowledge of the witnesses – not belief, but knowledge – that the brief absence of the suspect occurred so far from the scene of the crime that the absentee could not possibly have had anything to do with it. A five-minutes' absence, say, could safely take place at a spot half an hour or so from the scene of the murder by the quickest route.

To establish the perfect alibi, therefore, it was necessary somehow to give two normally intelligent and honest witnesses the unshakable conviction that they and the suspect were in one place, when, in fact, they were in another.

Cross was pleased with the neat logic of that proposition, and had a whisky on the strength of it. But as a practical step it got him no further. He ran a nervous hand through his hair. If only he could have had a couple of hours with Mussfeld, his old chess partner at the camp. Mussfeld, sitting back with his steel-rimmed glasses up on his forehead and a looted Havana between his thick lips, would have worked something out in no time. Odd how easy it had been to kill thousands of people, Cross reflected, and how risky it was to kill one. His thoughts were off on an old track now, and the lines deepened in his dissolute face.

On and off, for the best part of a fortnight, Cross chewed over this problem of the alibi. Unless he could solve it, there seemed no sense in going on with his plans. The need for speed was urgent, but there was no sense in courting one danger to escape another. There must be an answer. It was a straightforward enough question – how to be in two places at once? Just a problem in logistics!

What *would* convince an ordinary sensible person that he was somewhere where he was not? And not merely an ordinary person, but the sceptical police? Surely only some very substantial material thing – something very much more than suggestion. Not just the evidence of the senses – it wouldn't be enough for the witness to say "I know I was there because I heard something" – like a factory hooter or a tram bell. There was too much room for honest error. Or "I smelt something" – like a brewery, or wet timber, or a bonfire. These things wouldn't identify a place with sufficient certainty to save a man's neck. The only sense that juries took much account of was the sense of sight. The witness must be able to say "I know I was there because I saw". A particular neon light, perhaps, or a building, or the name of a fish-shop. But how could a witness be made to see something which wasn't there? A murderer could hardly be expected to erect a neon light or open a fish-shop specially for the occasion. Or could he? At least no one would ever suspect him of having done it. Cross was groping vaguely, but was there not the germ of an idea here? Camouflage. Many a bomb-aimer had released his bombs on to a dummy target, and been convinced that he had demolished his objective. If a familiar scene could somehow be transformed . . .

This central problem, the foundation of the whole enterprise, proved the most difficult of all to overcome. The answer came to Cross by accident one afternoon when he was out on the business of the firm, and it came because the soil of his mind was fertile. Uncle Charles had bought for his use – though nominally it was the firm's property – an almost new Vauxhall 14, and Cross had driven over to Epsom to see a client who lived at a place called Mulberry Drive. He had a lot of trouble finding the place, and twice stopped passers-by to ask the way. Finally he turned into the road to which he had been directed only to find, to his extreme annoyance, that it was called Acacia Drive.

He drew up by the kerb, and waited for a young woman to overtake him. He caught a glimpse of her in the driving-mirror, and saw that she was pretty and desirable. He thought he might kill two birds with one stone. He opened the car door as she approached and called out: "Excuse me, but *can* you tell me where Mulberry Drive is? I seem to be going round in circles."

"This *is* Mulberry Drive," said the girl, smiling.

"But it says Acacia Drive."

"I know. The name's been changed. There's an Acacia Lane on the other side of the hill and people got mixed up. They haven't got around to changing the name-plate yet, that's all. There've been a lot of complaints."

"Thanks very much," said Cross. He held the door open. "Can I give you a lift?"

"No, thanks – I live quite near." Cross watched her walk away with regret. After all, there were things in life besides murder.

Even then the seed nearly failed to germinate. It was thinking about the girl again, late that same evening, that took his mind back to Mulberry Drive. And suddenly, in a flash, he had the answer to his problem.

If he and his two hypothetical witnesses had been in that road that afternoon, and had not talked to anyone, they would certainly have believed that they were in Acacia Drive. People naturally believed they were in the street which was named on the plate at the corner of the street. If two people were to swear in court that at a certain time they were in a certain street, which they had identified by the name-plate, the jury would accept their testimony.

If only it were possible to alter the name-plate of a street!

Over supper in the comfortable restaurant on the ground-floor of Alum Court – the block where he lived – Cross took the problem a little further. This new idea might seem fanciful at first, but the more fantastic a plan was, the less likely was it that it would occur to the police. Who would ever imagine that in order to commit a murder a criminal would temporarily change the name of a street? Provided there was no material evidence, the thought would never occur to anyone. It was a brilliant scheme, a stroke of genius!

There remained the technical difficulty, and it might prove insuperable. Even with a car it would be most difficult and dangerous to detach and re-fix a couple of street name-plates, and to carry them about unobserved. It might be possible to make and substitute a dummy, instead of exchanging two existing ones, but it would still be necessary to do a lot of work actually in the street. And it would be fatal to be seen, for the whole point would be to make sure that no one knew the change had been made. Besides, not all name-plates were accessible. Some were high up on walls, though they varied from district to district.

The first thing, clearly, was to have a good look at one of the local name-plates. After dinner Cross went off in the car, called in at a pub for a double whisky, and on his way back drew up under a lamp at the corner of a road of semi-detached houses and closely examined the plate.

There was a single post driven deep into the ground, and a flat wooden cross-piece, bolted to it with three iron bolts, the whole forming a T. The metal plate, with the lettering on it, was screwed to the cross-piece with four screws – no doubt well sunk in paint and rust. To remove a plate, let alone exchange it for another, would take a long time. It could only be done in the dark, and still the risk of being spotted would be considerable. If there were ever an investigation, it would be obvious that the thing had been tampered with. To uproot the whole post and carry the sign away bodily would be quite impossible without heavy tools and plenty of time. Cross gazed at the sign despondently. The whole plan had been hare-brained, impracticable.

Then he had a new idea. He got out of the car and quickly examined the cross-piece. The slab of wood was rectangular, about three feet long, nine inches broad and a little over an inch thick. The sides were smooth, and slightly bevelled at the front edge. Might it not be possible to make a dummy plate and hook it on in such a way that it covered up the real one? Or, better still, a canvas dummy – a canvas dummy shaped like a very shallow bag, which could be slipped bodily over the cross-piece in a couple of seconds? In the daytime, of course, such a dummy would be noticed, but if it were a tight fit and carefully painted, who would be likely to detect the difference for a short period on a dark night?

At last Cross felt that the plot was beginning to take shape. The more he thought about the canvas cover, the more he liked the idea. It had one enormous advantage: it could be rolled up and stuffed into a coat pocket. Provided he could make such a cover, skilfully painted on one side in black and white, and work out the necessary movements, he had no doubt that he could deceive his witnesses. He went home feeling quite pleased with himself.

Back in the flat, he went to work on some of the details. The killing would obviously have to take place at Hollison's house in Welford Avenue. Somehow it would have to be arranged that Uncle Charles should be at home on the night of the murder, and alone. Cross took a sheet of paper and made a note under the heading, 'Things to see to'.

Suppose the murder were timed for eight o'clock. At that hour, Cross would have to be in Welford Avenue. At approximately the same time he would have to be persuading two witnesses – by means of a dummy name-plate affixed at a suitable moment – that he and they were, in fact, in quite a different street a long way away – a street not yet selected, but which for the time being could be called 'X Avenue'.

What about these witnesses? One thing was clear – he could not possibly do the murder first and rely on securing his witnesses afterwards. The Avenue might be empty. It wasn't a main thorough-fare, by any means – it was a rather quiet road of medium-sized detached houses set back behind gardens. Anyone happening to pass at that hour would very probably live near by, and would know that it was Welford Avenue, not X-Avenue, whatever the name-plate might say.

No, the witnesses would have to be complete strangers to the district, and they would have to be 'in the bag' – in this case, in the car – before the murder, all ready to do their stuff. But on what pretext could he pick up a couple of total strangers, whose presence in the car must be made to seem both unplanned and explicable? And on what pretext could he leave them in the car while he went inside the house in Welford Avenue and killed his uncle? Dare he take that risk at all – and yet wasn't it an essential part of the plan? Again, by what stratagem, short of a clumsy and obvious one, could he draw their attention to the faked name-plate and leave on their minds the erroneous impression that they had been in X-Avenue?

The questions were now running far ahead of the answers, and for the moment Cross contented himself with making a note of them. They must be dealt with one at a time, and in due course everything would fall neatly into place. He had still to decide how to get hold of the witnesses – that was the next step.

In what circumstances, he asked himself, did a motorist normally pick up strangers? Usually on quiet roads, where there were no ordinary means of transport, or main roads – arterials and by-passes – where a car was so much faster than a bus. Even then the pedestrian usually had to make the first sign. In the closely-packed suburbs around Twickenham and Richmond it wasn't likely that motorists would do much casual picking up. Only of young women, of course, and a floozie would hardly make the sort of alibi he was after. He felt certain that he could stooge around in the car all day long – and all night, too, for that matter – without being asked for a lift in this district. It looked as though the initiative would have to be his. He could always stop and ask a pedestrian the way, and then it would be only courteous to suggest a lift. But the pedestrian would probably have local knowledge, and so would be useless. You couldn't take people far out of their way, even at night, and get away with it. Not even strangers – they would begin to get uneasy after a few minutes. Cross thought and thought, and after a quarter of an hour he had to confess to himself that he hadn't the foggiest idea how this particular problem could be solved.

The foggiest idea! Fog! Fog! Of course, that was the answer. You could blame fog for anything. People would feel lost in a fog, they would be grateful for a lift. He could get lost, too, and they wouldn't mind. Of course, it would have to be a fog of just the right kind – thick enough to excuse error and make the detection of a dummy name-plate unlikely – but not too bad to spoil the working out of a precise time-table. There might not be many suitable nights, but there were bound to be one or two, with winter coming on. Yes, fog was undoubtedly the answer. Cross could see now the infinite possibilities of well-engineered confusion.

He went to his writing-desk – a present from his uncle before the war – and took out a road map of the district. To make the alibi safe, X-Avenue must be at such a distance from Welford Avenue that it would take a car not less than half an hour to make the journey on a foggy night. The witnesses must be picked up at a point about mid-way between Welford Avenue and X-Avenue. At the Richmond roundabout, say, where buses would be discharging home-going crowds all through the evening. Many people would live ten or fifteen minutes' walk from the bus. There should be no difficulty in getting customers. They would sit in the back, not seeing much. He would pretend to drive them home – pretend that was the way he was going – but in fact he would drive them to Welford Avenue. This would be his second visit to Welford Avenue, of course, because he would have already fixed the dummy X-Avenue plate. As he turned the last corner he would slow down, pretend he was lost, and ask them if they could read the name of the street. They would all three peer out, and read X-Avenue.

That would establish the alibi. He could easily check the time with them by apologizing for losing the way and for keeping them so long. But he would still have to do the murder. He would need an excuse for leaving the car and going to his uncle's house. He could say he was going to call at a house and ask the way. Uncle Charles lived at the second house from the end where the name-plate was; it would be perfectly reasonable to make inquiries there. His uncle, alone in the house, would come to the door. Cross would strike him down, return to the car, say there was nobody in and that they must drive on and hope for the best. He would have to put on a pretty good act, of course. And he would have to make sure that one blow was sufficient – it wouldn't do to have any calls for help. But Cross had had a lot of practice with blunt instruments, and, anyway, the fog would muffle the sound. Soon afterwards he could pretend to discover where he was, and drive his witnesses home.

The weapon would be a complication. Whatever it was, he could hardly conceal it in the car beside him – that would be too great a risk. He'd have to hide it somewhere handy – perhaps just inside his uncle's gate – when he paid his first call to fix the dummy name-plate. Yes, and as soon as he'd done the murder he'd have to collect the dummy and stuff it into his pocket before he returned to the car. It would all need most careful rehearsing, perfect timing, an ice-cool head. There was a hell of a lot to remember – his list of 'things to do' already filled the sheet of paper.

He'd have to establish the time of death with a responsible person in order to perfect the alibi. It wouldn't be safe to leave that matter to the police surgeon – it was notorious that estimates of the time of death were subject to a wide margin of error. If the alibi was to be good, the time of death must be pin-pointed. That meant he would have to ring someone up from his uncle's house, with the old man lying in the hall. Dangerous – but a reasonable risk, if it were quickly done. Whom should he ring – the police? No, they might move a little *too* fast. A near neighbour would be better – in a disguised voice, of course. He made a note to pick a suitable telephone number from the residents in Welford Avenue or near by.

Thinking over the plan as far as it went, Cross was suddenly brought up very unpleasantly by another obstacle – and a major one. The fact that he could have overlooked it at all rather scared him. At eight o'clock – or whatever the time chosen – he would ostensibly be in X-Avenue, calling at a house to ask the way. That would be his story to the police; that would be the story told by the witnesses. The police would undoubtedly go to the real X-Avenue to check the story, to find out if he had, in fact, called at a house there. And they would find that he hadn't.

For the first time Cross felt a serious pang of doubt. Things were beginning to get rather involved. Was he going to trip up, to forget something vital, as murderers so often did? There were always the unexpected things, the absurd coincidences, to wreck good plans. But the doubt did not last long. This, after all, was only the initial stage; the dress rehearsal was far ahead.

He posed the new problem. How could he knock at the door of a house when he was half an hour away from it? Or how could he appear to do so? Was there any way in which he could get someone else to knock? His thoughts ranged widely – sending a parcel, sending a messenger, ringing someone up and telling him to go urgently to the address – absurd ideas, conceived only to be put aside. He must do this alone, all alone, or not at all. He had long ago learned to trust no one but himself. If the people in the house were out at the time . . . But he couldn't possibly arrange for them to be out. Things must seem to happen naturally. An empty house! – that was it. He could tell his witnesses that he had knocked, and that there had been no reply. He had gone round to the back, perhaps to see if there were any lights, but there hadn't been. Of course, there were always the people next door – they might say they hadn't heard a knock. But who would regard their evidence as conclusive? It was notoriously difficult to prove a negative. The real trouble was that X-Avenue would have to be a road where the second or third house – occupying a position similar to that of the Hollison house in Welford Avenue – was empty. To find such a road was going to be a pretty formidable task. There weren't many empty houses in London these days!

All the same, Cross felt that he had made real progress. However incomplete in detail, the plan had one outstanding quality. Practically all the things which might go wrong related to events *before* the murder. If the fog were too thick or too sparse, if the witnesses proved unsuitable, if they were too interested in the route, if they were suspicious or inquisitive or too helpful, if they were stupid or short-sighted and couldn't identify the street from the false name-plate, if the time-table broke down, or the car broke down, or his uncle had unexpected visitors – well, he needn't do the murder that night. He could simply pick up the weapon and the dummy, take the witnesses home, and try again another night. Indeed, he could go on trying until all the circumstances were favourable. Surely there could be no better safeguard than that?

He would not be committed in any way until the moment he struck the blow. All he would have to do then would be to report the murder, drive off and wait for the inquiry to reach inevitable deadlock.

Meanwhile, the two most urgent jobs were to select a suitable X-Avenue, and to see if he could make a dummy name-plate which would pass in a fog.

CHAPTER III

The next day was Sunday. Uncle Charles, who had a small hoard of pre-war golf balls, had suggested a threesome if the weather were fine, but Cross was anxious to get ahead with his plan and excused himself. Soon after breakfast he set off in the Vauxhall to look for his empty house. He had already studied the street guide, and he thought he would start by investigating the Twickenham district. He cruised about for an hour or so without finding what he wanted. It was going to be, he feared, a disappointing as well as a tiring day. As he had expected, there were very few empty houses about. His simplest course would be to go to an agent and get a list of houses for sale with vacant possession, but that would mean starting a trail which later on might lead to trouble. It was important that no one should know he had ever shown an interest in empty houses.

By lunch-time he had covered many miles. Altogether, he had found three 'empties'. Two had been in roads so different in character from Welford Avenue that Cross had to reject them at once as quite unsuitable. The third was in the right kind of road, but it was just about half-way along and too far away from the name-plates to be of any use.

During lunch at a pub down by the river, Cross considered the problem again. Was it really necessary that he should find this empty house? Could he 'get away' with less? Could he, perhaps, just pretend that he was going to make inquiries at a house and then come back to his witnesses after a few minutes and say that it was so foggy and there were so few lights about that he'd changed his mind and decided it was better to go on? Cross let his mind dwell on such a hypothetical scene. He decided that the story would sound awfully lame – he would have to be away at least five minutes to do the murder, and the police would expect those five minutes to be adequately accounted for. With an empty house he could say that he had walked up the path, knocked, waited, knocked again, walked round the back – he could easily explain five minutes' absence. But he could hardly expect the police to believe that he had 'dithered' in the fog for five minutes. They would want to know where he walked to, whether he actually opened a gate, why he didn't, what exactly he thought he was doing. Cross could vividly imagine that uncomfortable conversation with a sceptical inspector. No, his explanation of his absence had got to be convincing. That meant he must have a particular empty house in mind, a house which to some extent he could describe. He must know whether the gate was of wood or metal, whether the path was of concrete or gravel – even in a fog, it would be expected that some small detail would stay in his mind. There was, it seemed, no alternative to the empty house.

After lunch, therefore, he resumed the search. He had combed the Twickenham district pretty thoroughly in the morning, so he decided to go back to the Richmond roundabout and try the Kingston side during the afternoon. He drove up Kingston Hill and investigated several turnings which were ideal in the sense that they would have been just the kind of places he would have found himself in if, intending to go to Welford Avenue, he had accidentally taken the wrong turning out of the roundabout. But all the houses were occupied. Later on he found two more 'empties', one in the middle of a row and one at the bottom of a cul-de-sac. An elderly couple were looking over this last one, and Cross did not linger. He was feeling very despondent when he suddenly had a stroke of real good fortune.

He had turned into a fairly wide and pleasant road named Hamley Avenue. An estate agent would no doubt have described it as 'select'. The name-plate was of a type similar to that in Welford Avenue, though a shade shorter. As Cross eagerly looked across at the house which, by its position, corresponded with his uncle's in Welford Avenue, his pulse leaped. It was a bombed house!

Cross stopped the car. He could hardly have regarded the place with a warmer sense of ownership if he had been a young husband taking his first look at the new homestead. This house had everything that he could have desired. It was detached, and stood well away from its neighbours. It had just about the same amount of garden in front as his uncle's house. It had a path to the front door of well-laid crazy-paving, which would not show footmarks. And it was well and truly blitzed. Part of the roof was open to the sky, a gable was almost torn away, all the windows were smashed, and the front door appeared to be jammed half open. Broken tiles lay all around.

Cross took a quick glance up and down the road and decided to risk a closer look. He turned his coat collar up and pulled his soft-brimmed hat well down over his face. It would only take a moment. He walked quickly up the path. The garden was still in fairly good shape – the house must have been hit by one of the last of the fly-bombs. He slipped through the opening of the front door, broken glass crackling under his feet. He saw at once that the whole place was quite beyond repair – and that was all to the good, for it meant that the shell would stand untouched throughout the winter. It was the right-hand side of the house that had been most damaged. There was a lot of debris lying about – remnants of smashed furniture, torn books, some old sacks. In the first room on the left, which looked as though it had been a rather nice lounge, there was a settee with one foot off and most of the stuffing ripped out. Everything worth taking had, of course, been salvaged.

Cross was delighted. From now on X-Avenue was Hamley Avenue. The place was perfect for his needs. Looking for a house at which to inquire the way in a fog, he would be just as likely to pick a blitzed house as an occupied one. He could imagine himself telling the story – how he had groped about in the dark and found the front door open and tried to knock, and then realized it was a bombed house and damned nearly broken his neck getting away. He could be in an infernally bad temper. That would cover up any natural agitation he might feel after killing his uncle, and would help to make his story sound convincing. He went home with a comfortable sense of solid achievement.

Now came the practical task of making and testing the dummy name-plate. Cross had enjoyed pitting his present ingenuity against the skill and persistence which the police would undoubtedly show in due course. Now he had to do something with his hands, and he had no special aptitude. Still, it shouldn't be a very difficult job, and his confidence was growing. If the name-plate were a failure, the whole plot failed, too. If it were a success, all else seemed possible.

The first thing was to get hold of a suitable piece of canvas. It should not be too thick, because the paint would tend to stiffen it. Cross had noticed that there was a roll of canvas aboard *Truant*, and both he and Geoffrey had keys to the boat. But there was really no need to run that risk. For the same reason, it would be better not to take paint from the Works. At lunch-time on the Monday, therefore, he ran up to town in the car, stopped at Gamages, and bought a roll of deck-chair canvas, a pot of broken-white paint, some white undercoat, and a pot of black paint. He also bought a selection of brushes.

Making the dummy took a lot more time than he had expected. First, he had to get the exact measurements of the name-plate in Welford Avenue, over which the dummy was to fit. That meant an expedition after dark, with the car parked a couple of streets away, and some rather nerve-racking fumbling with a tape-measure under the light of the street lamp. He took a two-way measurement of the cross-piece and ran a piece of string right round it to get the circumference. He had made up his mind that if he were seen and accosted during any of these rather peculiar operations he would say that he was working on an invention for a new and cheaper sort of street sign. But he took very good care not to be seen, for in such an event he doubted very much whether it would be safe to go on with the undertaking.

Having taken the measurements of the Welford Avenue plate, he had to go back to Hamley Avenue and make a sketch. He did this by daylight, sitting in the car with a newspaper at the back of his sketch-pad. The lettering was very plain and simple, and he decided it would be quite sufficient if he could get the spacing approximately correct. It took only a moment to measure the size of the type. One or two people walked along the road while he was sitting in the car, but no one gave him more than a passing glance, and certainly no one would connect him with the name-plate.

In the flat that evening he locked the door, spread newspapers all over the carpet, opened up his paint-pots, and went to work. The letters on the real sign were embossed, but he hoped that nothing so complicated would be necessary for his purpose. First, he carefully pencilled in the letters HAMLEY AVENUE, copying the sketch which he had made in the car. Then he painted all round the letters with the white undercoat, brushing it well into the canvas.

It dried overnight, and Cross was glad to see that the paint had stiffened the canvas appreciably. Next evening he put on the top coat of white and again had to wait for it to dry. There was still the lettering to be blacked in, and a black line to be drawn as a border round the whole of the lettering, giving it a neat and authentic finish. Finally, he painted in four dummy screw marks. Even then the most difficult part of the job was still to be done – the cutting of the canvas and the bending and sewing of the edges to make it a shallow tray of the exact size. Not until the fifth night was the task completed. Cross surveyed the finished product with a craftsman's satisfaction. Even in the bright light of the flat, it looked remarkably like what it was supposed to be. He rolled it up tight, and just managed to squeeze it into his overcoat pocket. He unrolled it again and examined it carefully. The paint, thinly applied and well soaked into the canvas, had not cracked. The lettering was as good as it had been before.

Now the dummy had to be put to the test on the spot. Cross took even greater precautions on this occasion to make sure that he was unobserved. On a dark and drizzly night, he drove through Welford Avenue and the roads on either side of the avenue and made sure there was no policeman about. When he felt satisfied that he would not be disturbed, he approached the name-plate, pulled the rolled-up dummy from his pocket, and began to ease it over the cross-piece. It was a bit of a squeeze, but that was a good fault. After he'd wriggled it about a bit, it slid home. He found that he had scratched his hands a little on the garden hedge which pressed against the name-plate at the back. On the night he must wear gloves.

He walked to the kerb and inspected his handiwork. Perfect! In the murky lamplight it was quite impossible to tell that the name-plate wasn't real. Even though he knew it was a fake, he could detect no flaw at that distance. An unsuspecting stranger would certainly never dream of doubting its genuineness. The only risk was that it might be difficult to decipher in a fog. Cross made a mental note to bring a torch with him on the night.

He eased the dummy off the plate, rolled it up carefully, and thrust it back into his capacious pocket. Elated, he strolled back to the car. There was still one risk, he realized, against which he could not guard. Since he would have to put the dummy in place before he arrived with his witnesses, it would mean that for something like half an hour on the night of the murder Welford Avenue would be Hamley Avenue for any passer-by. But if a policeman, or any person with local knowledge, happened to spot it in the fog – which seemed most unlikely – such a person would undoubtedly go right up to the sign to see what had happened, discover the dummy, and take it off. And naturally, if it had been removed when Cross arrived with his witnesses, the whole plan would be washed out. There remained the outside chance that a stranger might be confused by the sign and report the fact as a curious incident after the murder had been discovered. But that was really such a remote possibility that it could be ignored.

The time now seemed to have come for the drawing up of a draft schedule for the night of the murder. Cross worked on it with care.

7.15 p.m.   Leave flat at Alum Court by car, with dummy, weapon, torch, gloves, rubber soles.

7.30 p.m.   Arrive Welford Avenue. Hide weapon inside Uncle's gate. Fix dummy on name-plate.

7.45 p.m.   Arrive at roundabout. Pick up likely witnesses.

8.00 p.m.   Arrive Welford Avenue (now marked Hamley Avenue) with witnesses. Draw their attention to name-plate and time. Call at Uncle's on excuse of asking way, and bump him off. Ring neighbour and report accident. Remove dummy. Put weapon in pocket. Drive away.

8.20 p.m.   (approx.). Arrive at witnesses' destination, establish identity with them (under lamp?), make note of their address.

So far, so good, Cross thought. He was beginning to feel a reassuring familiarity with the plot, so much had he lived with it in the past week or two. He was well aware of the mass of detail still to be dealt with – he had several pages of notes. Little things like getting rid of the weapon, for instance – the river would probably be the best place for that. And disposing of the dummy – the deadliest piece of evidence. He would have to burn that, and see that the ashes were scattered. He could burn it in his fire-grate, if he were very careful not to leave any trace.

A few dress rehearsals were needed now. He might find in practice that his timing was too optimistic for a foggy night. He must get to know the district perfectly so that he could find his way with precision, however bad the conditions. That meant that he would have to make a mental note of landmarks rarely observed by drivers. He might even have to provide special landmarks of his own. He must make himself master of the streets. When he had done so he would test the whole time-table again and again, until it worked so smoothly that nothing could go wrong.

Meanwhile, he must be very careful. He locked up the dummy and his notes in a drawer of his bureau. The unused part of the canvas he burned, piece by piece, in his grate. And one evening he drove out into the country and threw the paint-pots and brushes into a pond. Clearing up as you went along – that, he told himself, was the way to make a success of premeditated crime.

*

He was well aware that his plan had one great and ineradicable weakness. It could not be put into operation until the weather was suitable. The sort of fog he needed was not likely to occur before late November, and even then it certainly couldn't be relied on. He could remember whole winters when there had been no fog to speak of in London. Not many, but one or two. However, it was reasonable to hope for at least one fairly thick patch, and he would have to be as patient as he could until it came.

That was the trouble – being patient! How could he be patient, knowing what was hanging over him? In the daytime he could sometimes believe that he was exaggerating the danger – that his luck might be in, that it might be years before the facts were discovered, even that they would never be discovered. But that was in the daytime. At night his thoughts became unbearable. Sometimes he would wake wet with fear, shaking and struggling, and crying out. Uncle Charles had asked him how he was sleeping and had suggested tablets. Cross preferred alcohol. He drank heavily, and usually alone. The difficulty was, he'd done so much drinking at the camp that small quantities had no effect on him. He guessed there wasn't much blood left in his alcohol stream!

Also, drinking was very expensive. Buying all the whisky he needed in the Black Market was ruinous. His flat was costly, too, and so were all his tastes. It irked him to be short of money, and he found two thousand a year, after tax, quite inadequate. What he needed was a capital of a hundred thousand pounds, which he could spend at the rate of five thousand a year for twenty years, with a bit of interest thrown in. The way he was living now, twenty years would probably see him through! That didn't worry him. The main thing was to have a good time now, before youth slipped away and hot blood cooled.

The thought of his uncle, looking so healthy and with all that cash at the bank, was unendurable. It wasn't even as though Cross had any interest in the Works – the whole thing bored him. It seemed intolerable that he should have to go along there every day, putting on an act, just to keep on the right side of the old boy. He loathed the sight of his office, the smell of linseed oil, the drab monotony of business and the faces of all the people he had to deal with. Wealth and freedom – they were the only things that attracted him. And neither was any good without the other.

In this frame of mind, the perfecting of his murder plan was a recreation. It occupied his thoughts, it was exciting, and it offered some hope of an early release. With anything like normal luck the night of the murder should fall within the next three months – perhaps even in a week or two. At least, he must act on that assumption. One of the things he still had to do – and he must do it quickly – was to set the scene domestically at Welford Avenue. It had to be arranged that his uncle should be at home and alone on the night; that Cross should be expected, and – preferably – that Geoffrey should arrive just after the kill.

In the course of one or two social visits that Cross had paid, without any great enthusiasm, to his uncle's house, he had been able to make some useful discoveries. It appeared that Dorothy, the daily girl, arrived at the house each weekday morning except Saturdays and finished her work around five. That meant that she was not likely to be an obstacle, and could be ignored. There had been a maid as well, but she had been called up during the war, and after several unsatisfactory attempts it had been decided not to replace her. The housekeeper, Mrs. Armstrong, was a woman of regular habits, as befitted a former hospital sister. She had come to take charge of Uncle Charles's establishment soon after his wife had died, and 'taken charge' she had. In Cross's view she was a dragon. She had never taken to 'Mister Arthur', and 'Mister Arthur' had never taken to her. It was essential that Mrs. Armstrong should be safely out of the way.

Cross soon found out that Thursday was her evening 'off', and that it was her routine habit to visit her sister at Ealing. Instead of giving Uncle Charles a hot meal on Thursdays – as she did with conscientious regularity on other nights – she always left something cold for him and departed soon after tea. She never returned before ten, and never after ten-thirty. That left the way clear for the murder, with an ample margin of safety. But it also meant that Cross needed not just a foggy day, but a foggy Thursday. He felt that the opportunities were becoming dangerously narrowed.

When he first realized how seldom Mrs. Armstrong was away, Cross almost felt like abandoning his cherished plan and starting again from the beginning. Was it not more important to play for a quick decision than for safety? What persuaded him to wait and see was the discovery that Geoffrey, now living with his father, was also away during the early part of each Thursday evening. The lectures he was giving at the Staff College had been fixed for Tuesdays and Thursdays throughout the winter. It seemed that he lectured between five and six-thirty, had a drink and dined in the Mess at Greenwich, and then drove himself home, arriving soon after eight-thirty.

This arrangement fitted in so perfectly with Cross's scheme that it seemed to him like an act of Providence, of which advantage must be taken. If Hollison were killed at about eight o'clock, and Geoffrey turned up soon afterwards, he might have some trouble proving that he had not done the murder himself. In any case, the more suspicion that fell on Geoffrey, the less the police would be able to concentrate on Cross.

It was still necessary that Cross's projected visit to his uncle on the night should be accounted for in a natural manner. It would not do for him to have arranged to call on his uncle on that particular evening if such a visit were an unusual event. Cross therefore set to work to make it usual. On the next Thursday he suggested that he should drop in at Welford Avenue after dinner. Hollison was delighted, and the evening proved a success. Cross arrived about eight, having dined early at the flat. His uncle had just finished his meal, and Geoffrey came in soon afterwards. They had a glass or two of port and then, at Hollison's suggestion, played cut-throat until midnight.

After that it was the easiest thing in the world to make the Thursday meeting a regular one. Hollison liked to feel that he could rely on a definite evening each week for the family gathering that had always been his wish. Sometimes they played cards; sometimes – if Geoffrey was tired after his lecture – Cross and Hollison would play chess; sometimes they just sat around, smoking, drinking and chatting. Geoffrey, full of zest for life and work, always had plenty to say.

Cross realized that he had better establish from the beginning the sort of procedure which would be necessary on the night. He made a practice of dining early at Alum Court – always a good thing to do if you wanted anything decent to eat! – and of arriving at Welford Avenue punctually at eight.

There was one subtlety which rather pleased him. On the night of the murder he would be supposed not to have called at his uncle's at eight o'clock. But the murderer would have called, and presumably would have knocked – and the knock might have been heard. With this in mind, Cross got into the way from the beginning of announcing his arrival on Thursdays by tapping on whichever window was lighted as he stood in the porch – the dining-room being on one side and the lounge on the other. Uncle Charles's hearing was still acute, and he never failed to hear the tapping. Always he would open the door with an eager, welcoming smile, giving Cross's arm an affectionate grasp as he went in. The unusual knock on the night of the murder would suggest a stranger.

As the weeks went by the three men settled securely into the Thursday routine. Cross felt it was like running in an engine before putting a car on the road. Sometimes, as he sat drinking Hollison's whisky, he felt quite jubilant at his own cleverness; but occasionally he became morose, for the weather remained mild, and week after week he had to listen to the hale old man enthusing about his dreary business or ridiculous plans for sailing in the summer.

Talk of sailing turned Cross's thoughts to *Truant*. He was planning his campaign like a military operation, and good commanders always provided for withdrawal in case of defeat. He would probably not have bothered about this if *Truant* had not offered an obvious way out, but since this means of escape from a tight corner was all ready for him, if was just as well he should know how to take advantage of it. He began, therefore, to show a rather more intelligent interest in the yacht. One Saturday he even suggested that he and Geoffrey should go down to the river and run the engines for a while, and he took the opportunity to make sure that all necessary stores were really aboard. He knew that his knowledge of chart work and coastal navigation was negligible, but in a real emergency, and if the weather were good, he thought he could probably motor the boat over to France or Holland. At least it was a comforting illusion.

CHAPTER IV

The mild weather persisted until the end of November. Cross felt that there was no point in making trial runs yet, since the timing would be completely different in fog. But repeatedly he drove over the ground at night to get used to the route. The roundabout proved to be an ideal starting place for the main journey. Five important roads ran out of it, and it would be readily understandable that he should take the wrong one on a thick night. His difficulty, indeed, would be to avoid taking the wrong one. He decided that the best pick-up point for his witnesses would be just beyond the three bus-stops. From there, moving on round the circle, the second road was the one which led in the direction of Hamley Avenue; the third was the road for the Welford Avenue district. He had to take the third, and let it be supposed that he had taken the second. He would need, of course, witnesses who wanted to go in the general direction of Welford Avenue, otherwise it would be difficult to explain to the police afterwards why he had been so generous as to pick them up.

Cross now began to take a great interest in kerbstones – his main guide in a fog. He already had a fog-lamp fitted low down on the Vauxhall, which threw a beam on to the edge of the pavement. Inspecting the roundabout on foot in daylight, he discovered that just before the Welford Avenue turning there was a broken kerb. But could he identify a broken kerb in fog? Even with the greatest care the chance was that he would miss it.

He decided on bold action. One fine dry night he stopped the car at the roundabout. Choosing a moment when no one was passing – it was nearly midnight – he carefully opened the near-side door and emptied a small pot of white paint over the broken kerb and dropped the pot in the gutter. The whole thing took only a few moments. Next day, on his way to work, he drove past the roundabout to see if his plan had been successful. The kerb was a bit sticky, but a good deal of the paint had dried. Twenty-four hours later the thick of the paint had been wiped off – presumably by a street-cleaner – but the effect had been achieved. The kerb stood out from the others, and would probably remain white for months.

There was really no reason, Cross decided, why this method of marking the way should not be used on a greater scale. A careful inspection of the route between the roundabout and Welford Avenue showed two turnings each way where he might easily become confused. Again, therefore, he set out – this time with a larger pot of paint – and in a short time had decorated four bits of kerb. The empty paint tin he threw into the river. He wondered whether by any chance the fact that five kerbstones had been splashed with white paint would arouse any local comment, and he studied the next issues of the district newspaper with some care. But nobody had taken any interest. Painting a kerb, after all, was not like painting a statue. No doubt there had been some rude remarks among the employees of the Highways Department of the Council, but the matter went no further. Cross could have hugged himself for his daring and resourcefulness. He made a few more night runs and decided that except in an absolute pea-souper – which would be useless for his purpose, anyway – he could find his way from the flat to the roundabout, and from the roundabout to and from Welford Avenue, with complete assurance.

He now felt ready for a dress rehearsal. He had never tapped the barometer so often; never studied the weather reports so closely. Towards the end of November a cold spell set in, and visibility dropped sharply. The outlook was 'Continuing cold, some fog'. Cross set off on what he mentally termed 'a spin over the course'. After an early dinner at Alum Court he left at 7.15 p.m., wearing a heavy grey overcoat and a soft grey hat. In a fog they would provide some protective colouring. In one pocket he had the dummy name-plate; in the other a ten-inch steel spanner. The fog was not as thick as he would want it to be on the night, but it was bad enough to make a fog-lamp useful and ordinary white lights troublesome. He reached the roundabout at 7.20, and with the help of the whitened kerb picked up the turn for Welford Avenue with ease. He drove slowly through to the Avenue without a hitch, arriving there at 7.34. The fog was a little sparser here, and he decided not to go through with the name-plate and spanner drill. Instead, he waited a minute or two and then drove back to the roundabout, arriving at 7.48. He parked just beyond the third bus-stop for fifteen minutes. That seemed a reasonable allowance for picking up his witnesses. He noticed with satisfaction that all the buses were very crowded, that long queues were standing at the stops, and that there were plenty of people walking by on the pavement. At 8.03 he again set off for Welford Avenue, arriving at 8.16 – a bit late, he decided, for safety. It would never do to run into Geoffrey as he left the house after doing the murder! He would have to put the whole schedule forward a bit.

As he sat in the car in Welford Avenue he mentally rehearsed the part he would have to play on the night. He would say something to his passengers about asking the way; he would get out, walk to his uncle's gate, pick up the spanner and hold it in his right-hand pocket, tap at the window, wait, go in, shut the door, hit his uncle over the head, put the spanner back in his pocket, ring up a neighbour (he had still to choose one – he must remember that), walk quickly to the name-plate, remove the dummy, return to the car, curse about the bombed house and drive away. Round a couple of corners, and safety! Time, 8.21. Say five minutes for the whole operation. After that he could take his passengers to their destination at his leisure.

Back home, Cross revised the schedule. He would leave Alum Court at 7 o'clock instead of 7.15, and then he should arrive at Welford Avenue at just about 8.

There remained the problem of the neighbour to be rung up. It was not as simple as it seemed – in fact, Cross could see several dangers. Once the killing was done, it was imperative that he should get out of the house quickly. Indeed, it might be better to phone from a call-box. Cross considered that possibility. He could make some excuse to his passengers, but it would be straining their patience – he would already have been away five minutes. And it would come out that he had telephoned – he would be asked whom he had rung up. He could invent something – an engaged number – but why should he want to ring anybody up at that hour, when he was on his way to see his uncle? Of course – he'd lost his way, and was late, and was ringing up his uncle. There would be no reply. Perfect! He would be puzzled, of course, but . . . No, that wouldn't do, though. Ostensibly he would be in Hamley Avenue, using a call-box there. It might turn out that such a call-box had not been used during the period from 8 to 8.30. A quiet district, a foggy night – that was quite possible. And then where would he be? How tricky it all was!

Then the call must be from the house, after all. He must ring up someone who could be relied on to be home at that time. The police would be ideal in many ways, but they might move too fast. They were very much on the alert with their 999's and radio cars, particularly as there was what the newspapers called a 'crime wave' just at the moment. Deserters, the papers said. Cross wanted to be well clear of the neighbourhood before the police got busy.

Whom could he ring? He called at a post-office and consulted the local street directory. He looked all through the list of residents in Welford Avenue without inspiration. Most of them had telephones, but there was no certainty that they would be at home on the night. Even if he equipped himself with alternative numbers, he couldn't afford to be phoning one house after another with a corpse lying in the hall and his car outside with passengers in it. He glanced down the list of residents in the next road – Pargeter Avenue, backing on to Welford Avenue – and suddenly he knew he had found the very thing. A doctor! Even if the doctor himself weren't at home, there would be a nurse or someone to take a message. Whoever answered the phone would be a responsible person, and would certainly see that help was on its way within a few minutes. Cross carefully memorized the doctor's telephone number. And, just in case the number should be engaged, he found another doctor a street or two away who would serve as a second string.

The next day was Thursday, and the fog was thickening. The blueprint was finished, and the time for action had come.

Strangely enough, Cross slept better that night than he had done for a long time. There was no more need for him to scheme and plot; to lie awake, as he had so often done, until three o'clock in the morning, devising alternative ways of dealing with various situations. Now all was plain and settled. Anything that might go wrong now was, he believed, unforseeable. Obviously, there were dangers, but he had no doubt whatever that in his particular circumstances they were worth taking. This frame of mind, aided by half a tumbler of whisky, brought a quiet night.

He woke at eight, a little liverish but with rested nerves.

Between gulps of tea and puffs of cigarette smoke, he gazed with an appreciative eye at the raw November scene. There was a rime of frost on the window-sill, and fog hid the building across the way. It was thicker than it had been the day before; if it held like this until the evening, it would be perfect. He switched on the radio for the weather forecast. "Fog service in operation on all lines . . . motorists warned of difficult road conditions . . . rather cold, continuing foggy." Splendid!

He was completely engrossed by his one idea. It was in no way a repellent idea. On the contrary, he was really looking forward to the evening. For so long his only interest had been in building up this plan, item by item, to its present state of perfection. He was excited by the thought that he was now going to put it to the test. He was eager for the inevitable duel of wits with the police; all his faculties were sharp for the contest. What was important now was the technical execution of the plot. The mere death of his uncle was just an incident in the plot. An important one, of course. Cross wondered how long it would be before he could get his hands on the cash. Lawyers were so slow.

At the Works the hours dragged. Uncle Charles, fussing in and out with his talk about Cambridge blue and eggshell finish, was more than usually trying. "I'll give him an eggshell finish," thought Cross. How on earth did the old chap manage to keep such a tan on his bald head in November? Or was it a yellow skin and blood pressure? Surely he couldn't really feel as fit as he looked?

There was one bad moment. Hollison, popping in with his hat and coat on just before six o'clock, said: "It's a foul night, Arthur, and it seems to be getting thicker. Perhaps you'd sooner not come over tonight?"

"Oh, I don't know," said Cross, cool and cautious. He took a look out of the window at the dim light of the street lamp. "It's not as bad as all that. I bet Mrs. Armstrong won't stay and cook your supper just because it's foggy."

Hollison laughed. "Not she. You won't catch her missing her weekly jaunt."

Cross laughed, too. "If she can face it, I can. I suppose Geoffrey's lecturing as usual?"

"Yes – but he'll probably be a little late with all this fog."

"That's an extra reason why I should come. We'll have a game – I'll give you a rook and a bishop tonight. I'm feeling in form."

"You're getting above yourself," said Hollison, with a grin. "Well, I'm off. See you later."

"Be careful how you drive," said Cross. "We don't want any accidents."

On the way home he stopped to get the Vauxhall's petrol tank filled up and the oil level checked. Thank goodness he never had any difficulty about petrol – these 'E' coupons for business use were a wonderful idea. The car, as usual, was running splendidly. He couldn't afford any breakdowns tonight. He left the car outside Alum Court while he had a quick snack. He would have liked to ring Geoffrey, just to assure himself that his cousin was actually at the College and going through his usual routine. There was not the least reason to doubt it, but – well, illness or a cancellation! Cross shrugged and put the thought behind him. It would be just too bad.

The time was ten minutes to seven. He popped up to his flat to get the dummy name-plate, had one short drink to steady himself, and went down to the car. The fog was a beauty! It was thick enough to make route-finding difficult, to make it seem reasonable that a driver should get lost. At the same time it was still possible for traffic to move. The white frost crackled a little under his feet; there was no breath of wind. He drew his coat up round his ears and pulled his woollen muffler a shade tighter across his narrow chest. Not much good coming into a fortune if he got pneumonia doing it. He climbed into the driving seat, picked up the spanner from the well at the back, and slid it into his right-hand pocket with the torch which he had already put there. All set! His luminous watch showed exactly seven. He started the engine and turned carefully into the main road.

There was rather more traffic than he had expected, but it came bunched up, with big gaps in between the convoys. Most of the vehicles were buses, crawling one behind the other with their fog-lamps on the kerb. They seemed ghostly and remote. In a fog, people were always intent on their own problems. There was no idle curiosity, no one to stand and stare and wonder. Everyone wanted to get home as quickly as possible. The police probably had their hands full with the traffic and the petty crime that always came with fog. In short, it was a grand night for a murder.

Cross had no trouble with the route. He had been over the ground so often that he almost knew when to turn the wheel and how much. The painted kerbs, yellow under the fog-lamp, were as reassuring and helpful as buoys at sea. It was 7.17 when he cautiously turned into Welford Avenue and drew up a few yards from his uncle's house. The road was silent and deserted; through the murk it was just possible to see a faint light at Hollison's window.

Cross slipped out, leaving the car door slightly open and the engine ticking over. Without opening his uncle's gate, he slid the heavy spanner on to the concrete close to the gate-post. Then, without a pause, he walked quickly to the corner by the lamp. There was still a faint crackle of hoar frost under his rubber-soled shoes. He glanced round the corner. There was nothing to be seen except grey vapour. Nothing to be heard. It took him hardly a moment to pull the dummy from his pocket, unroll it, and slip it over the plate. Once again he stepped back to the kerb and examined it. HAMLEY AVENUE. It was convincing. The marks of the dummy bolt-heads painted on the canvas gave it the final touch of authenticity.

The car was a dim shape across the road. Listening intently, Cross thought he could hear footsteps somewhere in the Avenue, but as he drove along he passed no one, and decided that he had been mistaken. He was keyed up, but his nerve was all right. Tomorrow a fortune!

Fifteen minutes later he was back at the roundabout. A glance at his watch told him he was keeping to schedule pretty well. He drew up at the kerb, twenty yards or so beyond the bus-stop, and opened the near-side window. People were plodding by. He could allow himself ten or twelve minutes to get his witnesses, and if he failed to find suitable candidates in that time, he must call the show off for the night. This was one of the worrying bits – particularly unpleasant because success did not depend solely on his own efforts. But surely someone would be glad of a lift on a filthy night like this. The thing was to make it seem natural, not to force anything. He peered through the fog, wondering whether he should speak to someone or wait a while.

He had not been at the kerb more than three minutes when a figure took shape out of the fog and bore down on him. It was a woman, a young woman, with a scarf over her hair. She was a little diffident. "Excuse me," she said, "but *do* you happen to know if there's a taxi rank anywhere around here?"

"There's one by the station, about half a mile ahead," said Cross, studying her. "But I don't suppose there's a cab on it on a night like this. Isn't it shocking? I'm lost myself. I'm trying to get to Welford Avenue. That's not your part of the world, I suppose?"

"Oh, no," said the girl hastily, retreating. "I'm going in the opposite direction – to Kew. The buses are all full – it's most awkward. I suppose I'll have to walk." She disappeared into the gloom.

"Silly bitch!" muttered Cross, lighting a cigarette with fingers that shook just a little. Time was passing, the suspense was very trying. Perhaps he ought to have pressed her to accept a lift – but *would* a man trying to find his way to Welford Avenue give a lift to an uncomely young female who was going to Kew? It would really sound most unlikely. Whatever he did, he mustn't allow himself to be stampeded into taking foolish risks.

Seven minutes to go! It looked as though he would have to take the initiative after all. Several people glanced in his direction as they passed, but no one else stopped. About ten yards back he could just make out the figure of a man selling newspapers near the bus-stop. There were also two men standing talking in a shop doorway almost opposite him. One of them looked towards the car. Cross was just about to call out and ask them if they knew the turning for Welford Avenue when they came over. They were both young men, and they looked as though they might have been recently demobbed. Both wore dark overcoats and coloured scarves, and both had nondescript soft hats. In the poor light it was not easy to see anything of their faces.

"Sorry to trouble you, mister," said the taller one. His voice was a little hoarse, as though the fog had got into his larynx. "Any chance of a lift?"

"Depends where you're going," said Cross. "I'm trying to get to Welford Avenue."

"That's a stroke of luck," said the short man. "We're going up that way – Angel Road. You could drop us off." ·

"Okay – jump in the back," said Cross, opening the door for

them. "I don't guarantee to get you there, mind. Do you know the way?" He waited anxiously for the reply. If they did, he was probably sunk.

"Not exactly," said the hoarse man. "On a clear night, yes; but not in this muck. There's a turn on the left here somewhere, isn't there, Fred?"

"Somewhere," said Fred unhelpfully.

"I expect we'll find it," said Cross, more cheerfully, swinging the car round by the familiar painted kerb.

"Anyway," said Fred, "it's a bloomin' sight better gettin' lost in a car than walkin'. I know – I've got a bad foot. Copped it in Sicily."

"Just out?" asked Cross sympathetically.

"Yus, couple of months back. Wish I was still in Sicily, with this damned weather. Fair snorter, ain't it?"

"It's a bad night for going places," said Cross. "Angel Road, you said; any particular number?" He must know where they were going.

"Trade union meeting," said the hoarse man. "*And* we're late. But I reckon they'll all be late – don't you, Fred?"

"Sure," said Fred.

Cross looked at his watch. He was well on time. "Good honest working chaps," he thought to himself. "Just the thing. No nonsense about them – they'll stick to their stories. Any jury would believe them." He swung out to pass a stationary bus and crawled back to the kerb. "I believe we're all right," he said hopefully. "What do you think?"

"Blowed if I know," growled Fred. "It all looks alike to me."

"Do you live in these parts?" asked Cross. Time was running short – he must make sure that his witnesses would be traceable afterwards.

"Kingston," said the tall man. "Both of us."

"Anywhere near the river? I've got a boat down there."

"You don't say! Lucky feller. It's hard enough to get a house these days. My missus is on a waitin' list for one of them prefabs. They're nice."

"Whereabouts on the list?" asked Fred.

"There was eighty-nine thousand seven hundred and fourteen people in front of her last Tuesday week," said the tall man.

A wave of irritation swept Cross. They were getting very near to Welford Avenue and the whole thing was damned unsatisfactory. Where the hell did these chaps live in Kingston? Why wouldn't they open up a bit? In five minutes, he had to kill his uncle. Was it safe to wait until afterwards to find out more about his witnesses? He didn't like it – he began to have doubts whether he ought to go on with the plan.

Suddenly he had doubts no longer. Something hard was pushed sharply into the back of his neck – it hurt even through his coat collar – and the hoarse voice said: "Stop the car, mister, and keep quiet. This is a stick-up!"

"You swine—" began Cross, violently.

"Take it easy, mister. Pull in to the kerb."

"You've been seeing too many films," said Cross between his teeth. He wasn't worried by the hold-up, but by the total ruin of his evening. He stopped the car.

The hard object was still pressing into his neck. "This is a gun, mister," said the hoarse voice, unnecessarily. "We're desperate men. One sound, and you're a goner."

"What do you want? You'll get ten years for this."

"Shut yer trap! We're takin' the car and your wallet. Wallet first – and any loose notes you've got. Come on, make it snappy. Come *on*!" The point of the gun jerked menacingly.

Cross took out his pocket book and handed it over. "It's got all my papers, addresses, everything," he said. "They're no good to you. There's about ten pounds – take the money and give me the wallet back."

"Orl right, mister – if there is ten pounds." There was a moment's silence while the hoarse man fiddled with the wallet. "Right you are, mister, catch hold. Now hop out. This side. Step lively. Fred, get in the driving-seat. Steady, mister – I'm a dead shot. Lots of practice, you know! Open the door. All right, Fred, shove 'im out. You needn't bother about yer car, mister. She'll look quite different when we've fixed her." The engine revved, and the Vauxhall shot away into the fog.

Cross stood motionless on the pavement. One or two cars had passed, but there would have been no sense in calling out. It had been a real gun, all right. He stood and cursed. He was deflated, wretched, suddenly cold. He'd lost a good car, and what was far worse, his splendid plan had come to nothing. "Damned crooks!" he ejaculated.

What should he do? Obviously he must report the hold-up, but how? The fog which had been better than a spring day to him a few minutes ago was now just a fog. It was difficult to adjust his ideas. He had been concentrating so hard on his plan – now his mind felt empty. Funny that he should be calling in the police! He could have wept with frustration. He ought to have known those chaps were up to no good, skulking about in doorways. If he hadn't been so full of his own affairs . . . A trade union meeting! Prefabs!

He must go to Welford Avenue, of course. It was quite close – ten minutes' walk at the outside. He would report the theft of the car from there. He could use a drink, too. Suddenly he remembered that the dummy was still on the name-plate. He had nearly forgotten it in this new excitement. If he'd left it . . .! He quickened his pace. In a few minutes he swung round the last corner and crossed the road to the lamp. HAMLEY AVENUE. It was still there, all right – nobody had noticed. Everything would have been so easy – it had been such a good plan. He rolled up the dummy, retrieved the spanner from beside the gate-post, and walked up his uncle's path to the front door. He tapped on the lighted lounge window, and Hollison let him in. The smooth bald head shone temptingly in the light of the hall lamp. Cross's fingers were gripping the spanner which he could not use. It was an agony of anti-climax. Sweat stood out on his forehead.

He went in. "My car's just been pinched," he said curtly. "Two chaps held me up with a gun. Catch me giving anyone a lift again. I'd better phone the police."

He went into the lounge and rang up the local station, while Uncle Charles hovered in the background, pouring out a stiff whisky and making indignant noises as Cross told his story.

The rest of the evening passed wretchedly. Geoffrey arrived in good spirits just before half past eight – just as he should have done. Presently a police officer called from the station to get a more detailed description of the two men, and Cross told him all he could remember. The officer seemed quite hopeful that the men would be picked up, or at least that the car would be found, but Cross was indifferent. He found it difficult to be civil to anyone, drank a lot of whisky, and departed early. He was disgusted with himself and with his luck. He had had a fortune within his grasp that night – now it was as far away as ever. For the moment he had lost faith in his plan, and all his anxieties about the future came rushing back. Alone in his room, he steadily drank himself into a stupor.

CHAPTER V

Cross brooded over his disappointment. If things had gone right, he might now be booking his air passage to Rio. His temper became shorter, his drinking heavier. He clung desperately to the thought that at least no structural defect had appeared in the plan itself. It was just a question of time before he picked the right witnesses. He really needed three or four chances. The trouble was that the odds against several foggy Thursdays were enormous. For the moment, anyway, opportunity had passed. The weather had cleared up, and people were talking hopefully of a mild winter.

The situation was even more awkward for Cross than it had been before, because his cost of living was rising. Soon after the fiasco with the Vauxhall, he had picked up a bedworthy but expensive young woman at a West End theatre. He was having fun, but his financial position had sharply deteriorated. Every time they went out for an evening it cost him a fiver. That couldn't go on, unless somehow he could raise the wind. The business was doing well, and he thought of asking for a higher expense allowance. He felt sure that if he were to tell his uncle he needed money it would be forthcoming without any unpleasantness. But you could never be sure. Hollison had made what he considered a generous arrangement – he would certainly be surprised, perhaps pained, if his nephew seemed to be turning out a spendthrift. It was most important that nothing should be done to spoil the present excellent relationship, and equally important that Cross should not seem to be hard-pressed for cash just before his uncle died. The idea was that he should appear to be managing adequately on his income and that when Hollison was killed someone should say to the police: "Poor Mr. Cross – he must be cut up. He and his uncle got on so well together."

Meanwhile the police had been working on the 'hold-up' which had robbed him of the Vauxhall, but so far they had had no success. His description of the two men would have fitted almost anyone. Nor had any trace of the car been found. The police view was that the thieves were probably running a regular 'grab and repaint' business, and that the car had been re-cellulosed at once and sold second-hand with new plates and a registration book belonging to another car of the same make. It was quite easy to do that with these popular models, particularly as people rarely bothered to check engine and chassis numbers. The thieves had probably cleared six or seven hundred pounds from their haul – a good night's work. Not that Cross was concerned about the car. His insurance company had paid up nobly, after some rather trying inquiries, and Cross – with the help of an unsought gift from his uncle – had bought himself a Rover 12 of pre-war vintage. It had an excellent performance and an attractive body – always a point with Cross – of a rather striking light blue. On the whole, therefore, the episode had not ended too badly, though Cross still felt sore over the ignominious way he had been treated. He wouldn't have minded a few more minutes alone with Fred and his companion – if this time he could be the one with the gun. He could have shown them a trick or two!

The Thursday night sessions at Welford Avenue remained a disagreeable chore. Cross had come to dislike Geoffrey intensely – the man seemed to have no worries and to be thoroughly enjoying life. Christmas came and went – revoltingly green and sickeningly festive. There was a party for the staff at the Works, which Cross naturally had to attend, and at Welford Avenue Uncle Charles kept open house. Geoffrey brought several naval types home on Boxing Day, and the naval types brought three Wrens, and everybody was frightfully jolly. Cross had no friends; he had been too busy to make any. He could hardly take his young woman along to his uncle's; he felt that the old boy wouldn't have approved of her sort. In any case, Cross was thinking of changing her. Women became so tedious after a while. By the New Year, the financial situation was becoming critical. The first week in January had brought in a surprising number of unpaid bills and one or two of them were pressing. Cross could not see how a fresh approach to his uncle could be avoided much longer. There were always the risky ways of making money, of course – like forging a cheque – but that seemed no way to smooth the path to fortune. It might be all right if he could be certain of getting out of the country soon, but not otherwise. It was really ridiculous that a man of his expectations should be stumped for a few hundred pounds. Perhaps he might be able to persuade a moneylender to advance him something on his prospects.

Then the weather changed. In mid-February an iron frost clamped down on southern England, and as it eased the fog returned. Cross felt all his old enthusiasm for the murder plan rushing back. Every detail was etched in his mind; he could almost go through with it in his sleep. He took out the dummy name-plate from the bureau where it had lain for three months, and it looked as fresh and convincing as ever. He took a run over the route to refresh his memory just for safety's sake, and looked in at Hamley Avenue to make sure the bombed house had been left alone. He put a larger bulb in the Rover's fog-lamp.

Day after day the fog held – a little thin in the daytime, but always thickening up nicely towards evening. Thursday came, and once more Cross looked from his window with satisfaction. He could barely see the pavement.

All the preliminaries were accomplished without a hitch. Mrs. Armstrong was in good health and unlikely to depart from her weekly routine. Uncle Charles this time took it for granted that his nephew would be coming over. Geoffrey was certain to lecture – Cross knew that he had been working hard that very morning on notes for the first of a new series.

Once again Cross carefully filled up the tank of the car and checked the oil and water. Once again he wrapped himself up warmly, with the heavy spanner transferred from the tool-kit to his pocket, and the dummy name-plate comfortably tucked in the other pocket. Gloves, torch – yes, he had everything.

The evening was very similar to that earlier unlucky one as far as the fog was concerned. The first run to Welford Avenue went smoothly. The white kerbstones had weathered a little, but they still made good landmarks. Welford Avenue was empty apart from one pedestrian who disappeared quickly into the gloom. Slipping the spanner under the gate and the dummy on the name-plate took only a couple of minutes. Cross was confident; he had a hunch that this time everything was going to be all right. It was just after half past seven when he returned to the roundabout and parked in the old familiar spot.

This was the test. His heart was beating fast, in spite of all his efforts to calm down – or perhaps because of them. He was out of training, he told himself, for these tough jobs. The soft life! He lit a cigarette from the last stub and inhaled deeply. He could do with a drink – but that would have to wait. Afterwards he could soak in alcohol if he wanted to.

He had waited a few minutes, scanning the passers-by and seeing no one particularly suitable, when he noticed a man and a woman stopping a few yards away, apparently in some doubt about what to do. The man was talking and pointing across the roundabout into grey opacity. Cross heard the girl laugh – a pleasant laugh, good-tempered and amused in spite of the filthy night – and then the man said something again and they both walked over to the car. Cross leaned out and opened the door on the near side as they approached.

"You don't happen to know where Hailey Crescent is, do you?" the man asked. His voice was friendly, courteous; his accent cultured.

"Hailey Crescent?" Cross repeated. He remembered that he had seen the name during one of his many exploratory journeys round the district. Yes, of course – and the right direction, too. "Isn't that somewhere up near the Park?" he asked.

"That's right, darling," said the girl. "Don't you remember John boasting about his early-morning walks?"

"Of course," said the man. "Can you tell us how we get there?"

"If you like to take a chance," said Cross amiably, "you can jump in. It's roughly the same direction that I'm going – I'm making for Welford Avenue. I thought I knew these parts like the back of my hand, but I'm a bit stuck myself. It's this roundabout that's the trouble. I was just trying to get my bearings."

"It's very good of you," said the girl gratefully as she got in. "We've a dinner date at eight – rather an important one. And there's no sign of a taxi anywhere. I do hope we shan't be taking you too much out of your way."

"I don't guarantee anything," said Cross cheerfully, "but you'll never get a taxi. There's a rug there somewhere – you may as well make yourselves as comfortable as possible."

"That's lovely," said the girl. "It really is kind of you."

"Not at all," said Cross. The more he put them in his debt, the better.

The man leaned over. "Smoke?" he said.

"Not just now, thanks," said Cross. "I've just finished one. If I take my eye off the kerb I'll be sunk. Shocking, isn't it? Let's see, there should be a turning somewhere here. I'm afraid it's impossible to hurry."

"You're doing fine," said the girl, peering out a little anxiously. Cross could see her in the driving-mirror as she drew on her cigarette. She was smart, good-looking. Excellent types, both of them. His luck was in! No gun in his neck this time, or knife in his back. Civilized people. He hummed softly to himself, concentrating on the kerb.

"Do you live round here?" asked the man after a few moments.

"Not far away," said Cross. "Actually, I'm going over to spend the evening with my uncle, Charles Hollison, the paint manufacturer. You must have heard of Hollison's paint."

"Rather," said the man. "We used it all over the kitchen, didn't we, darling? I say, it *is* thick, isn't it? I'm glad you're doing the driving, I must say. Do you recognize anything at all?"

"I wouldn't put it as high as that," said Cross. "Now and again I think I do, but I'm not too sure. If we took the right road out of the roundabout – that was where I picked you up – we ought to pass a lighted pub soon. I'll recognize that all right."

The girl laughed softly. "I could do with a drink, darling. I hope John has some good strong cocktails laid on."

"What's the number in Hailey Crescent?" asked Cross, turning by a painted kerb.

"I don't think there is a number," said the man. "It's a big white house, standing back, with a white gate. Should be easy to spot, but don't you bother. We can find it easily once we know we're in the right road. It's Sir John Lutimer's house – I should think anyone would be able to tell us when we get close."

"Isn't he in the Foreign Office?" asked Cross, recalling newspaper headlines.

"That's right – one of the Permanent Secretaries." The man was winding down his window, staring out. "No sign of that pub. I say, I do feel we're imposing on your good nature."

"Nonsense," said Cross. "It's nice to have company on a night like this." He swung the car into Welford Avenue and drew up beside the dummy. "Anyway, you've nothing to thank me for. I'm afraid I'm lost." He wound his own window down. "If we could only read the name of the street it might help . . ." He peered out; they all peered out. "Half a minute, I've got a torch." He switched on and directed the beam towards the dummy. There was a lot of dazzle, but it was visible.

"I can see – I think," said the man. "H – A – M – something – E – Y – Hamley, that's it."

The girl leaned across him. "That's right, Hamley Avenue," she said. "Does that help?"

"Damn!" said Cross. "We must have taken the wrong turning at the roundabout. Hamley Avenue – let me see. We'll have to get back to the roundabout, somehow." He slipped the car into gear and drifted slowly forward past his uncle's gate, as though still cogitating. Suddenly he jerked on the brake. "I think I'd better try and get directions at one of these houses," he said. "Otherwise we'll be wandering around all night. Sorry, folks. I'll only be a minute or two."

"Don't worry," said the girl, "after all, we should never have got there on our own."

Cross walked back ten yards. The fog had already swallowed up the car. Suddenly a thought hit him like a blow. Suppose someone were to pass the car while he was in the house? His passengers would be sure to stop any pedestrian and ask the way. They might discover it wasn't Hamley Avenue. For a second Cross stood hesitating. Should he go on? Alternatives swept through his mind – grim alternatives. Murder and discovery; retreat, penury, fear. He would take the risk.

Softly he opened his uncle's gate, picked up the spanner, and approached the door. There was a light in the lounge window. He was braced for action – it should take no time at all. He gave a loud double knock on the iron knocker. They could hardly fail to hear that in the car, if they were listening. He heard his uncle moving in the lounge, the padding of slippered feet in the hall. The door opened.

"Here I am," said Cross.

"*Hello,* Arthur! I felt sure it was someone else. You don't usually knock. Come in – my word, what a night!"

"Wicked!" said Cross. "Lead me to a drink – I'm frozen."

He closed the door quietly behind him. Uncle Charles turned towards the lounge. His smooth head gleamed. At last, thought Cross, at last! He drew himself up on his toes and brought the heavy head of the spanner down on Hollison's skull with all his strength. The blow was fearful, and Hollison slumped down with hardly a sound. A faint inarticulate gurgle – that was all. He lay still.

Cross was cool. This was the crisis – he must move fast. He bent over his uncle and made sure that he was dead. There was a huge rent in the skull, and a lot of blood. Cross stepped over the puddle, and hurried into the lounge. He wiped the spanner on a corner of carpet and slipped it back into his pocket.

He sat down by the telephone and dialled RIC 51423. He waited impatiently for the click and the ringing tone. Waiting, his eye fell on a pile of papers on the telephone table. One of them was in Geoffrey's handwriting. Diagrams and things. It looked like a page of lecture notes.

A woman's voice said, "Dr. Whitworth's house."

Another moment of risk! Cross had practised this – he felt certain that a disguised voice over the telephone could never afterwards be identified with assurance. He pitched his tone high, made it quaver. "There has been a bad accident at Charles Hollison's house – 12A Welford Avenue, quite near to you. For heaven's sake send round at once."

The woman said: "I'm afraid the doctor's out, but I'll attend to it. 12A Welford Avenue. I know the house. Don't worry." She rang off.

Cross replaced the telephone receiver carefully. He was still wearing gloves. His eye swept the room. Keep cool, keep cool, he told himself. These are the moments of decision. This is life or death. There was no blood on the carpet, no footmark. His shoes were clean. So were his clothes. There was nothing to show that he had been there. Those notes of Geoffrey's – should he? – shouldn't he? It was unplanned, but why not? At worst they would help to confuse things. He carried the paper into the hall and slipped it under the body. Stepping once more over the pool of blood, he softly opened the front door, listened, left it ajar behind him, walked rapidly to the name-plate at the corner, dragged off the dummy, rolled it and thrust it into his pocket. He thought he heard a car starting up in the next road but it could have been his imagination. He was clammy with perspiration – his shirt was clinging to his back. A near thing – it had taken longer than he had expected. A good five minutes.

He reached the car and climbed in. The man was just saying something about 'protocol'. Evidently they had not been talking about Cross or the fog, anyway.

"Any luck?" asked the girl.

"Hell, no!" said Cross. "Sorry I was such a while. Our luck's out tonight. Of all the damned silly things to do, I picked on a bombed house. Did you hear me hammering away at a door that was off its hinges? I fell over something and came an awful cropper. That's why I was so long." He let in the clutch and the car moved off. "I hadn't the heart to try anywhere else – the whole street's as quiet as the grave."

"It's all our fault," said the girl sympathetically. "I *am* sorry. I do hope you're not much hurt."

"Oh, it's nothing, really. No bones broken." For a second, as they passed the end of the road, he had another bad moment. The name-plate at this end said Welford Avenue. But the fog was too thick for his passengers to notice, and the spasm passed.

"We'd better ask the first person we see," he said. "Or maybe I can find my way back to the roundabout. Once I get on the right road it won't take long. What's the time – will you be very late?"

"It's ten past eight," said the man, flicking on his lighter to examine his watch.

"John won't mind," said the girl, "not on a night like this. I shouldn't think anybody will be very early."

"I think the fog's lifting a trifle," said Cross. It was not true, but it might seem to explain his better progress, and it passed without comment.

Blessed silence! Relief from talk! He'd done it – he'd done it. No mistakes. No one had seen. He'd played his part – his witnesses even liked him. It was a cinch. Murder was easy!

They negotiated the roundabout and Cross picked out the road that led to the Park. He was pretty sure this was the way to Hailey Crescent. He could ask now – he was out of the danger zone. He passed a couple of men. He slowed, and called out.

"Is this the way to Hailey Crescent?"

"Straight on!" shouted one of the men. "Third on the left, if you can find it."

"Oh, good," said the girl thankfully. She began to make up her face. Cross watched the kerb. That would be the second – the next turning must be theirs. He took the corner slowly, looking for the name-plate. How sick and tired he was of name-plates! Yes, it was Hailey Crescent. Phew, he could do with a drink!

"Isn't that a car light ahead?" said the man. "Stationary. That's probably it. Yes, look, it's a white gate." Cross pulled up and they bundled out.

"We really can't thank you enough," said the girl. "We'd never have found it without you, would we, Charles? You've been a real good Samaritan."

"You certainly have," said the man. "We're most grateful. You see, we're flying to South America tomorrow, weather permitting, to take up a new job. It would have been most awkward to miss this date. Well, good night. Hope you manage to find your own way without too much trouble."

"Good night," said the girl. They turned quickly into the gate-way.

Cross, caught up in panic, began to call after them. "I say . . ." he cried desperately, not knowing what he *would* say. But they didn't hear.

Cross slumped back into the driving-seat, exhausted. Flying to South America! A fine pair of witnesses he'd chosen!

CHAPTER VI

Cross's moment of near-panic was soon over. It was extremely awkward, of course, that his witnesses might not be around to answer questions, but there could hardly be any real danger. Sir John Lutimer would be able to give all particulars about his guests, including their destination in South America – even if the police did not decide to take a statement from them tonight. There might be delay, but the evidence was secure enough on a long-term view. Indeed, it might even be better that the police should have to make an effort to get it – the harder they had to work for it themselves, the more value they might attach to it.

Suppose the plane crashed! The horrid thought had no sooner passed through Cross's mind than common sense reasserted itself. He could hardly require that his affairs should be exempted from the normal hazards of life, just because he was a murderer. As far as he could see, that sudden flash of fear in the car had been quite unnecessary.

He came back to the immediate tasks. There was a lot to be done. The most pressing thing was to destroy the damning evidence of the dummy name-plate – the only thing in the world which might give a clue to the real events of the evening. It must be destroyed at once, before inquiries and searches began – and it was not an easy thing to destroy. It certainly couldn't be thrown away, like an empty tin of paint, nor could it be safely hidden. Obviously, it must be burned, and for that purpose he must return to the flat. If the time had to be accounted for afterwards, he could say he had been shaken by his fall at the bombed house, and had felt in need of a clean-up and a drink. He set course for home.

Inside the flat, he drew the curtains and poured himself a stiff whisky. Then he cut the canvas dummy into small strips and soon had a nice blaze crackling in the grate. The paint-soaked canvas burned fiercely, leaving a stiff ash. It made an abominable smell.

He took the scissors into the kitchen, washed them carefully with hot water and soap, and replaced them in their drawer. Then, with a small dustpan and brush, he carefully collected every scrap of ash from the grate and wrapped it in a piece of stiff brown paper. Then he put the brown paper parcel into his coat pocket. He would deal with that in a few minutes.

He made sure that no ash was left in the dustpan or clinging to the brush, and returned them to their place in the kitchen cupboard. The lingering smell was the most worrying thing. There must be some reason for it – burned paper would be better than nothing. He found some old letters in his bureau and set alight to them.

He had already wiped the spanner on the carpet at Welford Avenue, but perhaps it had better be washed. He could see no mark on it, but it was impossible to be too careful. When it was dry, he put it back in his coat pocket alongside the paper parcel.

As he threw the grey coat over a chair back, he suffered another of those little shocks which for a short period were so unnerving. On the front of the coat, near the bottom, there was a dark streak. He touched it with his finger – it was drying blood. It hadn't been there when Cross examined the coat in the lounge at Welford Avenue; it must have been picked up while he was bending over the corpse to secrete Geoffrey's notes.

Hell! For a second, his mind seemed utterly confused. He sat down, trying to concentrate.

It was clear that he couldn't just put the coat away for the time being and say nothing about it. He must be prepared for an early search of the flat. In any case, it was just possible his witnesses might remember he had been wearing a grey coat; that the police might ask why he had changed it, and where the other one was. They would be sure to interest themselves in what a man was wearing when there was so much blood about.

He would have to pretend the blood was his – to be quite frank about it. Fortunately, he had already told his witnesses that he had hurt himself at the bombed house. Now he must really hurt himself. He could say he had put his hand on some broken glass . . . This wasn't going to be very pleasant.

He looked round the flat. The cut mustn't be too sharp or clean. Those scissors would probably do. He snatched them quickly from the drawer, chose a spot in the palm of his left hand, set his teeth, and jabbed. He had to do it twice, because the first jab wasn't hard enough, and it hurt like hell. Even then there wasn't much blood, but there was enough to account for a spot or two. He tied his handkerchief round the wound, feeling a little sick. Injuring oneself deliberately and brutally was much more unpleasant than having it happen by accident . . . He had another drink, and once more washed the scissors.

Now he must get the stains out of the coat. The police were devils these days with their scientific tests. They would certainly test a stain for its blood-group, and his own blood-group might be different from his uncle's. And hadn't he read somewhere about its being possible nowadays to identify exactly any particular specimen? He couldn't take any chances – all this was far out of his depth. He carried the coat to the wash-basin and soaked out the stain in cold water. It didn't really amount to much – it hardly coloured the water at all. After a few minutes, he felt satisfied that the coat was free of all trace. After he had squeezed out the water, and just to make quite sure, he splashed petrol from a bottle of lighter fuel over the place where the stain had been. Whatever was there now should defy analysis. His behaviour would no doubt seem a little odd, but there would be no positive evidence.

He hung the coat over the back of a chair to dry, after transferring the contents of the pockets to his black coat. He gave his shoes, his socks and his suit a meticulous examination, but found no more stains. He carefully cleaned out the bowl in which he had washed out the blood. He glanced round the flat – everything seemed in order. He opened the window to air the room.

He felt better now, though his hand still throbbed painfully. At least he could account for everything. He hurried down to the car and put the spanner back in the tool-box.

Now he must phone Welford Avenue. It would be only reasonable to do so, since it was nearly nine o'clock and he was practically an hour late. His uncle would have expected a call. Also, it would be a little easier to behave naturally at the house if he had first been told the news by telephone.

He stopped at a box just before the roundabout. It was an odd feeling, ringing that house where his uncle lay dead on the floor. It was Geoffrey who answered the call, with a low, curt, "Yes, who is it?"

Cross hastened to say his piece first. "Hello, Geoffrey," he said quickly, "this is Arthur. Isn't it a hell of a night? Listen, I'm sorry I'm so late, I've had an awful time in the fog, will you tell Uncle . . . What's that? . . . What do you say?"

He held the receiver a little away from his ear. The words that Geoffrey was saying were just a part of the working-out of the plan – they carried no human message. ". . . Bad news," the telephone-distorted voice was saying, ". . . very bad. Father's dead . . ." The receiver crackled. "Better get round quickly."

Cross took a deep breath. "Oh, Geoffrey! Oh, my God!" He hoped it was competently done. "I'll be over as soon as I can." He rang off.

The fog was really lifting a little now. Cross stopped once more on his way to Welford Avenue. Making sure that he was alone, he emptied the contents of the brown paper over a low wall into someone's front garden. He rolled the piece of paper up into a ball and threw it out into the street as he drove along. He had disposed of the last of the evidence.

The Avenue looked very different from when he had last seen it. There was a whole row of vehicles drawn up outside the house – Geoffrey's little Morris, and a couple of police cars, and an ambulance. One or two curious people, probably neighbours, were talking in low tones on the side of the road opposite the house. There was a police officer outside.

As Cross approached the gate, a girl came out of the house. Cross had no idea who she was. He just caught a glimpse of a pale, attractive face and chestnut hair under a kerchief, and she was off into the fog.

"Good evening, officer. I'm Arthur Cross."

"That's all right, sir – they're expecting you."

Cross walked up the path and rang. Another policeman opened the door. "Can I come in? – I'm Arthur Cross."

"Yes, sir – be careful, sir. Terrible business." He indicated a hunched-up pile on the floor in the passage, covered with a table-cloth. There was still a lot of blood around.

Cross was staring down at the body when Geoffrey came out of the lounge. He was grey and drawn. "Come in, Arthur – mind where you step. This is Superintendent Jackson of the local police. A Yard man is on his way."

"I don't understand," began Cross, looking bewildered. (How *did* people behave when they were told to step over a close relation lying in a pool of blood?) "You said he was dead, but—"

"Murder, Mr. Cross," said Jackson. "Better sit down. You don't look so well yourself." Jackson was a large florid man with a friendly expression.

"Have a drink," said Geoffrey, pouring whisky. "One for you, Superintendent? No?" He passed a glass to Cross and drained his own.

"I still don't understand," said Cross. "For heaven's sake, what are we all sitting around for? Why can't that – that ghastly mess be cleared up? Why isn't anybody *doing* anything?"

"Take it gently, Mr. Cross," said the Superintendent, soothingly. "Everything's being taken care of. The coroner's officer and the police surgeon have been and gone. Death was practically instantaneous. We've taken photographs and done all the routine jobs. Inspector James, from the Yard, will be here any moment to take over. Until he's had a look round, we can't move anything."

"What happened?" asked Cross.

"Some swine hit him on the head," said Geoffrey, very slowly and quietly. "Smashed his skull in." His fingers were working, his face was twisted with pain. "If I ever get my fingers on him—"

"Now, sir, easy does it . . ." said Jackson. "You'll only work yourself up again. We'll find the chap who did it, never fear."

"Who was the girl I met as I came in?" asked Cross, lighting a cigarette.

"Dr. Whitworth's daughter," said Geoffrey wearily. "Apparently someone rang up from here – it looks as though it must have been the murderer – and as the doctor was out she came round herself. She's a medical student. She . . . she made sure he was dead. She put the tablecloth over him, called the police, took charge. She was here, alone, when I arrived. She was a brick – she told me what had happened before she'd let me in at the door. She even insisted on making me a cup of tea." Geoffrey gave a mirthless laugh. He looked 'all in'.

"What time did you get here?" asked Cross.

"Just before half past eight. The police followed me in. What happened to you?"

"I got completely tied up in that damned fog. It's a long story. And I might have prevented this if I'd been on time! Listen, that must be the Inspector – I heard a car door slam."

There were noises without and the Inspector entered. He greeted Jackson with a friendly "How d'ye do, Super?"

"These gentlemen are the relatives," Jackson told the Inspector. "Geoffrey Hollison, the deceased's son; Arthur Cross, the deceased's nephew."

Inspector James nodded gravely. Like most Scotland Yard inspectors, he might just as easily have been anything else. He was broad, grizzled, fiftyish, with keen grey eyes under thick grey brows. He looked quite human.

"This must have been a very great shock to you," said James, taking off his overcoat. "Before we start all the unpleasantness, may I offer my sympathy?"

Geoffrey said: "Thanks, Inspector. I only hope you're successful in finding the man who did it."

"We'll do our best," said James. "If you'll excuse me a moment, I'll just take a look round. Everything as it was, Superintendent?"

"Pretty well, sir. I'll give you the details." And he went out with the Inspector, closing the door behind him.

"I still can't believe it," said Cross. "Fancy this happening to *us*! Who was it – a thief, do you think? Anything stolen?"

"No sign of anything," said Geoffrey indifferently. "Oh, God, it doesn't make sense – who would want to bump off the old man? He never did anyone any harm."

"Neither did I," said Cross, "when those chaps pinched my car." Geoffrey grunted.

Presently there were more sounds outside. Geoffrey put his head round the door. Two policemen were taking the body away on a stretcher; another was swabbing the floor with a cloth and a pail. In a few moments, the ambulance drove away to the mortuary, and James and the Superintendent came back into the lounge.

James sat down. "Well, gentlemen," he said, "it's a bad business. There's very little to go on at the moment. All we know is that someone called, killed Mr. Hollison with a blunt instrument, rang for help, and disappeared. There's no sign of any weapon, no useful finger-prints, nothing disturbed in the house."

"No prints on the telephone?" asked Cross.

The Inspector sighed. "There are confused prints all over the telephone, of course. They probably belong to everybody in the household, and to the young lady who called the police. There are also marks of gloves. They'll be the murderer's."

"I suppose gloves don't leave distinctive marks," said Cross.

"I'm afraid not," said the Inspector.

"What time did it happen?"

"According to Miss Whitworth," said the Inspector slowly, "she was rung just after eight. She found the door open, and the body in the hall. Mr. Hollison must have opened the door himself to the murderer, because the lock wasn't broken. Well, you'll have to leave it to me, gentlemen – we've only just begun our inquiries. Don't worry – we know the ropes. Now do you mind if I ask *you* a few questions?"

"Not in the least," said Geoffrey. "Go ahead."

"The usual question first, then. Did your father have any enemies? Can you tell me anything at all that would be likely to help me?"

"I'm sure he didn't," said Geoffrey. "He wasn't the sort to make enemies. He was the most kindly man I've ever known – sympathetic, generous, treated his workpeople well. I think everybody liked him."

"Is that your view, Mr. Cross?"

"I agree absolutely," said Cross. "As a matter of fact, in the six months or so I've been working with him since I was demobbed, I don't think I've ever heard him exchange a cross word with anyone."

"I understand you lived here with him, Mr. Hollison? And there's a housekeeper?"

"That's right," said Geoffrey; "Mrs. Armstrong – she'll be back soon. Thursday's her night out. It'll be a dreadful shock for her."

"So as far as you know," pursued the Inspector, "there was nothing in his life which could have accounted for this tragedy. You understand, I'm relying upon you to tell me if there is. No mysteries, no – complications, money, anything like that? No secrets?"

Geoffrey shook his head. "I'd help you if I could, Inspector, willingly, but his life was an open book – this last six months, anyway. I'm sure I'd have known if he'd had any worries. We were very close to each other. I'm positive there was nothing. He enjoyed life enormously. He was almost always cheerful, his health was good, he was absolutely normal in every way."

"No strange callers, ever? – nothing that seemed odd at the time?"

"Nothing!"

"Was he away from home at all?"

"Not recently. I believe in the war he occasionally went on short business trips but there was never anything unusual about them, as far as I know."

"No letters that upset him, Mr. Hollison? Nothing in his past life – domestically? Forgive me trespassing like this, but it has to be done."

"I can't help you, Inspector," said Geoffrey emphatically. "To the best of my knowledge, there was nothing at all. I've always understood that he got on excellently with my mother – he was very grieved when she died and he has treasured her memory. Frankly, I doubt if you could find anywhere a less complicated life."

"Well, that's that," said James. "It makes it all the more difficult for us. As you know, in these matters we always have to look for a motive. If a man has lived a tangled life, there are often all sorts of hidden motives. In this case . . . Anyway, let's get on. What about theft? The Superintendent tells me you had a look through the house at his suggestion. You're sure there was nothing missing?"

"Nothing of any significance, I'm sure," said Geoffrey, "or I'd have noticed. There are a few jewels of my mother's – he was keeping them in case I ever married – they're all intact in a dressing-case in his room. His bureau has not been disturbed, his clothes are all in order, everything seems just as it always was. As you can see for yourself, Inspector, this is a comfortable, but not a luxurious, house. My father didn't go in for *objets d'art* or anything like that. His main interests were his business and his boat – he's got a motor cruiser on the river, you know. He didn't collect anything – no valuable silver, no pictures. It's hardly conceivable he could have been knocked down for the money in his pocket?"

"He wasn't," said the Inspector. "There were several notes still in his pocket book."

"Another thing," said Geoffrey eagerly, "how would a thief, a complete stranger, dare to take the chance of finding him alone?"

"A stranger might have known the family habits, I suppose," said the Inspector, though without conviction. "He might have seen Mrs. Armstrong go off, and felt confident that the coast was clear."

"Pretty dangerous," said Cross, "considering Geoffrey and I were both on our way here."

"'Why would a stranger telephone a doctor directly he'd committed a murder?" said Geoffrey.

"Why would anyone, for that matter?" said the Inspector. There was a moment of silence. "And why would a complete stranger bother to wear gloves, unless of course he had a record already and knew that his finger-prints were at the Yard?"

"As far as I can see, Inspector," said Geoffrey suddenly, "this 'stranger' theory doesn't make any sense at all. I'm sure you don't believe in it."

"It's early days, Mr. Hollison," said the Inspector cautiously. "Tell me about Mrs. Armstrong."

"Good heavens," ejaculated Cross, "you surely don't suspect her?"

James looked at him severely. "Mr. Cross," he said, "don't please get the idea into your head that everyone I ask questions about is a suspect. I've got to know *everything* about this case. It'll be Mr. Hollison's turn soon – and yours. How long had Mrs. Armstrong been housekeeper here?"

"Oh, years and years," said Geoffrey. "Twenty-five years, I should think. She's a most respectable and admirable lady, I assure you. She came in answer to an advertisement after my mother died. She had been at a hospital or nursing home or something – anyway, a most respectable place. She has devoted herself to my father. She'll be dreadfully upset. Besides, she's been at her sister's all the evening – always does go there on Thursdays, it's a regular thing. She's bound to have a complete alibi."

"That's all right," said James. "I don't doubt it for a moment. What about this other young woman – what's her name – Miss Whitworth? The girl who was called in. Know anything about her, either of you?"

"Not I," said Cross. "I never saw her in my life until I met her going out tonight."

"Nor did I," said Geoffrey. "She seemed very charming and competent. I'm sure my father didn't know her. He may have known *of* her – Dr. Whitworth was his doctor, and no doubt they chatted. Not that Father needed much doctoring – it must be ages since Dr. Whitworth was here. Mrs. Armstrong would know more about that. Anyway, Inspector, it's ridiculous – this isn't a woman's crime."

The Inspector grunted non-committally. "There are women and women," he said. "I've not seen the young lady yet. She sounds as though she had her head screwed on tight."

Cross put in a word. "Didn't the position of the body tell you anything? I mean, was the blow struck from behind? I'm trying to visualize the scene. If it were a stranger . . ."

"It *couldn't* have been a stranger," said Geoffrey angrily.

". . . But if it were, Uncle would hardly have turned away from him. On the other hand, if it were somebody he knew well . . ."

"The blow," said the Inspector, "was struck from behind. It *looks* as though he invited somebody in. It's difficult to be sure." James pulled out a curly briar pipe and began to fill it. "There's one other thing – again I must ask you to forgive me for raising a rather sordid topic, but the sooner I know all the relevant details, the sooner I'll see the picture clear. Was your father a very wealthy man, Mr. Hollison?"

"I always gathered that he was, Inspector. There was nothing ostentatious about him, though – he didn't spend a great deal."

"No doubt that's why he was wealthy," said the Inspector dryly. "Of course, I shall be able to get details from his solicitor. You might give me the name of the firm before I go. Do you know who – er – inherits? I suppose you do."

Geoffrey looked worn out. "You're bound to find out, Inspector, anyway, so I may as well tell you that – as far as we know – we both inherit. Arthur and I. We don't know the proportions, but my father made a new will just after we got back to England, and he told us he was dividing his estate between us. He gave us to understand that there'd be plenty for both of us. Personally, I don't give a damn, but there it is."

"Thank you for being so frank," said James. "I may tell you, in return, that we never jump to rash conclusions. Somebody always inherits. Anything to add, Mr. Cross?"

"Nothing," said Cross. He had always known that this financial motive would stand out bleakly in an otherwise motiveless desert. And so it did, whatever the Inspector might say.

"Right. Now, if you don't mind, I should like to know just what you two gentlemen were doing throughout the evening. You don't have to tell me, of course, if you don't want to, but – well, you're not under suspicion so I'm not giving you any formal warning."

"I don't like the way you put it, all the same, Inspector," said Cross.

"If you can think of a pleasanter way of putting it, Mr. Cross," said the Inspector, mildly, "just re-phrase the question to suit yourself."

"That's all right," said Cross.

James turned to Geoffrey. "Well, Mr. Hollison, I gathered from the Super here that you were lecturing at the Naval College. Can you tell me your movements briefly?"

"Very briefly," said Geoffrey. "I dined in the Mess at seven, and I left at seven-thirty. That's a good deal earlier than I usually leave, but I knew I should be delayed in the fog and the old car wasn't running too well. I wanted to get home."

"You actually got home just before eight-thirty – almost an hour. Does it usually take so long?"

"No, Inspector – I can usually do it in half an hour. But you know what the fog was like – and the engine let me down. I had to stop under a lamp and clean the carburettor." His tone was a little defiant.

"Let me look at your hands," said the Inspector sharply.

Geoffrey, taken aback, held out his large strong hands, palms upwards. Then he smiled wanly. "I'm afraid I had too much on my mind to wash my hands. You're smart, Inspector."

"Routine, Mr. Hollison – please remember that this is all routine, all of it. As a matter of fact, you could quite easily have made your hands dirty if you had wanted to – it wouldn't have taken you a moment. But if you *had* washed – well, I should have been rather surprised. Let's get back to your movements. You say you took an hour to do what would normally have been a half-hour journey, because of the fog and your car. Did you speak to anybody on the journey? Can you think of a single incident which would – well, corroborate your account. I wonder if anyone saw you tinkering?"

Geoffrey shrugged. "In the fog? Perhaps, but *I* didn't see *them*. I didn't stop for petrol anywhere. I didn't talk to anyone. Surely, Inspector, you don't think *I* killed my father?"

James threw up his hands. "Mr. Hollison," he said. "I don't think *anything*. My mind is practically a blank. All I want is information. I know you've had a fearful shock tonight, but please refrain from drawing these dramatic conclusions. Now where were we?"

"You were asking me for corroboration," said Geoffrey.

"Well, we'll leave that for the time being. If you think of

anything, let me know. Now, tell me, do you recognize this paper?"
He held out the single blood-stained sheet so that Geoffrey could
inspect it.

Geoffrey stared at it, puzzled. "How did it get blood on it?" he
asked. "What *is* this, Inspector?"

"I'm asking *you*."

"It's a page of notes for my lecture at the College today. The
second half of the course started today – I was at home this
morning preparing the first lecture. Actually, those notes are about
a particular operation I was engaged on in the Pacific – Okinawa.
It's all to do with the direction of fighter planes by radar from
carriers. Do you want me to go into details?"

"Heaven forbid!" said James. "I take it you had to do without
this page of notes today – or did you? I want the truth, Mr. Hollison,
quickly and plainly. Did you or didn't you?"

"Of course I had to do without them," said Geoffrey. "Look,
Inspector, I was working this morning over there by the telephone,
where the Superintendent is sitting. I had quite a lot of papers – a
whole wad of notes, and one or two maps – all spread out. When
I'd finished, I thought I collected all the notes together but I must
have left one sheet – this one – with some other papers on the
telephone table."

"I wonder if Mrs. Armstrong would have seen it?" said the
Inspector.

"You can ask her, but I doubt it. The girl had already done this
room before I settled down. I don't suppose anyone would come
in again."

"When did you miss this page?"

"When I was actually lecturing. I turned the previous page over,
quite happily, and came to the gap."

"What did you do – stumble, break down?"

"I didn't burst into tears, if that's what you mean! I don't know whether I gave any sign or not – I tried to remember what was on the paper, and skipped a few details – perhaps someone noticed. You'd better go along to the College and conduct an examination, Inspector."

"Perhaps I will," said James. "You see, it's rather important. This paper was found – by me – underneath the body. If you left it at home this morning it could hardly have got there without someone putting it there deliberately – perhaps to get you into trouble. It's often done, I believe – though usually it doesn't get the murderer anywhere, except into a mess. On the other hand, if you didn't leave it at home, if you used it for the lecture, and brought it back with you at about eight o'clock – as on a normal day you could have done – it's just conceivable that you could have dropped it in the hall under your father's body – before he fell . . . Now *don't* say it, Mr. Hollison . . . this is all supposition and I'm making no accusations of any sort. We'll go into the matter further." The Inspector wiped his forehead with a large white handkerchief. "Now, Mr. Cross, it's your turn. Just an outline, if you don't mind."

Cross, who had listened tensely to the conversation between Geoffrey and the Inspector, now sat back in his easy chair quite composed. "Well, Inspector, I left my flat at about a quarter past seven on my way here. It's become a regular thing for the three of us to get together on Thursday evenings. You know what the fog was like. I got lost at the roundabout – the Super knows where it is. Talk about the wide open spaces! I stopped the car, and thought I'd see if some pedestrian could put me on the right turning for Welford Avenue. Then a couple of people drifted by – they were lost too – they wanted to go to Hailey Crescent, which was more or less my way."

The Inspector looked at the Superintendent, and the Superintendent nodded to show that the story made sense so far.

"So we all three got lost together!" Cross went on. "We had a
terrible time. Just after eight, we found ourselves at a place called
Hamley Avenue. Miles off the route. I stopped and went into a
house to ask the way, but it was a bombed house. I didn't realize
it at first – I knocked and called 'Anyone at home?' and then I
stumbled over something and put my hand out to save myself and
jabbed it on to some broken glass. It wasn't funny." He half held
out his hand, still wrapped in a handkerchief.

"Yes, I saw you'd cut yourself," said the Inspector sympathetically.
"Better let me have a look." Cross unwrapped the handkerchief,
and the Inspector tut-tutted. "Couple of nasty jabs, Mr. Cross.
Better put some iodine on. There's all sorts of muck about in these
bombed houses . . . I suppose you didn't have a torch?"

"I'd left it in the car," said Cross. "Anyway, the fog was so thick
it wouldn't have been much use. After that, we stooged around a
bit and then I began to recognize the road and we got back to the
roundabout and finally found Hailey Crescent. I dropped my
passengers – very late for their dinner date, I'm afraid, but it couldn't
be helped. I rang up here to explain why I was so late, heard the
news from Geoffrey, and came right on as fast as I could. I got here
– oh, about nine, I suppose. And that's all."

"Most lucid," said James. "So, in fact, two people were with you
all the time from about seven-thirty until about eight-thirty. Do
you know who they were?"

Cross smiled ruefully. He was doing nicely. "I'm afraid I don't,
Inspector. Now if I'd known they'd be wanted as witnesses . . . I
know the man was called Charles – he was a University type,
something in the Foreign Office, I imagine. Oh yes, of course, I
know where they were going to spend the evening. They were

dining with Sir John Lutimer – he'll be able to tell you who they were. What's more, Inspector, in case you want to hear their story, they're leaving by plane for South America tomorrow morning – so the chap said."

"Ah!" said the Inspector, "I'm glad you told me. You'd better get on to them right away, Super. Tell them I'm coming round, and ask them to be so good as to wait. I'll be there in fifteen minutes, tell them." He stood up.

"Well, gentlemen, thanks for your help. I think that's enough for now. I shall be on the job again early tomorrow, and perhaps we'll have got a little further by then. You'll be available, of course, in case you're wanted?"

"You'll find me at the Works or at my flat," said Cross. "Or shall I stick around here tonight, Geoffrey? You look used up, and someone's got to break the news to Mrs. Armstrong."

"Thanks, Arthur," said Geoffrey. "I'd be glad. Good night, Inspector. Good night, Superintendent."

As the car moved off, he leaned heavily against the front door. "Oh, God!" he said. "What a mess!"

"Better get to bed," said Arthur.

In the car, the Inspector was pulling viciously at his pipe. "It looks like being a tough case, Super," he said. "A really nasty case. That young fellow is a bit too bright for my liking."

"Which young fellow?" asked the Superintendent.

"The one with all the answers," said James.

CHAPTER VII

Soon after ten o'clock the next morning, Inspector James walked into the Superintendent's office and helped himself to a chair. He looked fresh and cheerful, as though in spite of everything he had had a thoroughly good night's sleep.

"Well, Super," he began brightly, "what do you make of it all?"

Superintendent Jackson smiled his heavy good-natured smile. He was a slow-moving commonsense man, wary in his replies. He had progressed in the Force chiefly by not making mistakes. He said: "I don't make much of it, I'm afraid. It's one of the most cold-blooded, brutal murders I've ever been mixed up in, I know that – but there's not much evidence pointing to anyone, is there?"

"Not a jot, as far as I can see," said James, lighting his pipe and settling himself for a nice comfy talk. "Somebody's been very clever, and is probably hugging himself with delight at this very moment. What about the loose ends, Super? Did you get them cleared up?"

"Mostly," said Jackson. "I've been on the job myself since eight o'clock this morning. We called at the houses each side of Hollison's and across the street. A stockbroker lives at number twelve – a man named Forsythe. He was having dinner at eight o'clock last night – he *thinks* he may have heard a knock next door, but he couldn't be positive."

"Bright chap," said James.

"Yes," said the Superintendent. "I asked him about other noises – cars and so on – but he wasn't any use. At all the other houses I drew a complete blank. There was someone in all of them last night, but no one heard a sound that meant anything. An old lady at number fourteen said she heard someone singing a hymn in the street about six, but I gather she's nuts and converses with Mars in her spare time. Two people said they heard cars in the road during the evening, but they couldn't remember when – and why should they? I've got a man going through the rest of the houses in the road, and also those that back on to Hollison's in the doctor's road, but it's pretty hopeless. That fog muffled everything – thank heaven it's cleared now."

"There's plenty still hanging around the case," said James. "Plenty! Anyway, I didn't expect much from the neighbours. What about the young lady? Did you manage to squeeze anything out of her – any spicy bits of gossip about Hollison?"

The Superintendent grinned. "I could've squeezed her, all right! She's a peach, Inspector. If I hadn't been a respectable family man . . ."

"Tut, tut," said James. "I ought to have gone myself. Anyway, what did she have to say?"

"Nothing. Except what we know. She's a medical student at the South London – third year. Following in father's footsteps, and very keen. She said she'd seen Hollison once or twice but never spoken to him. Her father thought a lot of him – pillar of society and all that. First thing she knew about last night's affair was the phone going and a voice squeaking into the receiver that help was wanted. She hasn't any doubt it was a man. Apparently he said – here, I've got it down somewhere – oh yes, he said, 'There's been a horrible accident at Charles Hollison's house,' and he gave the address, 'quite near you,' he said. Then he said, 'For heaven's sake send round right away.' That's as near as she could remember anyhow. She's a good witness – very cool and sensible. She told the chap the doc wasn't in, but that she'd look after it for him. It seems she thought it would be a fine opportunity to be in first on a real case and get some practice, so she shoved a coat on and a scarf over her head and rushed round on foot to the scene of the accident."

"Nasty moment for her when she pushed the door open," said James. "I bet she wished she'd left it to daddy!"

"Not a bit of it, Inspector. She said it was horrible, of course, and she felt a bit queer for a minute, but she got down and felt the old boy's pulse, which wasn't there, and she saw right away that there wasn't anything could be done for him, which was true enough. So she didn't bother to call another doctor – she just rang the station. I gather she said, 'There's a man been murdered at 12A Welford Avenue,' which was so obvious it stuck out a mile. We sent Macpherson along right away and I followed in a second car. Mac examined the corpse. He said Hollison hadn't been dead more than twenty minutes or so. Miss Whitworth said, 'That's right,' and got a flea in her ear for her pains."

The Inspector grinned. "I'd like to meet that young woman some time. You don't think she could have done it?"

"What, her?" said the Superintendent. "Don't be funny, Inspector. She's only about five foot five, and Hollison was a big chap. If she'd lashed out at him, she'd have hit the back of his neck, not his head. In any case, she'd never have had the strength to smash his skull in like that."

"You've fallen for her," said the Inspector. "Your opinion is worthless."

"Oh, come, Inspector . . ." For a moment Jackson was open-mouthed. Then he smiled a bit sheepishly. "I thought for a moment you were serious."

"Well," said James, thoughtfully, "she *is* a bit small, of course. But the old boy might have been kissing her feet! Suppose they'd been having an affair, secretly, and she got angry with him because he wouldn't fork out enough dough. Crime of passion! After all, we've only her word for it that there was any telephone call at all. She could easily have found out the domestic arrangements and slipped round at a suitable moment."

"You don't believe all that, Inspector?" Jackson was horrified.

"No," said James. "I agree with you – she's too small and not strong enough. Now tell me, I suppose there's no doubt about the time of death. I mean, if it had been earlier – say, soon after Hollison had come in – it might make a difference to a lot of things. Forget the telephone call for a moment – that could have been made a couple of hours after the murder. Is the medical evidence watertight?"

"Better ask Mac yourself," said Jackson. "I daren't. He was positive. So was she. The poor old chap had barely stopped twitching."

"You put things very crudely," said the Inspector. "All right, we'll have to accept the time of death as fixed. Eight o'clock, as near as makes no odds. Now what about this chap's voice – the one who telephoned? Any chance of Miss Whitworth helping us there?"

"I pressed her on that, Inspector. She said it was high and squeaky – that it sounded disguised. She thought that out afterwards, of course, but she thought it sounded funny at the time. 'Funny?' I said to her. 'What do you mean – a bit like this?' and then I said something in a high voice myself. She said, 'Yes, very much like that.'"

"I wish you'd do it again, Jackson," said James earnestly.

"I won't, sir – you keep on making fun of me. It was all in the line of duty. I shouldn't think if you brought the criminal face to face with her and told him to speak, she'd be able to say for a certainty one way or the other. She doesn't think so either."

"This case is all dead ends," said James. "What about Mrs. Armstrong?"

"Poor old girl, she was knocked all of a heap, in spite of having been a matron or something. Mr. Cross broke the news to her when she came in last night at ten. She gave an awful shriek and they had to pour brandy down her throat. She's calmed down this morning, but she looks pretty ill and worried to death. She must have been fond of the old boy. After all, a quarter of a century is quite a while, and she'd looked after him like a mother."

"You did say like a mother?"

"Inspector, I'm surprised at you. You're full of nasty suggestions this morning. You should see her face! You can't tell where her neck stops and her chin starts. Just the sort of woman to make a good reliable housekeeper."

James guffawed. "Super," he said, "you're a man after my own heart. We're going to work well together. So she couldn't help at all?"

"She hadn't a clue, sir. Just went out as she always does on Thursdays, and was back quite punctual. I sent a man over to Ealing first thing this morning to check up with Mrs. Armstrong's sister and husband. She was there, all right – all the time. I'll show you the report."

"There are too many good alibis in this case," said James. "Damn it, somebody must have done it. *And* no stranger. We can rule that out. Can you imagine any casual passer-by with an itch for money knocking at a door, sloshing an old gentleman, reporting the murder, and going off without pinching anything? Of course not. It was somebody he knew – somebody with a personal motive. The position of that blow told its tale as clearly as if we'd seen it happen. Hollison came to the door, recognized his visitor, and got hit from behind as he turned to lead the way in. He wouldn't have done that with a stranger – or even with an ordinary guest. He'd have closed the front door behind them and let them go ahead.

From the evidence of that blow, I would say this was somebody he was expecting and somebody he knew so well that he didn't have to stand on any ceremony with them. A child could think that one out. Now there may be something in Hollison's life that we're in the dark about. He may have been expecting a man he knew intimately – a chap we know nothing about. But I don't believe it. He'd have had to tell his son or his nephew. In that case, we're left with young Hollison and Cross as 'possibles'."

"You saw for yourself, Inspector, Geoffrey Hollison hasn't got an alibi. If he'd taken some risks driving, he could just about have made it by eight. I admit that he's a nice-looking young fellow, good type, distinguished record and all that – but he comes into a rare lot of money now, by all accounts. Plenty of motive there – and about the only motive there is in this case. He could have fixed it, and gone away again, and come back at the right moment with his story of engine trouble and grease all over his hands."

"And a murder on his conscience? He didn't strike me that way."

"Nor me – as I said, Inspector. But, good lord, you know they often don't look what they are."

"I know." The Inspector puffed thoughtfully. "I agree his story might just as easily be false as true. Just as easily."

"There were those notes . . ." said Jackson.

"Well, now, look at those notes. Suppose he hadn't left that paper on the telephone table – suppose he'd had it with him all day and dropped it accidentally in the hall himself. Why should he? The notes would be in his pocket, a sheaf of them. There was no struggle – the old boy dropped like a log. Why should one page of notes get detached and fall under the body? I just can't see it happening. I don't think I've ever seen a phonier bit of evidence."

"You think somebody planted them there?"

"I should think so, though it was a pretty dumb thing to do. Maybe they got there by accident during the afternoon. Does Mrs. Armstrong know anything about them – or the girl?"

"Nothing at all – I asked specially."

"Well, I suppose I'll have to go along to the College and ask a few questions there. I don't relish the job. There's another thing, Superintendent, about Geoffrey Hollison. Just supposing for a moment he did it – why would he telephone for the doctor? What was the point?"

Jackson was silent. Finally he said: "Blowed if I know. It beats me, that does."

"Why should anyone do that?" the Inspector went on. "What possible purpose could it serve? Hollison was dead, no doctor was needed, and sticking around in the house or near it was a big risk for the murderer. It must have cost him valuable minutes, when all he wanted to do was to get away. He took that risk because he wanted to establish the time of death and disguised his voice because he was known in these parts. There couldn't be any other reason to make sense, not that I can think of, anyway. And you know why murderers so often like to get the time of death fixed?"

"Sure – alibi."

"As you say, Super – it's routine. These things mostly follow a pattern. But you don't try to fix a time of death if you haven't *got* an alibi. That would be just silly. And young Geoffrey Hollison hasn't got one. But Mr. Cross has."

"What about Cross, Inspector? Does his alibi stand up?"

"It stands up so straight, Superintendent, it might have been trained in the Guards! Either he didn't have a thing to do with it, or it's the finest alibi I've ever come across in all my life. Like to hear my tale of woe?"

"Yes," said Jackson, all ears.

"Well, you know I was at Sir John Lutimer's place. They weren't too pleased to see me, any of them, and I can't blame them. There was quite a party on. Lutimer is a big shot in the Foreign Office, and he was giving a fatherly farewell to two nice young people who left this morning – at least I think they left – for Buenos Aires ... The man was Charles Everton, and he's going out with his wife to take up his duties as First Secretary at the Embassy. By and large, he's about the most convincing witness you could imagine. So's his wife. They're clear-headed, quiet, and sure of themselves."

The Inspector leaned forward. "They both confirmed everything that Arthur Cross told us, and a lot more besides. They contacted him at the roundabout – it was they who approached him. They were lost, and he said he was. He said he was going to his uncle's at Welford Avenue and they said they were going to Hailey Crescent. He wasn't eager about taking them; just kind of browned off with the fog and pretty hopeless about finding anything, but ready for a try. They exchanged a few polite words in the car, with Cross feeling his way and nobody seeing very much, and then they stopped and Cross said he was lost. They all took a peek out of the car, helped by Cross's torch, and they were in Hamley Avenue, just as Cross said. I checked up very carefully and there's no doubt about it. Everton read the name, and his wife, too. I said, 'Are you prepared to swear to that name?' and Everton said, 'My dear Inspector, I'd swear to that before God Almighty himself,' and his wife said, 'Really, darling!' But she was just as emphatic – it was his language she didn't quite like. I said, 'What time was it roughly?' and Everton said, 'It was just about eight o'clock.' I said, 'How do you know?' and he said, 'We were due here for dinner at eight,' and old Lutimer grinned. Everton said, 'I kept on looking at my watch every few minutes – you know how you do if time is moving quickly and you're standing still and wanting to get somewhere. So if you're trying to pin something on our friendly driver, Inspector, don't pin it for eight o'clock!"

The Inspector wiped his forehead, which had got rather damp. "Then I asked Everton about the bombed house. He said he couldn't see a thing himself, but that it was apparently a few yards down from the corner of the street and that Cross was gone about five minutes. He said that he and his wife were talking Foreign Office shop and hadn't got particularly impatient. They both heard a loud knock and that was all. Then Cross came back in a frightful temper, saying he'd fallen and hurt himself. It was dark and they couldn't see whether he had or not. Everton said: 'I should think it was more than probable, Inspector. It wouldn't have surprised me if he'd said he'd broken his neck.' That young man will go far in his profession – he has plenty of confidence. After that they drove away, stooged around hopefully just as Cross said, and finally reached Lutimer's. I've got a note of all the times and they all make sense."

The Superintendent gave a low whistle. "That's certainly an alibi!"

"It's unbreakable, Jackson – absolutely unbreakable. I've taken sworn statements from the Evertons – my word, I was unpopular last night, I can tell you. Those statements are pure gold for Cross. He was undoubtedly at Hamley Avenue at eight o'clock last night, and in fog it's a good half-hour's run from Welford Avenue. So he couldn't have killed his uncle, and that's that."

"It's a pity," said Jackson.

"What's a pity?"

"That he couldn't have killed his uncle. I don't much like Mr. Cross."

"A most unprofessional remark," said the Inspector severely. "Are we going to hang a man because you don't like him? Come to that, I don't like him either. He's too smooth. His story's too good. But there it is – he's not a suspect – he's ruled out. And yet—"

"What's on your mind, sir?" Jackson made an excellent Watson.

"At eight o'clock this morning," said James, "I called at Welford Avenue and asked Cross if he'd mind going over to his flat with me, so that I could have a look round. He didn't exactly take to the idea – in fact he was very huffy – and of course I said he needn't if he didn't want to. Naturally, he came along with the best grace he could, grumbling about a bad night and early hours and business going to pot. We went up to his flat, and there was a distinct smell of petrol. I said, 'You've been wasting your coupons, Mr. Cross,' and he smiled sourly and said, 'It's my coat, Inspector. I got some blood on it from my hand last night and called back on my way to my uncle's so that I could clean it off."

"Good lord," said the Superintendent.

"That's what I thought. I said, 'You were mighty quick doing that, weren't you – and why didn't you tell me you'd been back here last night?' He said it hadn't seemed important. I said, 'In a case like this everything's important and you ought to know that' – very severely. He looked ashamed of himself and said he was sorry. He said he'd been afraid the stains would stick if he didn't get them out right away, and that it was his best coat. He said he'd used water on them first and then petrol."

"Pretty fishy," said Jackson.

"Fishy? It stinks to heaven! I said, 'Did you come back here because of the stains or find them when you got here?' He said he came back because he'd hurt himself and needed a wash and a drink, and that he'd found them after he'd got home. Imagine it – here he was, nearly an hour late for an appointment, having a sort of private wash-day in his room just because of a couple of spots of blood!"

"I suppose we'll never know now whether it was his blood or not," said Jackson gloomily.

"I took the coat away on the offchance, but frankly I don't think there's a hope. That wasn't the only funny thing at the flat. His window was open a good eighteen inches – sash window. I said, 'Do you usually leave your window like that on foggy nights?' He said he was trying to get rid of the smell of petrol. Then I saw that the grate was full of ashes. I said, 'What have you been burning here?' He said, 'Midnight oil, Inspector.' I told him not to be funny and he said, 'Inspector, I've been burning papers. As far as I know, it's not a crime, but you're welcome to the ashes.'"

"And what did you do?" asked Jackson.

"Super," said the Inspector, "I'm a conscientious man. I don't like leaving anything to chance. I took a sample of those ashes, though I felt pretty foolish. Cross just stood there with a sneer on his face. If you ask me, he's a damned nasty piece of work!" And the Inspector, who was more annoyed than he ever liked to be, blew his nose violently.

"So now where are we?" he went on more slowly. "Cross has been behaving in a rather peculiar way – I would say definitely a suspicious way – but that alibi can't be got round. He wasn't there, so he didn't do it. So who did? Who was the man who was friends with Hollison, who socked him for a reason we don't know, at a time which showed he knew all about the domestic arrangements, who telephoned to establish an alibi, who disguised his voice because it was pretty well known around here, and who then vanished into thin air? Who?" And Inspector James thumped the Superintendent's desk.

"Search me, Inspector. I haven't an idea."

"Neither have I," said the Inspector, "but we'll find him. It's just routine – we'll stick at it and we'll find him."

CHAPTER VIII

About the same time that the Inspector was calling on the Super-intendent, there was a knock at the door of the Hollison house in Welford Avenue, and when Mrs. Armstrong went to see who it was she found a young woman on the doorstep.

"Good morning," said the visitor. "I'm Pamela Whitworth. I wondered if there was anything I could do for you."

Mrs. Armstrong, tight-lipped and outwardly composed again after the shock of the night, looked Miss Whitworth up and down carefully, but could find nothing to disapprove of.

"It's very kind of you," she said. "Mr. Geoffrey's in – I daresay he'll be glad to see you. He needs somebody to take him out of himself. Won't you come in?"

"Thanks," said Pamela.

"He's all right, of course – so far as anyone can be. It'll take us all some time to get over that horror. He was talking about you only a few minutes ago. He's very grateful for what you did."

"I'm afraid there wasn't much I *could* do," said Pamela. "You're sure I can't get you anything – take any messages? You must be terribly worried and busy, and I don't have to go to the hospital today."

Mrs. Armstrong smiled and shook her head. "Whatever has to be done, it'll do me good to do," she said finally. "If you can cheer Mr. Geoffrey up a bit you'll be doing us all a good turn."

Geoffrey came to the door of the lounge, looked out and said: "Hello, there. I thought it was you." He held out his hand. "Come on in. It's nice to see you." There were shadows under his eyes, and he was grave and subdued. Pamela felt deeply sorry for him.

"Don't hesitate to throw me out when you want to," she said, loosening her coat. "I expect you have a lot to do."

"As a matter of fact," said Geoffrey, "I was just thinking how quiet it was. I thought I'd better stick around today, in case the Inspector wanted me, but so far nobody's even telephoned. After last night's rumpus, the silence was getting a little unnerving. I say, do take your coat off – you look as though you're just going. Or are you in a hurry?"

"Not a bit," said Pamela.

He took the coat, folded it inside out and placed it carefully over the arm of a chair.

"I think it was spendid the way you took charge last night," he said. "I wanted to thank you. I'm afraid I was very offhand at the time – everything happened in such a rush and muddle. Cigarette?"

"Thanks," said Pamela. "What about you?"

He produced his pipe and sank into an easy chair opposite her. For the first time he really looked at her carefully. There was no doubt about it – she was quite lovely. Usually he found redheads hopelessly disappointing – they were marvellous from a back view, and then when they turned round they had thin pink-and-white complexions and plain features. This girl was quite different. Her hair was a deep Titian, loose to her shoulders; her complexion was creamy and her eyes were a warm brown. He had never seen anyone like her before.

He suddenly realized he was gaping, and smiled. "Sorry," he said, "that was very rude. The fact is – forgive my awful nerve – you're very good to look at. Really, quite a tonic! You'll have to be careful not to get your patients into trouble when you start doctoring. That's what you're going to do, isn't it?"

"That's the plan," said Pamela. "I've another two years to do yet before I qualify. It's rather an expense for Daddy, but he's keen about it, too."

"You like it?"

"It's fascinating. Very hard work, of course, but never dull. I like the theatre work. Watching, I mean – naturally I don't do it myself yet. But I'd like to be a surgeon. We've got some very good ones – women. After all, you don't need the build of a coal-heaver to remove an appendix, and I've a very cool head."

"You certainly have," said Geoffrey. "Of course, you don't *look* like a surgeon. You never *would* look like a surgeon. I don't know that I'm in favour of women doing jobs like that."

"Oh, you're just old-fashioned. When a patient's really ill, he doesn't care whether it's a man or a woman who operates. The more pain, the fewer the prejudices. Anyway, I beat a lot of the men in the Third Year lists. We'll see."

There was silence for a moment. Then Geoffrey said: "I've been thinking about last night. It's been a hideous business, but I was very glad that you thought my father died at once."

"There's no question at all about it. He couldn't possibly have known what happened."

"It's a great relief. I couldn't bear to think of the old boy dying there in pain and God knows what agony of mind. We've always been pretty good friends, you know. I shall miss him a lot."

Pamela nodded.

"Of course, we've not seen much of each other lately, because of the war, but he used to write regularly and we kept pretty close. The damnably tragic thing is that it should happen now, just when the war was over and he was beginning to enjoy life again. He was so proud and happy when Arthur and I came back – he looked good for ten or twenty years, he really did. But why should I worry you with my troubles?"

"Please go on," said Pamela. "It'll do you good to talk."

Geoffrey couldn't help smiling. "You sound terribly professional," he said. "But, as a matter of fact, it probably will. To you, anyway. No, the thing was he didn't act like an old man – he was interested in things. He was a fine sailor, you know, in his time. You wouldn't have thought it, seeing him cruising about the river in *Truant* – that's a boat he had on the river. All engine, no sail. But before the war he had a cutter, about ten tons, and he and I used to have wonderful fun round the coasts. I think he knew every creek from the Thames right up to Yarmouth – and they take some knowing. He really loved the sea, and that's how I came to love it. We had a few narrow escapes – you can't help that – but he really knew his stuff. I thought he'd live to a ripe old age and now—Oh, it doesn't seem right! A bloody end like that!"

"I know," said Pamela softly. "It's the way it happened that's shocked you so much. It's far worse for you than for him. You should see some of the old people who come in to us and die slowly after hopeless operations. He might have been like that. But I know it's no good talking that way. . . ."

Geoffrey re-lit his pipe. "Well," he said, "it's all over now. All except the damned inquest and the police inquiry and all the worry about who on earth could have done it. Lord knows what'll happen to the business. Have you met my cousin Arthur Cross, by the way?"

"I think I may have passed him as I went out last night. I didn't speak to him. How has he taken it?"

"He doesn't show his feelings much. Naturally, Father didn't mean as much to him. He's an odd chap – he was taken prisoner early in the war and had a bad time. It changed him a good deal. I expect you'll meet him. He's done very well in the business – probably it would be best if he took it over. I was going into it myself – the old man was very keen – but now—"

"Can't you go on being a sailor?"

"I'm too old for peacetime. Just passing on what I know and then passing out. The Navy likes to get 'em young – thirteen, isn't it? – and train them up. I say, did the police contact you today?"

"Oh, yes, I had a session with the Superintendent over breakfast. He was interested in the man who telephoned, but I couldn't help him much."

"Well, I suppose it's their job, not ours. I can't see a glimmer of light myself. Oh, must you go?"

"I think I ought to," said Pamela. "I've got to go and queue. That's what comes of having a free day."

"It's been so nice," said Geoffrey, helping her on with her coat. "Bit grim for you, but very kind. I must really stop feeling sorry for myself. Look, I suppose you're not free for dinner tonight?"

"I could be," said Pamela.

Geoffrey brightened at once. "Really? I say, that's marvellous. You'll probably save me from getting quietly drunk. Let's go up to town – I know one or two cosy places. We can drive up in the old Morris, if you don't mind. Suppose I pick you up at seven?"

"Lovely," said Pamela. Geoffrey went with her to the gate and stood watching her as she walked briskly down the road.

Early that afternoon Geoffrey rang the Superintendent's office.

"This is Geoffrey Hollison," he said. "Any news?"

"The Inspector's on his way round now, I think," said Jackson. "How are you feeling, sir?"

"Not too bad, thanks. Yes, you're right – his car's just stopped. Bye." He went into the hall and let the Inspector in.

"Good afternoon, Mr. Hollison," said James, in reply to Geoffrey's greeting. "I hope you'll forgive me for troubling you again."

"Forgive you! I've been waiting for you. Nobody tells me anything. Even Miss Whitworth knows more than I do."

"Ah – Miss Whitworth's been calling, has she? Nice girl. The Superintendent has quite lost his head."

"It wouldn't be hard," said Geoffrey. "Well, what's your news, Inspector – if any?"

"The inquest will be on Monday," said James. "You'll be there, of course – I've rung Mr. Cross and told him. We shall want Mrs. Armstrong as well, and Miss Whitworth."

Geoffrey nodded. "You haven't . . . you don't know yet who did it?"

"I'm afraid not, sir. The trouble is that if we rule out the possibility of a complete stranger being responsible – as we must – there are very few people in this case."

"I know. I lay awake last night doing mental arithmetic. Unless there's a completely dark horse somewhere you could count your 'possibles' on two or three fingers."

"Two," said James. "But there's no evidence."

"There's a first-class motive, Inspector. You were frank enough yesterday, and I'm not blind. Who in the whole world benefited by my father's death? Myself and Arthur. But Arthur couldn't have done it. Do you think *I* did – now that you've had a night to reflect on the situation?"

The Inspector smoked stolidly. Presently he said: "I went over to the College this morning, Mr. Hollison. About those notes."

Geoffrey nodded. "I don't suppose you've made me very popular there, but it couldn't be helped."

"I don't know," said the Inspector; "I don't think you'll find your reputation's suffered. I called on the Director of the School."

"I'm sure he was most helpful."

"Yes, he was. He – er – he said some nice things about you. Not evidence, of course. No use in a court, but still quite helpful. He said he hadn't heard your lecture yesterday, but that as it was nearly lunch-time and the morning session was over we'd go and have a drink in the wardroom and talk to the chaps who had heard it."

Geoffrey grinned. "I bet they did you well."

"They were most hospitable. Important people, too – captains, commanders, lieutenant-commanders – I've never seen so much gold braid all at once. It took quite a while to get around to the subject of your lecture. Anyway, in the end I said: 'Well, gentlemen, I understand you were all at a lecture given by Lieutenant-Commander Geoffrey Hollison yesterday afternoon. There's just one question I want to ask you. Did the lecture seem to go quite smoothly, or was there a break in the continuity at any point?'"

"Well," said Geoffrey, "what did they say?"

"One of them, Mr. Hollison, said your lectures never go smoothly. Another said, 'What was the fellow talking about yesterday? – dashed if I can remember.' A third – an American commander, very nice fellow – said, 'Have another drink, Inspector.'"

"Damn!" said Geoffrey. "I wish I'd been there."

"I thought you'd feel like that. I said to them: 'Gentlemen, Mr. Hollison's life may be in some danger. If you can answer my question, you will probably help him.'"

"God!" said Geoffrey softly.

"There was a dead silence – it's a wonderful building, that – very quiet. Then a young lieutenant said: 'I don't know what you're getting at, Inspector, but *if* you're serious, I was up near the front and at one point he seemed to have lost something. It wasn't very obvious but I saw him shuffling through his notes. Is that what you mean?' I said: 'That's exactly what I mean and I'm very grateful to you. Mr. Hollison will be giving his lecture next week as usual.'"

Geoffrey bit hard on the stem of his pipe. "You are a damn fool, Inspector, why the devil couldn't you tell me that in the first place?"

"Just routine, Mr. Hollison – my routine. Anyway, I think that disposes of the notes as far as you're concerned. I should think it's a thousand to one that the murderer put the notes under the body just to make things more difficult. But he must have known the significance of them."

"Nobody could have known – except my father – and Arthur."

"And we know that Mr. Cross didn't do it. Of course, if we were willing to – what shall I say? – enter the realms of fantasy we should have to admit that you could have left the notes at home, and still have put them under the body as a sort of double bluff in the evening – or picked them up from the telephone and then dropped them again. Crime can be such a very complex thing."

"And I was just beginning to think you'd let me out," said Geoffrey reproachfully. "I can't take that last idea of yours very seriously."

"I wouldn't like you to lose sleep over it. There's just one question I wanted to ask you, while I'm here – I hope you won't resent it. What's your financial position?"

Geoffrey looked surprised. "My financial position? I – er – I don't know. It's all right, I suppose. Do you want to borrow some money?"

"No, Mr. Hollison, I just wanted to find out whether you were solvent. You're sure you haven't been gambling heavily, or running into debt, or entertaining too many Wrens?" There was a disarming twinkle in the Inspector's eye.

Geoffrey sat back, relieved. "My dear Inspector, I haven't time. I'm officially attached to the Admiralty, you know, and I have some duties there as well as at the College. We're kept at it pretty hard. I get my pay – you can look up what a lieutenant-commander gets after deductions. Then my father insisted on making me an allowance of a thousand a year, though frankly I didn't need it. I've no idea what my balance is at the bank, but I'm sure it's adequate. I'll ask the manager to let you know."

The Inspector nodded. "You're really too good to be true!"

"I resent that. Just because you live in a world of crime . . . I've been at sea for six years, remember, and you can't get into much trouble there."

"I suppose not. Anyway, I'm glad you're in the clear financially."

"I wish I were in the clear altogether. You know, I believe you still think of me as a suspect in spite of everything you've said."

"I'll be quite honest with you," said James. "You *could* be the murderer. There is – how shall I put it? – a lack of evidence that you didn't do it. You could have got there in time. You could have had a motive, though in your case it isn't as strong as it might seem, because you're not the sort that's primarily interested in money. On the other hand, there's not a shadow of evidence that you did it. Not a particle. At the moment I can't go beyond that. All I can say is that if I were thinking of arresting you I shouldn't be telling you this."

"That's decent of you, Inspector. I should be happier if you could tell me whom you were thinking of arresting. It's not going to be awfully pleasant living under a question-mark."

"We're doing all we can," said the Inspector. "I should try to forget about this business now, if I were you. Why don't you – er – take Miss Whitworth out to dinner? It would do you good."

Geoffrey laughed. "Inspector, I'm going to."

Sharp at seven that evening Geoffrey drew up outside Dr. Whitworth's house and tooted twice. He watched the door eagerly, and was just getting out to knock when Pamela appeared. She looked very snug in some sort of fur coat – Geoffrey was quite untutored in female clothes – and she was hatless. As she got into the car and snuggled down, he thought he had never seen anyone so lovely. He said, "You know, someone ought to paint you."

"Someone has."

"Not really?"

"Aha! One of my father's patients. I believe it's hanging somewhere now."

"You want to be careful with those artist chaps," said Geoffrey. "They're an untrustworthy lot."

"Do you know any?"

"I've read about them."

She laughed. "You're sweet. Where are we going?"

"I booked a table at Taglioni's – off Greek Street. It's quieter than most, and the food isn't bad. I can leave the car there, too. All right by you?"

"Lovely."

"Got your thermometer?"

"No, why?"

"My temperature's rising."

"You'll have to go to bed."

"What did you say?"

"I said you'd have to go to bed."

"Oh! I say, I apologize for the car. I'm afraid it hardly does you justice. Don't be scared if she swerves a bit – one of the front hubs is out of alignment. Today's her twelfth birthday."

"She seems to have plenty of go in her still."

"I think she'll get us there." Geoffrey suddenly felt that he didn't want to talk any more. He didn't want to think, either. He just wanted to enjoy the incredibly exciting adventure of taking Pamela out.

They had crossed Putney Bridge before he spoke again. "I'm

glad you called today," he said. "Sorry to be so banal – but I really am glad. I wish I'd known you longer. I can't imagine how it was we never met, living so close. I've been at Welford Avenue almost six months."

"And to think I didn't know!" said Pamela, and Geoffrey laughed.

Taglioni's was just comfortably full, and their table was pleasantly secluded behind a pillar. They had gin and vermouth, and Geoffrey ordered a bottle of hock. He also handled the menu efficiently.

"This is really a great treat for me – going out to dinner, I mean," said Pamela. "I see so little of Daddy, and I like to be at home on my free evenings whenever I can, in case he's free too."

"I'd like to meet him," said Geoffrey.

"I dare say it could be arranged," said Pamela. "It would do him good to talk about something besides medicine. You could tell him all about your adventures."

"What adventures? I didn't have any."

"You must have done – in six years. How did you get into the Navy in the first place?"

"Well – I was a little tired of the paint industry and just applied – usual way. They found I had particularly good eyesight and normal intelligence, so they accepted me for the Signals. Just a rating, of course. I spent some time up on the east coast playing about with morse lamps and semaphores. I wanted a commission, and that meant getting experience at sea. Time passed, and I finally got to Chatham, and then we heard we were going to a depot ship. It turned out to be a station in Bermuda."

"And that was where your adventures began?"

"You're pulling my leg. In Bermuda we lay about on a veranda in shorts, peeling potatoes. We also carved a tennis court out of coral limestone. One day the Chief Petty Officer sent for us and told us there was a job to do inland, but there were seven of us, and he only wanted six. He said I'd better stay behind. 'I know you're disappointed,' he said, 'but don't worry, we'll find you another job. We shan't send you to sea.' I blurted out, 'But that's what I've come out here for.' He said, 'What? – pack your things and report here at two o'clock.' And that afternoon I was posted to a cruiser. Just luck, you know." He raised his glass. "Cheers. Am I talking too much?"

"I love it. Do go on."

"Well, she was a pretty teased-out ship, but we had some fun in the Pacific. We were supposed to be hunting a German armed merchant cruiser, but we did a three-months' tour and never saw anything of it. The thing I remember most about that trip was a picnic we had in a sandy desert in Peru, outside a little oil town. Two hundred ratings, salted peanuts, hamburgers and beer, and a dance in the evening with two hundred lonely wives from every township within fifty miles."

"Yes, I suppose you'd remember that! What about your commission?"

"Well, I got home eventually, went on a lot of courses, and finally finished up a sub-lieut. I'd heard some of the chaps talking about radar, and got interested, and so I asked to be put on Fighter Direction Control. I was posted to an escort carrier, then to a light fleet carrier, and finally to *Incorrigible*. We were in all the big shows – Iwojima, Okinawa and right up to Japan. Actually I had some aircraft out bombing Tokyo when the news came through on the commercial radio that Japan had surrendered. It was grand fun saying, 'Come back, boys, it's all over.'"

"The way you tell it, the whole thing sounds like a holiday from beginning to end."

"Distance lends enchantment. We sometimes worked twenty-three and a half hours at a stretch!" He relaxed in his chair, as though the mere recollection made him tired. "I don't know whether it's the wine or whether it's you," he said, "but everything seems so much better tonight. Even though I am suspected of murder."

Pamela nearly dropped her coffee-cup. "Don't be ridiculous," she said.

"Oh, I am, you know. The Inspector was awfully kind and did his best to set my mind at rest, but I'm a suspect all the same."

"You have an inflated ego," said Pamela.

"No, I mean it. You see, my father left me some money."

"There's nothing unusual in that."

"But *I* can't prove that I didn't do it. Everyone else can."

"I've never heard anything so absurd in my life," said Pamela, and she looked quite cross.

"I told you you'd never make a doctor," said Geoffrey.

"What *do* you mean?"

"If they brought in a young man with blue eyes and curly black hair, suffering from an acute appendix, you'd take one look at him and say: 'He couldn't have an acute appendix. He's much too nice. Take him away and give him an aspirin.' "

Pamela laughed. "Don't be absurd. I know it's very easy to make mistakes about people, and I know that an attractive man may be an absolute swine. But if you're trying to persuade me that you could be a murderer – well, I wouldn't believe it unless I'd seen you do it with my own eyes."

"It's most unscientific, that's all I can say. The Inspector is less impressionable. He asked me some very probing questions."

"I expect it's just routine."

"I'm getting tired of that phrase – that's what he says. Anyway, I'm afraid a lot of people are going to believe that I did it."

"A lot of people!" Her scorn was biting. "Do you mind?"

"I'd give anything to have the case cleared up."

"You must go on trying to forget it. Keep on working, and take me out to dinner now and again, and pretend it didn't happen."

"A counsel of perfection – but if you'll help, it'll make forgetting easier. You're not – engaged or anything?"

She held up her left hand. "Not a thing!"

"I've been trying to see all day."

"Well, that's one worry off your mind, isn't it? I'm only twenty-three, you know."

"That doesn't mean a thing. You can do an awful lot in a year or two."

"I'm fussy," said Pamela, "and busy."

"I thought medical students—"

"That was when they were all men. I thought sailors—"

Geoffrey laughed. "There's not much on my conscience. Maybe I'm fussy, too."

"I think we're being rather stupid, anyway," said Pamela. "I blame the wine. I shall be very angry with myself tomorrow when I recall this conversation."

"I shall treasure it," said Geoffrey, "always."

"Good heavens, you are becoming sentimental, aren't you? Positively maudlin! I think we ought to be going. It's been a most pleasant evening. Thank you so much." She got up more briskly than was necessary.

Geoffrey drove back very carefully, indeed – and very slowly. He said, "Everything I want to say sounds ridiculous before I say it."

"Then why bother?"

"I think I've fallen in love with you."

"Nonsense. We only met twenty-four hours ago."

"*I* counted them, too! Why shouldn't I be in love with you? You're beautiful and clever and good. . . ."

Pamela wriggled. "I wish you'd stop," she protested. "You don't know me a bit. What an impetuous man you are! It's . . . really, it's quite absurd."

Geoffrey was silent.

Presently Pamela said, "I'm sorry."

"Don't be. I *am* impetuous. Off my rocker a bit today. But I don't take a word of it back," he added defiantly.

"I wouldn't want you to," said Pamela. "I like you. I don't believe in pretending. I wish I could help you."

The cloud settled on Geoffrey's face again.

They passed the end of Welford Avenue and stopped outside the doctor's lamp. He looked at her. "Good night, Pamela," he said. "You don't know how I hate your going. It's been so wonderful." He leaned towards her, his arm on the back of her seat. Then he hesitated and said 'Good night' again.

She said, "Good night, Geoffrey," and got out.

"Damn!" said Geoffrey.

Pamela paused. "What's wrong?" she asked.

"I wanted to kiss you. My nerve's gone!"

She put her head inside the car and gave him the lightest of kisses. "Good night, my dear," she said.

She ran up the steps to the front door and quickly let herself into the house. A voice within her said: "You shouldn't have done that. It was stupid. It was – too soon."

Another voice answered defiantly, "But it was nice – and so is he."

CHAPTER IX

Geoffrey awoke next morning to a mixture of sensations. There was still the consciousness of tragedy, the oppressive thought of another grim day ahead.

But today there was something else as well. He felt stirrings of cheerfulness. He told himself that he ought to be ashamed of himself, with his father only two days dead and still unburied. But he couldn't help it, and he couldn't feel ashamed.

As soon as he had bathed and shaved, Geoffrey went downstairs in his dressing-gown to phone from the lounge. Mrs. Armstrong was not moving yet – it was only eight o'clock, and she was making up lost sleep. Geoffrey had to look up the number in the book. He dialled it with a quickened pulse.

"Is that Dr. Whitworth's house?" he asked. "Is Miss Whitworth about yet, please?"

There was a pause, and then Pamela came on the line. "Who is it?" she asked.

Geoffrey took a deep breath. He even liked her voice over the telephone – a searching test. He said, "It's me – Geoffrey Hollison."

"Oh!" said Pamela cautiously. "Good morning. You *are* an early bird."

"I thought I might not catch you otherwise. I suppose you're going off to play with your skeletons today?"

"You suppose quite right."

"It is *Saturday,* you know."

"Hospitals don't close down on Saturdays."

"You sound frightfully severe and business-like. I really rang to know when I could have another consultation!"

Pamela hesitated. "Well . . ."

"It *is* the weekend," Geoffrey pleaded. "It's the first of March tomorrow, and the glass is high. I believe March is going to come in like a lamb."

"You can't expect everyone to follow March's example," said Pamela.

"Please! Will you or won't you?"

"Perhaps tomorrow—"

"All tomorrow! I say, that's wonderful . . ."

"No, not *all* tomorrow. Heavens, you're impossible. Perhaps we could go somewhere for tea if it's a nice day?"

"I know," said Geoffrey, "let me show you *Truant* – you remember, the boat. I'll take a few things and we'll have tea afloat. What do you say?"

"I'd like that," said Pamela. "All right, say three o'clock. How are you this morning, Geoffrey? Did you sleep all right?"

"I'm fine, thanks. Slept like a log. Right, I'll call for you at three. Oh, and Pamela—"

"What?"

"It wasn't the wine last night. I *am* in love with you."

"I'll see you tomorrow," said Pamela.

In the Superintendent's office an hour or so later, Inspector James was studying with intense interest a report which had come in from headquarters during the night. Apparently there had been a car hold-up on the Southend road on the previous evening. Two men had stopped a Morris 12 and asked for a lift. They had then made the driver get out at the point of a gun and had driven the car away. A passing lorry had taken the owner to a telephone-box and the flying-squad had got busy. The hold-up men had been seen near Walthamstow, and chased at high speed to the Blackwall Tunnel. There, the Morris had crashed on a corner and one of the men had broken his back. The other, practically unhurt, had talked.

"It seems they had quite a flourishing business," said the Superintendent. "Smart work, catching them."

"I think you might have told me before about Cross having his car pinched," the Inspector said reproachfully. "If this chap hadn't spilt the beans I'd never have known."

"Sorry, sir – I'd almost forgotten it myself. It didn't seem to have anything to do with the case."

"I don't suppose it has," said the Inspector. "All the same, I think I'll pop over this morning and have a word with the fellow they've caught. You never know. We seem to have exhausted all other lines. The report on the bloodstained coat doesn't get us anywhere at all. I knew it wouldn't. The ashes are just paper and rag. By the way, I went over and had a look at the bombed house before I came here. It's an important part of Cross's story."

"It stands up all right, doesn't it, sir?"

"The house doesn't; the story does. The place is just as he described it. The door's off one of its hinges. There's broken glass everywhere. The house isn't too bad inside – not the ground floor, anyway – but the roof's badly damaged. There's a lot of rubbish about – bits of smashed furniture and oddments. There are one or two footprints beside the concrete path, but they're not very clear. I think one of them is a woman's. They're no help to us, though. If Cross walked up the concrete he wouldn't have left any trace."

"Too bad," said the Super sympathetically.

"Yes," said the Inspector, "our luck seems to be out on this case. Look, while I'm over at Barking will you ring Cross for me and ask him if he could make it convenient to be at his flat after dinner tonight? I think I'd like one more talk with him."

Jackson made a note, and the Inspector departed rather despondently. It didn't look as though there were going to be any bouquets for him as a result of this job.

If Geoffrey's feelings were mixed that morning, Cross's were even more mixed. On the one hand he was a successful murderer. The plan had worked perfectly. The alibi would stand. The inquest on Monday would result in a verdict against some person or persons unknown, and they would remain unknown. Vague suspicion would cling to Geoffrey – it was a pity he hadn't been able to implicate his cousin more deeply, but it would have been fatally easy to try something a shade too clever. It was better as it was. The case would be pigeon-holed, and a fortune was in the bag. It would be quite proper to get in touch with the solicitors after the inquest. There would no longer be any need to go to that wretched paintworks every day. He could begin to make tentative inquiries about a plane. The wide world would be open to him, rich and safe.

And yet Cross was not entirely easy in his mind. The Inspector had not been friendly. Cross himself had kept his temper with difficulty during the search of his flat. Those confounded bloodstains had given him a sleepless night. Throughout the day, as he sat in his office, the thought of what modern analytical methods might achieve with the coat still nagged at his mind. At least they hadn't asked for a sample of his own blood – that was a good sign. A rather peremptory invitation to be home that evening did not add to his mental comfort.

When he did get back to the flat he bathed and had a couple of short drinks and dined in the restaurant and felt a little better. He was very comfortable, with a box of cigarettes and half a bottle of whisky at his elbow, when the Inspector rang just before eight-thirty.

"Come in, Inspector," said Cross cheerfully. "Take your coat off and make yourself at home. Have a drink?"

"No, thank you," said James. He removed his coat and settled himself in a chair.

"You look as though you've got a lot on your mind," said Cross. "Can I help? By the way, did you have fun with the ashes?"

James puffed stolidly at his pipe. What a revolting young man! He said, "Whatever it was you cremated in the grate, Mr. Cross, there's nothing to be learned from it now."

"There never was, Inspector. Just some old letters."

"And some rag or cloth. What was that?"

"Just a bit of old rag from the car – I used it to get the stains out of the coat. I'm afraid I can't give you its pedigree."

"You seem to be unnecessarily hostile," said the Inspector.

"Surely that's a good sign. If I were a murderer I would probably be fawning around you with offers of assistance. You know, you haven't been exactly pally yourself, Inspector. I don't know how we've got across each other like this. I've nothing to hide, I assure you. You've been sniffing around for days like a cat round a mouse-hole, and it gets a bit tiring. Are you thinking of returning my overcoat, by any chance?"

"I'll have it sent round in the morning," said James.

"Did it – enlighten you?"

The Inspector smiled grimly. "Well . . ." he said. He was watching Cross's face closely, but there was nothing to read there. It was a worried, anxious face, but James had never seen it otherwise. "That coat might have told us something before you cleaned it, but you did the job pretty well. We shall have to assume that the blood was from your own hand."

"That's a pretty insulting way of conceding the truth, I must say." Cross was beginning to feel better. "Look here, Inspector, why have you come here today? Not just to exchange wisecracks, I'm sure."

"You're quite right, sir. As a matter of fact, I've come to bring you a bit of good news."

"You've found the murderer?"

James shook his head. "I'm afraid not. But we've found the men who stole your car."

"My car? Good lord, you mean the Vauxhall? Well, you people are smarter than I thought. How did you manage it?"

James told him briefly of the chase and its results.

"Which one was it that broke his back?" asked Cross. "The tall one?"

"That I couldn't say."

"I hope it was the tall one – he's the chap who stuck the gun in my neck."

"It may be a little difficult to get the car back."

"I'm not really interested – though the insurance company may be. Did you talk to the man who wasn't hurt?"

"Yes," said the Inspector, "and he talked to me."

Cross nodded. "So what? You're so credulous, Inspector, that he no doubt persuaded you *I* pinched *his* car!"

"No. But he started me thinking about the interesting subject of coincidence. It's the oddities of a case like this that are so intriguing."

"What you mean, Inspector, is that when you've quite failed to get to the heart of a case you like to kid yourself you're making progress by messing about on the outskirts."

"Put it that way if you like. What caught my attention was that you seem to make a practice of picking up people at the roundabout on foggy nights."

Cross poured himself out a shot of whisky. "I've done it – let me see – twice. I'd hardly call that a practice. Blessed if I see what you're driving at. If you think it's strange that I should have stopped there – though for the life of me I don't know why you should – all I can suggest is that you should try driving across the roundabout yourself on a foggy night. Just where do you think you're getting, Inspector?"

"We shall see, Mr. Cross. There's one straight question I'd like to ask you. How are you fixed financially?"

"Could be worse, Inspector."

James raised his eyebrows. "No money troubles?"

"Are you really entitled to go into this?"

"I think so," said James. "You don't have to answer."

"Well, I get a couple of thousand a year from the firm, and pretty good expenses."

"And how much do you spend?"

Cross grinned. "About a couple of thousand a year and expenses. I'm not the saving type."

"You've no large debts?"

"Afraid not. No one would lend money without security, and I haven't much property. Being in a P.O.W. camp isn't a very lucrative racket, you know."

"Overdraft at the bank?"

"It's curious you should mention that, Inspector. I have, as a matter of fact, a small overdraft. About – er – let me see, seventy or eighty pounds. Nothing much."

"Quite a bit without security. Has the bank been pressing you at all?"

"Not really – you know what they're like. I had a polite note from the manager a few days ago, but he must know I've got a good job."

James looked round the flat reflectively. "You do yourself very well on it. I quite envy you. Well, thanks for telling me all this."

"The bank manager would have done if I hadn't. Is that all?"

"Pretty nearly. I thought perhaps you could give me just a little more detail about that bombed house. Would you mind just re-calling again exactly what happened?"

Cross sighed. "Here we go – round and round the mulberry bush! It was dark, Inspector, and foggy. You surely don't expect a vivid word picture?"

"Tell me just what you did, saw, heard and felt. That's all – it's quite simple."

Cross lay back with his fingertips together, his eyes closed, a scornful smile on his face. "I opened the gate. It had a patent catch. I walked up the concrete path. I reached the door. I felt for the knocker. I knocked loudly – twice. Then I realized the door was open. I called out, 'Anyone there?' I had another look and saw the door was off its hinges. Then it began to dawn on me that the house had been blitzed. I stepped back from the door and stumbled over an obstruction. I fell and put my hand on something sharp. It hurt a lot and I felt it bleeding. I wrapped my handkerchief round it. I felt a bit sick. I waited a minute or two and then I went back to the car."

"We didn't find any blood near the house," said James. "And yet your hand was bleeding enough to spot your coat."

"It could hardly go on the coat and on the ground," said Cross.

"Perhaps not. Well, we'll have to leave it at that."

"Finished, Inspector?"

"Yes."

"Then do you mind if I ask you a question?"

"It depends," said James, "but go ahead and see."

"My uncle," said Cross, "was murdered forty-eight hours ago.

Have you made any progress with the investigation? Are you getting anywhere? It seemed a straightforward crime, in a way, and the police had a hot trail. I'm just naturally eager that you should find the chap. For one thing you'll stop looking sideways at me."

"If I look sideways at you, as you put it," said the Inspector, "it's because in certain respects you fill the bill. You had a motive – money. You knew about the household arrangements. Your uncle would have turned and let you follow him in, because he knew you well and was expecting you. You would have had to disguise your voice on the telephone. You would have had to fix the time of the murder by telephoning, because you have an alibi. You got blood on your coat, and made sure it was all cleaned up before the police could have a look at it. You burned something in your grate when you ought to have been keeping an appointment. One way and another, Mr. Cross, I think I may say that if it weren't for the fact that you have an alibi which I can't break, I would have arrested you twenty-four hours ago."

Cross was pale. "Then it's a very good job I have an alibi, isn't it? Otherwise you might arrest an innocent man."

"A very good job," said the Inspector. "It's an alibi that I have to accept. As far as I'm concerned, you didn't do it. So where am I? Apart from your own rather curious behaviour, there's nothing to go on. You talk about a trail, but there never was a trail at all. For once a murderer doesn't seem to have made any mistakes."

"Then what hope is there of your finding the man?"

"Well," said James slowly, chewing on his pipe-stem, "we often come up against this sort of situation. Everything seems quite hopeless, and we hold the inquest without getting anywhere, and the victim is buried, and the neighbours soon find something else to talk about, and the murderer thinks he's okay. Then, when it all seems forgotten, something happens. Have you ever accidentally dislodged a boulder on a hillside and been surprised at all the upset it causes as it tumbles to the bottom? Murder's a bit like that. It starts things happening. Because of the murder all sorts of human relationships are changed. Sometimes the murderer himself changes. Maybe his conscience gets to work. Maybe he's afraid. Maybe he talks in his sleep. He thinks he's got what he wants, but it doesn't always satisfy him. One way or another he nearly always loses in the end."

"You're a philosopher, Inspector. I think you're kidding yourself. What it amounts to is that you've fallen down on your job, and you're trying to pretend you haven't. I'd love to hear you reciting that piece to your boss! It seems to me that you've reached a point of complete deadlock, and that, to all intents and purposes, the case is closed. Isn't that so?"

The Inspector got up. His expression was inscrutable. "This case will be closed," he said, "when you and I hear the foreman of a jury say 'Guilty'. Not before. Good night, Mr. Cross."

CHAPTER X

"You're not much of a weather prophet," said Pamela on Sunday afternoon, as Geoffrey opened the door of the Morris for her. There was a boisterous wind, with small scudding white clouds in a pale blue sky. Pamela was wearing grey slacks, a sweater, and a green suede jacket. "We shall be blown away on the river."

"It'll be warm enough in the cabin," said Geoffrey, as she settled herself. "There's a paraffin stove if we need it. I say, what fun this is! I hope you don't think I'm a callous brute, enjoying myself as though I hadn't a care in the world. It worries me a bit."

"Do you want my professional opinion?"

"No," said Geoffrey, "I want your good opinion."

"It wouldn't help to mope," said Pamela. "Would it, now? Shall we be able to go for a run in the boat?"

"Why not – you're well wrapped up." He glanced across at her. She was looking straight ahead, with the faintest of smiles – hardly more than a glow of satisfaction. The cheek that Geoffrey could see was slightly flushed. Her hand was resting on the seat between them, and Geoffrey put his own hand over it.

"That's wonderful," he said. "I'm crazy about you, Pamela. I've never felt like this before."

Pamela gently took her hand away. "I do want you to be sensible," she said. "I don't think I like being swept off my feet."

"That's an admission," said Geoffrey eagerly.

"It's not – it's a warning. I like to think things over. I just don't know you at all. You might be – well—"

"I told you – I might be a murderer."

"Geoffrey, you're not to *say* that. It's not funny. You know that's not what I meant at all."

"You're used to taking a detached, scientific view of everything, I suppose. You'd like to spread me out on a slide and look at me through a microscope. Pamela, where are your emotions? I believe you're afraid of them."

Pamela smiled, very self-possessed, and shook her head. "Not afraid. As a matter of fact, I'm rather interested. A bit surprised, perhaps. After all, when you're thinking of devoting your life to medicine, it's – well, a little disturbing, to find suddenly that you want to hold hands with a man you hardly know."

"Pamela . . .!"

"No, don't let's be silly any more. The world isn't going to end tonight. Let's be very practical. I feel like rushing around and being shown things and watching you being frightfully competent. You pretend to be a lieutenant-commander, and all you can do is to make love to me."

"The two things aren't necessarily incompatible," said Geoffrey. "Anyway, here's the boathouse and there's *Truant*. Do you know anything about boats at all?"

"Not a thing, except that they float."

"They don't always do that! This is our dinghy. Wait a moment, I'll put a plank down. We really need gum boots for this job. All right, Queen Elizabeth!"

He helped her over the mud and shoved the dinghy off. The tide was high and slack, and rowing was easy, though the wind kept snatching drops of water from the oars and blowing them aboard.

"I wouldn't like to be at sea today," said Pamela. "*Truant*'s a nice shape, but she's not very big, is she?"

"She does roll a bit in a seaway. But, on the whole, you'll be surprised how well she rides. Okay – I'll go aboard first and take off the cockpit cover. I should hate you to fall in. Can you swim, by the way?"

"Of course. I once did two lengths under water. Can you?"

Geoffrey grinned. "I shouldn't be here if I couldn't." He unlocked the cabin. "Let me show you round – you're luckier than I am, you can walk under the beams without bumping your head."

"It's rather cosy," said Pamela cautiously. "There's a lot more room than I expected. And the fittings are lovely. Quite a little home, isn't it?" She opened a long hanging cupboard and peeped inside. "It's a bit damp, though."

"I know – you can't prevent that unless you live aboard all the time. I'll open the ports and let some fresh air in. Now, ma'am, you say you want to buy a boat? Well, here we have just the thing. Nice neat table – you see how the legs fit into sockets on the floor. That's so it won't come adrift in bad weather. Oil lamps for light – there are electric lights as well, of course, but it's difficult to keep a battery charged up when the boat's not being run much. Here's the paraffin stove – would you like me to light it?"

"No, thanks – not just now. It's really very warm down here."

"Boats are much less draughty than houses." He opened a little door. "Here's the galley. Stainless steel sink. Fresh water pumped from a tank in the starboard locker. Crockery here. Pots and pans. Toilet in here. Canned food under the starboard berth. Nice, isn't it?"

"It grows on you," said Pamela. "Are there just two berths?"

"No, there are two more forrard." He showed her. "And that's the chain locker in the forepeak."

"What's the chain for?"

"For the anchor. This end it's fastened to the bitts. Hence the phrase 'to the bitter end'." He grinned. "Isn't language fascinating? I know ever so many things like that. Frightfully well informed!"

"I thought it was the boat you were trying to sell me. Please go on."

"Well, of course, she's not really very modern – no chromium and streamline. But she's solid – teak and oak and a good keel and a buoyant bow. She's made for the sea, not just for cruising about the river. The pump, by the way, works from the engines to clear the bilge, and there's a hand rotary as well under the companion. The wheelhouse gives just enough shelter for the helmsman in bad weather without catching the wind too badly. Now, ma'am, what do you say?"

"She'd be ideal for lazing on in hot weather," said Pamela. "I can just imagine her fastened to her anchor—"

"Lying at anchor."

"Lying at anchor, on a flaming June day, in a quiet blue sea. And me getting brown in a two-piece."

"Yes, I can imagine that, too," said Geoffrey. "Or on a pitch-dark night, in half a gale of wind, with the engines conked and the anchor dragging and a hard shoal to leeward. Or something a little less dramatic – an exposed anchorage, wind against tide, the boat rolling and tossing and groaning and tipping you out of your berth and making you feel like hell. . . . It's after a night like that, my girl, that you really enjoy a snug berth and a quiet cup of tea."

"Let's go somewhere," said Pamela suddenly. "Have we time? It gets dark so early – it's nearly four o'clock now."

"You may remember," said Geoffrey reproachfully, "that I suggested the whole day. I'll tell you what, we'll take a short run downstream, just so that you can see her paces, and then we'll come back and moor again and have tea by lamplight. All right?"

"Perfect," said Pamela. "Can I do anything?"

"You can press the self-starters," said Geoffrey, "if you're *very* good." He showed her the two knobs. The port engine sprang to life at once, but the starboard one took a little coaxing. When it was running smoothly Geoffrey checked the gauges, made sure the cooling water was going overboard, and wiped his hands.

"The joy of boats," he said, "is that you can get filthy without anyone minding. Right – stand by the wheel and I'll slip her moorings."

There was no other craft in sight, and as Geoffrey let go *Truant* began to drift gently downstream on the tide. He came back over the cabin top to the wheelhouse, throttled up and slipped her into gear.

"You can steer. It's not difficult – just the same as a car. That's it, a bit over to port. Port is left, starboard is right. You'll soon get used to it. By the way, when you turn the wheel don't forget that it's the stern that swings – that's different from a car. Think of a woman walking!"

"How dare you!" said Pamela.

"No offence, ma'am – but it's very important, otherwise you might hit something. We've plenty of time to get through the half-tide lock and back again for tea. *Truant* only draws five feet."

"What's the half-tide lock?"

"Oh, that's a contraption at Richmond that lets boats through when the water has reached a certain height. There's an ordinary lock beside it, but most boats watch the tide and go straight through."

"It's all a little bit technical," said Pamela, clinging to the wheel as though it would fall overboard if she let go.

"You'll soon get used to it – wait until we've been on a trip or two. You'll be talking like a Thames bargee in next to no time. It should be easy for you – you're a technician. Of course we *could* re-name all the parts of the ship in anatomical terms—"

"For heaven's sake!" said Pamela hastily. "You would have fun, wouldn't you? Look, Geoffrey, there's a bridge. What do I do?"

"Don't panic – we're at least five minutes away. Starboard a little. Good, now keep her steady. Don't move the wheel backwards and forwards as though you'd got St. Vitus' dance. It irritates the rudder. Okay – I'm going to open her up." Both engines suddenly roared, and the big propellors bit hard into the water. *Truant* seemed to give a great leap forward, and a very presentable bow wave curved away on either side.

"Are you quite sure I'm all right?" asked Pamela, hanging on grimly. "It seems terribly fast."

"That's just an illusion – we're actually doing about nine knots, not as fast as a bicycle. We'd better slow for those boats at moorings – there might be someone else having tea aboard, and it's darned annoying to get the wash of another boat and pour boiling water into your shoe instead of the teapot."

Pamela smiled. "She slows down very quickly, doesn't she? I'm beginning to get the feel of her now. What would happen if the engines suddenly stopped?"

"They're not both likely to stop at once. If they did we should just anchor. There's a forty-pound C.Q.R. – that's a sort of patent anchor – rather good. You can see it forrard there, by the windlass. I think she carries fifty fathoms of chain, so she should hold almost anywhere. There's a spare anchor in the stern locker, and a smaller one in the locker by your feet. That's in case we should ever have to kedge off."

"Oh, I do hope we never have to kedge off," said Pamela, teasing. "It's fascinating – but there's so much to learn. Honestly, it's worse than medicine."

"I'll buy you a nice easy book to read," said Geoffrey. "You can swot up your nautical terms in the operating theatre. You'll soon make a sailor. I say, we'd better be going back or we shan't be able to spot the mooring buoys."

"Oh, dear, there's a ship coming."

Geoffrey guffawed. "If it's the *Queen Mary,* give her a wide berth."

"I think you have a horrible laugh," said Pamela. "Tell me what to do."

"Just take it easy – it's only a string of barges. Keep over to starboard – no, *starboard* – that's better. Think of it as tibia major or something! Open her up a bit – you've plenty of time. Easy. Now you're all right. Don't go too near the bank or we'll run aground and be stuck there all night. Then you'll say I planned it that way."

Pamela was concentrating and ignored the remark. The tug chugged by, twenty yards away. "Now swing her round to port," said Geoffrey. "A nice steady sweep – she'll turn almost in her own length but there's no point in laying her on her beam ends. Round she goes! Open her up again now, and pass the tug on the outside. Cold?"

"Not a bit," said Pamela. "It's exciting – it keeps me warm." But as they approached the mooring she began to get nervous again. "What about stopping her?"

"Easy as pie, my dear. Just shut down both engines – no, don't switch off, just close the throttles and let them idle. That's right. We're against the tide and she'll soon lose way. She's all set to run in. Gently does it – there's plenty of time. Never hurry anything in a boat unless you have to. There's a reverse gear, of course, but there's no point in using it if you can do without. There, she's just right. You're a born helmsman!"

"Blarney," said Pamela.

Geoffrey grinned. "I'm going to leave you now."

"What do you mean?"

"I'm only going forrard to moor her. Keep her straight for the buoy. I'll show you how to moor another time. It's a bit tricky in a bad light." He walked swiftly along the deck and soon had her tied up. "Switch off now," he called. The engines died, and the river was quiet again except for the wind and the water.

He clambered back and joined her in the cockpit. She was flushed, wind-blown but triumphant. "Well?" he asked.

"You're not a bad teacher."

"I know a lot more things—"

"But you're not very well behaved. What about some tea?"

"Go ahead," said Geoffrey. "I'll watch. You'll find cups, plates, knives, spoons, teapot and milk jug where I showed you. Condensed milk in the port locker – sorry, that's the best I can offer today. You'll have to get used to hardships afloat! I believe there's a tablecloth under the starboard berth. A place for everything and everything in its place – we hope. I'll light the primus."

He fiddled happily with methylated spirits and filled the kettle from the fresh-water pump. Out of a parcel that he had brought from the car he took bread, butter, jam, and a tin of crab. "I hope you like crab," he said. "I pinched it from Mrs. Armstrong, so you'd better."

"I'm ravenous," said Pamela. "If you'll hand me the loaf and butter I'll cut some nice thick slices. Can I light the lamps?"

"I think I'd better," said Geoffrey. "They're rather messy, and the chimneys crack very easily."

"You're a bit bossy, aren't you?" said Pamela.

"Aboard ship someone has to be bossy, ma'am. If you give any trouble I can clap you in irons." He fixed the lamps, sprawled out on the berth, and watched her cutting bread.

"I shall cut myself," said Pamela.

"You're lovely," said Geoffrey. "There was a film star who was something like you, but I've forgotten her name. Same red hair, same shaped mouth, same high cheek-bones. I saw her in technicolor on Okinawa. The boys all went, 'Phwee – phweeoo.' Like this." He whistled vulgarly.

"The kettle's boiling, Lieutenant-Commander. Don't forget to warm the pot in the excitement of your reminiscences."

"I always warm the pot," said Geoffrey. "I'm really very dom-esticated." He made the tea and turned out the primus.

They ate like children at a party. When they had finished they stretched out on their berths on either side of the table. Pamela had a cigarette and Geoffrey was filling his pipe.

"Perfect peace," said Geoffrey. He gave a sigh of deep content-ment. "You know, next time I think we ought to go down to the Nore."

"Do you mean it?"

"Why not? The weather will soon pick up, and we've got plenty of fuel. Of course, we'd need a whole day. *And* we'd have to sleep on board."

"Don't be absurd, Geoffrey."

"Well, we'd have to get married first, of course," said Geoffrey, unabashed. "No, seriously, I'd just love to spend some time with you in the Estuary. It's a fascinating place. If you like it busy there are ships and wharves, and if you want to be alone there are hundreds of quiet creeks and wind-swept islands behind seawalls. It isn't everybody's cup of tea, I suppose – grey grass on the saltings, and miles of mud flats, and wild ducks from the marshes, and gulls and curlews. But there's a wide sky and wonderful sunsets, and no one to push you around. It can be very exciting, too – actually the approaches to the Thames are just about the most dangerous in the world. It's a miracle there should be a port of London at all."

"I know something's always happening on the Goodwins. Twice last week I heard wireless reports about a ship aground there."

"That's farther south. They do say that on one occasion a ship went aground on the Goodwins in a gale and when the sandbanks dried out at low water people on the cliffs could see the crew walking about on the sand. They were alive and well, and yet they were as good as dead, because the seas were so rough that no boat could live in them. The next high tide washed them all away."

"What a ghastly story!"

"Pretty grim. Probably untrue. But there's always something getting into trouble on those shoals. The Estuary is littered with old wrecks – there are bits of ships sticking up out of the water at low tide that have been there fifty years or more. But the shoals are fun when you know them and when the weather's good. There's one sandbank I know, five miles off shore, where you can stand at low water and watch ships passing in the deep channel just like trains past a platform. But you need a shallow-draught boat to explore – I dare say we could get one down at Leigh or Benfleet."

"You know," said Pamela, "I never thought of the Estuary as full of sandbanks. It looks just plain blue sea on the map."

"My dear girl, let me show you – it's just like the land, all hills and valleys. Where's the chart?" He took a book down from the shelf over his head, enthusiastic as a boy. He went over and sat beside her. "This isn't a real chart but it gives an idea. Look – these long, shaded strips are banks. See how they point to London like fingers. Most of them dry out at low water – anyway, they haven't enough water over them for anything big. These are the channels in between – deep and safe – they're the arterial roads. The large ships usually keep to these lanes here – the Barrow Deep, the Prince's and the Edinburgh. Up and down, up and down, like clockwork. There are buoys and lights everywhere, of course – it's a world all on its own. I explored all over it in the old days. The Swin, here, is used mainly by coastal sailing barges and small tramps. These others – Middle Deep, Black Deep and Knock Deep – are pretty deserted."

"What fun for weekends!" said Pamela, bent over the book. "What happens if you do get stuck on a bank? I mean in a small boat. Is it all right?"

"It depends on the wind and the tide and the weather. If the tide's rising, you can probably float off all right. If it's falling, there's a very good chance of being marooned for a few hours. If the weather's bad, and there's a very high sea, the waves pick the grounded boat up on their crests and keep on dashing it down on the hard sand, and before long it begins to break up. It's a horrible sound."

"Has it happened to you?"

"I've never had a boat actually break up under me – I probably wouldn't be here – but I've been very close to it."

"And that's the sort of place you want to take *me* to!"

"Ah, my dear, when you're there the sun will always be shining, the tide will always be rising, and the sea will always be smooth and blue!"

"We'd better do the washing up," said Pamela, closing the book. "You can tell me more about the Thames Estuary another day. There's enough hot water in the kettle."

"I hate to move," said Geoffrey lazily. "It's so comfortable, and I like the way the lamplight shines on your hair. But I suppose it *is* getting rather late."

"What happens here when the tide goes down?" asked Pamela. "And where do these tea leaves go?"

"Overboard. Oh, she floats all the time. That's the whole point of the moorings and the dinghy – you can get away in any state of the tide."

"Does Mr. Cross use the boat much?"

"Now and again. He's not really very keen – he's a landsman. I think he's only been aboard once or twice in the past six months. But there's not the same attraction in winter. Funny thing, I don't know who she belongs to, now. I suppose we'll have to decide. Damn! – now we're back on the old subject. This is the first time for three hours that I've remembered it."

"It'll be different when the inquest's over," said Pamela. "Please go on being gay."

But the spell was broken. Geoffrey was quiet and serious as he went around the boat putting everything shipshape and closing up the ports. Soon he was fastening the cover and climbing down into the dinghy. He helped Pamela down, holding her tightly. She made an unwise show of independence and came down beside him with a bang in the stern of the dinghy.

"All right?" he asked anxiously.

"Perfectly," she said, composing herself. It was dark; her face beside him was a pale glow. He ached to have her close against him. "Darling!" he said softly. The wind blew her hair against his face. In a moment he was holding her, kissing her mouth. At first she didn't resist, but presently she wriggled and he let her go. She said nothing, and he went into the bows, a little blindly, and began to row. He could still feel the softness of her lips. She was silent as he helped her out; silent as he dragged the dinghy up the hard and tied it to a stake.

"You're not angry?" he asked her, full of concern, as they walked up to the car.

She drew her scarf more tightly round her blowing hair.

"Did you say anything?" asked Geoffrey.

"No," said Pamela, out of the darkness. "I just shook my head."

CHAPTER XI

The inquest on Charles Hollison drew a big crowd of acquaintances and sightseers, and the report of its proceedings was prominently displayed in all the newspapers of the district. It was not merely that Hollison had been a well-known and respected local figure; what aroused so much interest was that he should have been so brutally murdered – he, of all people – and that there should be no clue pointing to a murderer.

The coroner knew his business, and the inquiry was completed with dispatch. All the facts that were known were given in evidence by Pamela, Geoffrey, Cross and Mrs. Armstrong; no new facts of the least significance were added by the police, who had to admit, in response to a sharp question, that they had not really made very much progress with the case yet. The inevitable verdict was returned of 'wilful murder against a person or persons unknown', and the coroner formally expressed his sympathy with the son and nephew in their tragic loss. The reporters went off to write up their copy and the public dispersed for an enjoyable gossip.

Cross, after a few sober words with Geoffrey and Pamela, thought it best that he should return to the Works for the rest of the day. Geoffrey drove Mrs. Armstrong and Pamela home in the Morris. Geoffrey was grim, and Pamela subdued. Mrs. Armstrong was indignant.

"I don't know what the law's coming to, I'm sure," said the housekeeper. "It seems to me we're none of us safe in our beds these days. I'll be afraid to stay in the house alone, I really will. If a gentle peaceable citizen can't answer his own front door without being hit on the head by a murdering villain, it's a fine look-out. I don't know what the police think they're doing. That old Inspector, with his kind face and his 'I-know-more-than-I'm-telling-you' look! – why, I could have done as well myself. Don't you think so, Mr. Geoffrey?"

Geoffrey shrugged. "It must be very difficult. I imagine we all know pretty well as much as the Inspector, and we've none of us any idea who did it."

"Well, it's a shame, that's what I say." Mrs. Armstrong had her views and could not be easily turned from them. "They're paid to find murderers and they ought to find them."

"Look at that evidence we've just heard," said Geoffrey. "Listening to that, the only logical conclusion I could come to – being in my position – was that the murder never really happened. I could have done it, but I know I didn't; Arthur couldn't have done it because he wasn't there; you couldn't have done it, Mrs. Armstrong, because you were at Ealing—"

"I should think not, indeed!" cried Mrs. Armstrong.

". . . and Pamela here couldn't have done it because she isn't strong enough. There's no one else in the picture. A stranger couldn't have done it for about a million reasons."

"And yet there the poor man was lying dead," said Mrs. Armstrong. "It's a wicked, wicked shame. If there's a God in heaven, he'll punish that man. He'll find him and punish him, you mark my words." And Mrs. Armstrong eased herself out of the car and went indoors to take off her Sunday clothes and get back into her Monday ones.

Geoffrey drove Pamela on round the corner and stopped the car and the engine outside her house. "Well, that's that," he said. "Pretty foul, wasn't it?"

Pamela nodded. "I think it's very heartless to ask the next-of-kin to identify the body. Almost anyone would have done."

"I suppose it was my job. That thing in the box didn't seem like him, anyway." He leaned heavily on the wheel. "If only they could have found the man who did it! I don't see how the case is ever going to be tidied up. We've all been over the ground so many times. I don't see how there can be any new evidence now. The whole thing gnaws at me."

"You mustn't dwell on it, Geoffrey. You *really* mustn't."

"I – oh, it's so easy to say that. I'll never quite get over the feeling that I'm not cleared. I suppose it was my imagination, but when the coroner offered his sympathy I couldn't help thinking one of the jurymen was looking at me with an odd expression, as much as to say, 'It's all very well, mister, but you could have done it, you know.' I bet at least half the people who were there today are now doing a simple problem in elimination."

"What do you mean?"

"Four 'possibles'. For various reasons three of them are ruled out. The fourth is therefore the man. It stands to reason."

"Oh, Geoffrey. . . ." Pamela looked very unhappy. "I'm sure you're wrong. If I'd been an ordinary member of the public I'd have been much more likely to suspect Mr. Cross if I'd suspected anybody."

"Against all the evidence? That wouldn't do for the lab!"

"Well, I didn't like him much. I'm sorry, but I just didn't. He looked me up and down with those flinty eyes of his as though he was wondering whether I'd make a good pick-up."

"Flinty? I've never noticed."

"You wouldn't. Now if he'd been a boat . . .! Anyway, I didn't like him. I thought he seemed all knotted up inside, and flabby outside."

"Sheer female prejudice. Oh well, I suppose I'd better drift along to the Admiralty. Funeral tomorrow, and then we'll try to forget."

"Let's go somewhere Thursday evening," said Pamela. "A show, or something. We must keep you occupied."

"All right," said Geoffrey. "You're an angel, and I'm a misery. Good-bye." He pressed her fingers and let her go.

The Inspector and the Superintendent were having a hardly less gloomy session in the Super's office. James had his feet up, his pipe alight, and a pair of spectacles on his nose. He was reading through his notes all over again. The Superintendent was sitting anxiously forward at his desk, his elbows on the table, waiting for the Inspector to have an idea. His faith in James was getting a bit ragged at the edges.

Finally the Inspector flung his notebook on to the desk and swore savagely.

"It's no good," he said. "Cross was right. In spite of what I told him. The damned case is as good as closed. The only real hope was that someone would come forward who'd seen something – and no one has. You'd think that at *some* stage *someone* would have noticed something funny, wouldn't you? People in this country mind their own business too much, that's the trouble. Too tolerant. See a man cutting his wife's throat in the street and put it down to eccentricity! . . . I've been through all the dead man's papers – there's not a hint of any trouble anywhere. I've seen his solicitor and his bank manager. Blanks everywhere. It's all *most* unsatisfactory . . . nags at you, that's what it does. All the little things point to Cross, and yet . . ."

Jackson tried to think of something helpful to contribute. "There's no smoke without fire," he said.

"No? I read those sworn statements again last night," said James wearily. "In the face of that evidence you wouldn't get a conviction even if Cross had told somebody that very day that he was going to do it, even if he'd been heard quarrelling with his uncle, even if he'd been found soaked in blood from head to foot!" James banged on the desk in his exasperation. "He wasn't there, blast his eyes! Hell – what's the good of bellyaching? I may as well admit that this is my worst failure. I'll have to report the case as a total loss. The only thing that can still save us is a stroke of luck. We deserve one – we haven't had any. Isn't it true that every murderer makes one mistake? No, don't say it – I know the answer. It isn't true. Some murderers get away with it. But when you think of all the complex details that go to make up a murder like this – the planning, the execution, the coherent story the murderer has to tell afterwards – you'd think that something would go wrong somewhere. Cross has an answer for everything – some of them aren't very good answers, but they serve."

The Inspector sighed and got up. "Well, I'm going back to the Yard to take the rap. Maybe the Assistant Commissioner will be able to see a little daylight through the problem. But I doubt it."

Cross was far from gloomy. The inquest had not given him a moment's worry. There had been no surprises of any sort. Whatever suspicions the Inspector might have had, he had given no hint of them. He had been completely stymied by the alibi. Cross had been too clever for him.

Now it was possible to begin planning ahead with some assurance. Sooner or later it would be necessary to sell out his share of the business – what he needed was limitless cash. But he mustn't be too hasty – there were currency restrictions for people going abroad, and the business might be a help. He could say he was off to South America to collect export orders or open a branch or something. Once he was there he would be able to find a way of getting round the currency regulations. Plenty of people did.

He let his imagination play with many attractive possibilities. Rio was a fine civilized city – by all accounts there wasn't a better place in the world for a man with lots of money. No food shortage there, no housing problem, plenty of red meat. He would get himself a dark-eyed Spanish mistress – as lovely as Geoffrey's little piece, but not so goody-goody and serious. A sophisticated woman – someone who knew what it was all about – someone you could have fun with. He'd rent a luxurious flat with a splendid view over the harbour. He'd have an enormous limousine and a fast sports car as well, of course, for getting around outside town. Then he'd have a ranch or villa, or whatever they called them – *haciendas?* – those brilliant white houses with sunny verandahs and flowers up the wall. And lots of servants. He'd entertain – perhaps become quite a figure in the place. There must be a large foreign colony, and he was good at the social stuff. He could always seduce some of the diplomats' wives if he got bored. He could travel a bit if he felt like it – Hawaii, perhaps, or the West Indies. Warm places, with golden beaches, exotic clothes, beautiful women, and plenty of leisure for everything. Swimming, surf-bathing, aquaplaning, speedboats. His imagination rioted. And he wouldn't need to worry any more – nobody would think of looking for him there, and if they did they wouldn't be able to touch him. How right he had been to take those few risks he had taken! A bit of a gamble, a reasonable gamble, and it had come off brilliantly.

He felt even more cheerful the next evening. Uncle Charles had been buried. It had been a bit tedious putting on an air of gloom

all day, but now one could relax a bit. Hollison's solicitor had paid
a respectful call on the two heirs at the house in Welford Avenue.
Uncle Charles had been as good as his word – Cross had always
felt that he could trust Uncle Charles. The old boy had been straight
– a decent, reliable type. There was more money even than Cross
had imagined – a whole string of first-class investments, as well as
the business, and a third of all of it went to 'my very dear nephew
Arthur'. The investments were as good as cash, and there would
be no difficulty now in raising an overdraft for any amount at the
bank. He and Geoffrey had talked about the business, and decided
to begin looking around for a buyer. Uncle Charles had not made
any provision about keeping the business in the family, bless him
– hadn't even expressed a wish. He had attached no strings at all.
There was a useful lump sum for Mrs. Armstrong, and a few jewels
for Geoffrey's wife if and when he married, and some personal
oddments for Geoffrey, and a thoughtful provision or two for old
employees. Cross didn't mind that – didn't even mind Geoffrey's
two-thirds. He could afford to be generous. Geoffrey, of course,
had tried to give the impression that he was indifferent about the
whole thing, but he'd find the money useful enough later on,
particularly if he married that girl. Lucky chap, Geoffrey – but
Cross wasn't jealous. One good-looker was very like another, and
she didn't give the impression of having much experience. She was
a peach, certainly, but there were plenty more on the tree and Cross
was in a position to give it a good shake.

Geoffrey had asked him to stay at Welford Avenue for a bite
of food, and Cross had agreed – reluctantly. The fact was that
Geoffrey's long face gave him a pain in the stomach. Absurd to
take these things so hard. Damn it, the old man had to die some
time, and it had been a nice quick death.

Cross returned to his flat about nine. He would have a quiet couple of hours with a book, and a few drinks, and then go to bed. After all, it *had* been rather an exacting day. He took a newspaper out of the letter-box as he went in, and after he had got himself a whisky he settled down to read it. It was one of the local papers – the *Gazette* – and it carried a verbatim account of the inquest. Cross read the report carefully, and found it entirely satisfactory. His own evidence, he thought, gave just the right impression. He had said neither too much nor too little. There had been no sticky questions or unpleasant innuendoes from the coroner. "Would you care to tell us, Mr. Cross, how you yourself spent the evening?" And Cross had told him, all right – just a shade off-hand, just sufficiently frank. "Thank you very much, Mr. Cross, for that very lucid statement." All the essential details, without too much padding. The newspaper had managed to get Geoffrey's picture and his own picture – heaven knew how – and there was a photograph of the house in Welford Avenue and a little sketch of the hall, with an X marking where the body had lain. There was no photograph of the bombed house, Cross noted with a smile. No one had seemed particularly interested in the account of his misadventure there – and why should they have been? It mattered to him, but not to anyone else. The paper was much more interested in Pamela Whitworth. It carried her picture, too – full length, taken just before the inquest, by the look of it. It did her less than justice, Cross thought – didn't show her curves. There was quite a chunk of biographical detail about her, too. It had certainly been a wonderful case for the Press.

He threw the paper aside and poured another drink. Peace, perfect peace! He was just toying with the idea of taking a leisurely bath and turning in with a new thriller when he heard a step outside his door, and the bell suddenly shrilled. Odd, since he wasn't expecting anybody – it was most rare for him to have callers in the evenings. Surely it couldn't be the Inspector again? If so the play-acting wasn't over after all. Or his past catching up on him just when everything was rosy? He opened the door with frozen features. It was a woman.

"Mr. Arthur Cross?" she asked.

"That's quite right."

"I wondered if I could speak to you for a minute."

"Of course," said Cross, disrobing her with an expert eye. Never let it be said that he had refused admission to a young woman! "Come in."

She walked in, self-consciously diffident, and Cross examined her. She was fairly young – twenty-five to thirty – and easy on the eye. She brought with her into the room the odour of cheap, heavy scent of a sort with which Cross was not unfamiliar. She wore a fur coat which had once clothed quite a number of rabbits. She was spectacularly blonde, with hair done up Edwardian fashion and surmounted by a hat consisting mainly of purple gauze. Three little blonde ringlets were carefully arranged across the upper part of her forehead.

"Have a chair," said Cross politely.

"Thanks," said the girl. "I don't mind if I do." There was a thin veneer of studied refinement in her voice, overlaying a solid foundation of Cockney. She sat back, loosened her coat and revealed a luscious figure. She crossed one leg over the other provocatively, and smiled. Cross noticed that she had a small button mouth, enlarged and re-shaped by thickly-applied lipstick.

"Lovely place you have here," she said, gazing around admiringly.

"Not bad," said Cross.

"I bet you have a good time here."

"What exactly have you come to see me about, Miss . . .?" He raised his eyebrows.

"Garton – Doris Garton. I live at Kingston. I work in Cutter's – you know, the dress shop in Market Street. Lady assistant."

"Oh, yes. Would you care for a cigarette?" Cross was feeling his way.

"Well, since you ask me I won't say no. Players? I reely prefer Luckies. Still, we can't be choosy these days, can we?" She took a lighter from a purple handbag and flicked it on before Cross could make a move. "Nice lighter, isn't it?" she said. "Came all the way from America. Given me by a gentleman friend."

"Reely?" said Cross. "Look, Miss Garton: do tell me why you've come. I'm most charmed, of course, but . . . well, it is getting a bit late. I was just thinking of going to bed."

"Don't let me stop you," said the girl impudently.

"You're a fast worker," said Cross. "Just feeling lonely? Or what?"

"Well, if you want to know, Mr. Cross, it's like this. You see, when I finished work last night I just happened to buy a paper, and I read all about the inquest on that poor man that was hit over the head."

"You mean my uncle?" said Cross. He sat down. Somehow he felt less interested in Miss Garton's legs than he had thought he was going to be.

"That's right. Wasn't it orful? I felt so sorry for his son – the naval commander. Such a handsome man in his uniform, with that curly hair and nice smile."

"Please go on," said Cross.

"Well, it was so interesting I read all through it – every word. All about that lady doctor, and the blood, and Mr. Hollison being on his way to the house, and you being lost in the fog, and no one knowing anything about what happened. It made me feel quite funny."

"I'm sure it did. I still don't see to what I owe the pleasure of this visit."

"Coo, how you talk! I'm just coming to that. I read everything you said to the coroner. About the people you picked up in your car, and how you got lost with them, and how you suddenly found yourself in Hamley Avenue by mistake. And how you got out to ask the way and found yourself in a bombed house, and fell over and hurt yourself. It was such an interesting story, with the fog and all – mysterious, just like the pictures. I love the pictures, don't you?"

"I think there's something to be said for a good murder now and again," said Cross coolly. "I still don't see what all this has got to do with you, Miss Garton."

"I'm coming to it – you mustn't hurry me." She giggled, and Cross winced. "You see, I wasn't a lady assistant till quite recently – I was in the A.T.S., you know. But I didn't like it – I always say a girl's figure never looks its best in uniform." She uncrossed her legs, and crossed them the other way. "Do you think it does?"

"Come on, Doris, tell me what's on your mind," said Cross.

"I say – bit familiar, aren't you? Anyway, what I was saying was that I was in the A.T.S., and I had a gentleman friend. He was an American, a sergeant. He always said he wanted to marry me. We got on a treat. It was him that gave me these nylons." She showed him a good deal more than her nylons. "And he taught me to chew gum." Again she giggled. "Well, to cut a long story short, he had to go back to America last week. He said he'd get everything ready for me and then I could go over in a liner and be a G.I. bride. We were reely going to the pictures when he told me, but he said he'd like a bit of a walk. I thought it was silly, because it was Thursday – ever so foggy, it was, and you could hardly see where you were going, but he said that was a good thing. He said he wanted to be alone with me. You know what men are – they all want the same thing. We walked about for a bit, and he said didn't I know anywhere quiet? I said I was cold, but he said he was steamed up enough for both of us. So then I said, since we were in Hamley Avenue – ooh, you've dropped your cigarette, Mr. Cross."

"That's all right," said Cross. "Go on."

". . . Since we were in Hamley Avenue, I *did* happen to know there was a bombed house where we could be quiet for a bit." She simpered. "I wouldn't like you to think I make a practice of that sort of thing, Mr. Cross, but – well, between ourselves I had been there just once before, with a Polish officer I felt sorry for, and it was fairly comfy, if you knew where the broken glass was. So we went in there. It was quite easy, reely, because he had a torch, and there was an old settee that somebody had left. Anyway, it *was* cold, but after all, it was his last night. He said he wanted me to have something to remember him by."

"Well?" said Cross.

"It's a funny thing, Mr. Cross, but in this paper you say that you were there as well. About eight o'clock, you say. Now Cy and me, we got there at half past seven and we were there till half past eight – I always say a girl shouldn't let a man have his way too quickly, even if it is foggy. And nobody came near us all that time. I mean, we should've known, shouldn't we? So when you told the coroner you were there, I thought maybe there was some mistake, and that I'd better come and see you about it."

Cross pretended relief. "If there's any mistake it must be yours, Doris," he said good-naturedly. "I was certainly there, as I said in the evidence. The two people who were with me know that I was. I can only suppose you were having such a good time that you didn't notice what was going on around you."

"Don't you believe it," said Doris sharply. "I'm not as silly as all that. Not with men, I'm not. Besides, there was always the chance a policeman might decide to have a look-see, and I don't want my name in the papers – not in that way. They wouldn't like it at the shop. I was keeping one ear open all the time, and there wasn't the tiniest sound. You say – " she picked up the paper – " . . . you say that you knocked twice on the door – loud, you say – and that you called out, 'Is anyone there?' Well, now, don't you think we'd have heard you if you'd done that – with the front door half open and all? And you say you fell over something. We'd have heard that, too." She held out a neat foot, and appeared to be admiring the shoe. "Why, Mr. Cross, I could swear on my oath that from half past seven till half past eight last Thursday no one came anywhere near that house except us."

Cross got up. "I don't know what your game is, Doris, but if you aren't very careful something worse is going to happen to you than getting your name in the papers. There's such a thing as slander and perjury, you know. The first costs you a lot of money, and for the second you go to jail. I was with two very respectable people that night – a man from the Foreign Office, for one thing – and they know perfectly well where I was and what I was doing. Either you've made a silly mistake, or else you're deliberately trying to make trouble – and that's dangerous."

"So that's your tone, is it?" said Doris shrilly, suddenly leaning forward and shedding the illusion of feminine softness like a coat. "Well let me tell *you*, Mr. Clever, that it doesn't look so good for you, either. I don't know what you were up to that night, but there were some very funny things going on. *Very* funny, if you ask me. And I know you weren't where you said you were."

"There's only your word for it," said Cross contemptuously. "Do you think anyone would believe your ridiculous story – that is, if you dared to tell it? I'd like to see you in court, explaining how you spent the evening in a bombed house with an American soldier."

"Be your age," said Doris. "It's always happening. Maybe I wouldn't like talking about it, but if I thought it was my duty—"

Cross laughed harshly. "Your *duty*! Don't be funny. Anyway, I tell you nobody would believe you."

"We'll see about that," said Doris. She got up and reached for her coat. "If you ask me, the police'll be *very* interested."

Cross took a deep breath. A great pit had opened in front of him, and he felt a little giddy. He could see there were two ways of handling the situation, but one was too dangerous to risk. He'd never be able to get rid of her body. He must play for time.

He said: "Look, there's no reason for us to quarrel. I'm sure there's some mistake. What about a drink? Whisky, gin?"

"Now you're talking! Gin and orange, please. Not much orange." She sat down again, and drew her skirt delicately above her knee. "I thought we should understand each other in time."

"I'm sure we shall," said Cross. "Cheers!"

"Mud in your eye!" The gin went down in one.

"That's better," said Cross. "Have another?"

"Coo, you going to try and get me tight? You've got a job on, I can tell you. Well, p'raps just a little one."

"Now," said Cross, when they were comfortably settled, "just tell me where you *think* I was that night. Cards on the table."

"Blowed if I know," said Doris. "But if you weren't where you said you were, maybe there was something you were trying to hide. Of course, I'm not a detective – but after all, there *was* a murder done that night."

"You think I murdered my uncle?"

"Ooh, I wouldn't say that! That's awful." The impact of the

idea seemed too much for Doris, but she made a swift recovery. "But I suppose you could've, couldn't you? You must have been somewhere."

"Tell me, what did Cy think about it?"

"Oh, he didn't know about this – he'd gone back home before the paper came out. Demobbed."

"What was his name?"

"Smith. He said there were a lot of Smiths in America, same as here. I guess there are, too. His first name was Cyrus – funny name, isn't it?"

"Very American." Cross was trying to be casual. "Know where he lives?"

"Oh, yes – Chicago. He hadn't got a proper address – been in the army so long, he said – but he said he'd tell me his new address when he wrote."

"Do you think he'll write?"

"Of course he will," said Doris. She caught Cross's eye. "Well, and if he doesn't, what of it? I should worry." She stroked her nylons. "Plenty of fish in the sea, that's my motto."

"You express yourself with admirable clarity," said Cross. "Of course, you're quite wrong in your suspicions of me. I was at the bombed house, in spite of what you say. I wouldn't in the least mind your going to the police, or anyone else, except that I really don't want the whole wretched business brought up again."

"I'm sure you don't," said Doris sympathetically. "I'm sure you'd like to forget it. Anybody would."

"Exactly. Well, what about us forgetting it together? You know what I mean. Your boy friend's gone to America, and I haven't got a girl friend. Suppose you hitch up with me for a while. We could have a pretty good time together. I've got – er – well, enough money to give you a good time. . . ."

"I'll say you have," said Doris greedily. "I read all about it in the paper."

"I hardly imagined you'd have missed it," said Cross. His fingers itched to strangle her. What a bitch!

"You don't have to be nasty. Fair's fair. If you treat me properly, I'll keep my mouth shut. But I can't stand mean gentlemen. Would you like me to stay here tonight?"

Cross looked at her – the shining hair, the kiss curls, the provocative breasts, the pink flesh above nylons, the crimson nails and the stilt-like shoes – and gave an inward shudder. In other circumstances, yes, but . . .

"I'm a bit tired tonight," he said. "I think you'd better go home."

"Lumme," said Doris, "you're a funny one. Still, have it your own way. I expect you'll be screaming for me before long. What time do I see you tomorrow, and where?"

"If you like," said Cross, "we'll go out to dinner. I'll drive you up to town and we'll go to a nice quiet spot."

"Not so much of the quiet," said Doris. "Sounds stuffy to me. Bit of dancing, I like, or a prize fight. I love prize fights. You'll soon get to know my tastes."

"Anyway," said Cross, "let's make it a quiet place tomorrow, just for once. Get to know each other a bit, eh?" His tone was wheedling.

"Okay, but I shan't be free till about seven, because of the job." She smiled. "Not that that matters so much now, does it?"

He stood behind her and helped her on with her coat. He saw that her hair was full of dandruff. She pushed her bottom against him and giggled. He put his hands on her shoulders, his fingers moved towards her neck. Then he thought of the lighted stairs and the porter down below, and he went and poured himself another drink instead.

"Greedy!" she said. "What about me? Just one for the road."

"A good long one?"

"No, you jerk, gin." She raised the glass. "Here's to us, big boy. You and me are going to enjoy life from now on." She pinched his cheek and he forced a smile.

"I'll pick you up at seven, at the roundabout," he said. He let her out, and he heard the lift coming up for her.

He went back inside and sank into a chair, his shoulders slumped. His luck had turned, all right.

CHAPTER XII

For hours that night Cross sat and wrestled with the new situation. The more he thought about it, the worse it seemed.

It had been all very well to tell Doris that the police wouldn't take her word – the word of a common little floozie – against the story of his own two reputable witnesses. But Doris had been damnably right when she had said the police would be interested. It might take them a long while to unravel the whole complicated and ingenious plot, but once they'd got a loose end in their teeth they'd never let go. Cross could just see the Inspector throwing himself into the case again. He could imagine only too well the interview between Doris and the Inspector, and the train of thought that it would start. James had been aching all along to get a wedge under a corner of that alibi. Doris would provide it. Taking Doris's story as a starting point, the Inspector would certainly have new inquiries made of the two witnesses in Buenos Aires. He'd want to know, in the greatest detail, what was the positive evidence on which they based their view that they'd been at the bombed house. When they were really pressed, they'd have to admit that they'd never actually seen any part of the house, even the gate: that the car hadn't even stopped outside it: that, in fact, they'd no evidence at all except Cross's words and behaviour and, of course, the name-plate.

The question was, would the Inspector ever be able to jump the big gap between knowing that the alibi had been faked, and knowing *how* it had been faked? Would it ever occur to him that the name-plate had been changed? The Inspector had plenty of imagination – what Cross had planned, he might well think of himself. Certainly, James could never prove anything. The evidence had been burned. There was no conceivable way in which he could demonstrate to a jury that Cross had changed the name-plate. He might suspect it, he might even outline possible methods. He might be astute enough to hit on the actual method that Cross had used. But he couldn't prove it.

There was another danger, though. Cross's witnesses had been sure enough that they had been in Hamley Avenue. But if another witness appeared – even one of such dubious character as Doris – equally ready to swear that Cross had not been there – with a lot of very human reasons why she was so sure – might not his own witnesses waver? Particularly if the Inspector had put the idea of a faked alibi into their minds? They had been certain enough at the time, but the sharpness of their visual picture would fade. Even if it didn't, and they stuck to their story, might not a jury argue that after all it *had* been foggy and anyone could make a mistake? Cross could just hear a skilful counsel examining his witnesses, and successfully introducing just a shadow of doubt into their story. And a shadow might be enough.

All the other evidence would fit. The Inspector would produce his little bits of jigsaw – the pick-up at the roundabout, for the second time on a foggy Thursday; the five minutes away from the car, long enough to do the murder; the telephone call, so essential for a man with a faked alibi, and the disguised voice, so necessary for a man who might be encountered later as a member of the family; the placing of Geoffrey's notes, which could have been done only by someone with inside knowledge; the blood on the coat and the hasty efforts to clean it up; the fact that something had been burned in the grate; the financial straits of the accused; the temptation of a fortune. By the time

a good counsel, briefed by the Inspector, had put all those bits
of the jigsaw in place, they would make a pretty damning pattern.
What verdict would a jury bring in on that evidence? Cross
simply didn't know. All he knew was that many a man had been
hanged on no more circumstantial evidence than that. He would
certainly, unquestionably, be arrested; he would have to stand
trial; it would take weeks, perhaps months. He would never get
abroad. Even taking the most optimistic view of the prospects,
Cross could see no future for himself in letting Doris go ahead
and tell her story.

So Doris must be silenced. That meant that he must either kill
her quickly, before she had been seen around with him, or he must
buy her off and go on buying her off.

Cross knew a blackmailer's strength. He would have made a
good blackmailer himself. He would have drained his victim dry,
without mercy. What would Doris be like at the game? There were
risks – you had to know the ropes.

He thought back to her visit. She had been astute enough to
realize the value of her knowledge, which meant she wasn't nearly
as dumb as she looked. Her approach had been clever. Her 'tastes',
as she called them, were probably not very expensive at the moment,
but they would no doubt mature in a suitable atmosphere. She was
unscrupulous, heartless and greedy. It was impossible to guess what
her ultimate demands might be, but it was reasonable to suppose
she would strip him pretty thoroughly before she'd finished with
him.

What was worse, she'd always be around – in the way. It would
be no good his paying her a good sum and then skipping off to
South America on his own – she'd tell her story to get her own
back, and extradition on a murder charge would be simple enough
to arrange. He might be able to change his name, disappear, go

underground – but that wasn't what he had killed Uncle Charles for.

No, she'd always be a millstone round his neck. Could he bear that – as an alternative to discovery? He could hear her talking now – a grating recollection. He could hear her giggling. He remembered that swift change from sexy wheedling to raucous shouting, when it had looked as though he wasn't going to play. She would drive him crazy. There would be no peace of mind, no fun, as long as she was alive.

Then he must kill her. It would be a pleasure. But it wouldn't be easy. In the case of his uncle, he had thought everything out carefully beforehand, made detailed preparations, covered himself against all – no, almost all! – contingencies. With Doris, he couldn't do that. He would have to act swiftly – within the next forty-eight hours. Even so it would be risky. The porter might remember her as the woman who had come up to the flat when her picture appeared in the papers. Cross would have to have some explanation for that visit. If a connection were traced between them, the police would be on to him like lightning. Two murders within a week – and he mixed up in both of them! Cross didn't like it at all – any part of it. He reflected grimly that army commanders must feel like this when their great offensives had not quite succeeded, and the relentless tide was beginning to run against them. Had he passed his peak? Would he be able to impose his will on events much longer?

He was so tired, so depressed. He would try to sleep on the problem. He would be meeting Doris the next evening, and he could decide then what to do. Perhaps she'd prove more manageable than he dared to hope.

Sharp at seven the next night he parked the Rover at the roundabout. He was glad it was dark – it was most unlikely that anyone would notice them. He knew the way that Doris would come, and kept a sharp look-out. At five past seven she came swinging along the pavement. He could see as she climbed in that she still wore the rabbit fur and that underneath she had a satiny mauve frock with a monstrous diamanté brooch. In the closed car her perfume was stifling.

"Well, big boy, I've given in my notice," she announced, almost before she was seated. "*I* told that old bitch a thing or two. 'If you think you can talk like that to me,' I said, 'you've got another think coming.' I said, 'Call yourself a lady,' I said, 'why, you wouldn't know one if you saw one.' You should've heard me. Coo, I could use a drink. What about stopping at the 'Monkey Puzzle', eh?"

Cross slipped the car into gear. "I don't think we ought to hang about here," he said. "I reserved a table at the *Moulin Vert* for seven-thirty, and they might not keep it if we're late."

" 'Course they'll keep it – for *you*. I bet you're a good customer." She gave him a nudge with her elbow.

"As a matter of fact, it's a new place to me – recommended by a friend. It won't take us long to get there."

"I hope it's good," said Doris. "It had better be. I say, I'd like to see that old cow's face if she knew I was going off like this with Mr. Arthur Cross, the paint manufacturer. Make her eyes pop, wouldn't it? The things she said! – talk about rude. Do you know what I told her?" Doris giggled. "I told her I was going over to Paris for the weekend. That shook her. Mind you, I always say you can't expect everyone to like you."

"Of course not. Did you actually tell her we were going out together?"

"Not me! People 'ud think something was up if I started talking about you."

"Good girl. It wouldn't help you much to kill the goose that lays the golden eggs, would it?"

"How do you mean?"

"Well, what you said – if anyone got suspicious about me, I'd be no more good to you."

"Don't worry – I know how to keep my mouth shut, when it pays. It'll be different in Paris – no one'll know you there."

"Paris?"

"Sure. We're going this weekend. I told you."

"My dear girl, we can't go off to Paris like that. You need passports and things."

"Go on, you can fix it."

"I could have a try, I dare say." Why should he argue? What did it matter what she thought she'd do in the weekend?

" 'Course you can, you poor fish. Why, Cy said he could get me over to the States right away, only there wasn't a house ready. You don't mind me talking about Cy, do you?"

"It's a pleasure," said Cross.

"He was such a nice boy. Knew his onions, too. You're not exactly hot stuff, are you? Need some pep putting into you, if you ask me."

"These murders take it out of one," said Cross.

"So could I, big boy. Just give me a break. I say, did you reely do your uncle in?"

"Of course I didn't. I liked him – what would I want to do a thing like that for?"

"Come off it! What about all that dough?" The car stopped. "Is this the place? Looks pretty dull, I must say. Why not the 'Trocadero'?"

"Next time," said Cross. He led the way in, quietly gave the name in which he had booked a table, and followed Doris to the corner. He helped her to slip the rabbit off her shoulders and winced under the full impact of the mauve frock. "Sherry or gin?" he asked.

Doris pondered. "I think I'll have sherry tonight," she said. She leaned over and whispered in Cross's ear. She laughed. "That's the one thing wrong with gin," she said. She turned to the wine waiter. "Oh, and then champagne, of course."

"Of course," said Cross. "The best you have, waiter."

"Believe it or not," said Doris, "I haven't had champagne since I went to Brighton with a Colonel just before Christmas. He was a real card – tried to get me plastered. But he didn't manage it. I said to him, 'Colonel,' I said, 'I don't need that to warm *me* up,' I said. And what d'you think he said next morning?"

"I've no idea."

"He said, 'I see what you mean, little girl.'"

"Witty fellow," said Cross. "Now what will you eat? Anything specially good, waiter?"

"I'll have lobster," said Doris with an air of finality.

"I'm sorry, madame – there's no lobster tonight."

"Those people are having lobster over there," said Doris in a loud voice.

"They brought it themselves, madame."

"Oh yeah? Do you believe that, Arthur? Tell him to bring some lobster. Tell him to fetch the head waiter."

"I'll call the head waiter, madame."

Cross controlled himself with an effort. "I'm sure they haven't got any," he said. "People do bring their own stuff here, you know."

"Then why didn't we? You're a fine sort to take a girl out."

"If you make a scene," said Cross, "you'll probably get our names in the papers and start a lot of trouble. What about some mushroom soup to start with? Or shall we see what the hors d'œuvres looks like?"

"I hate mushrooms. Filthy things. Lobster for me."

"Look, have some fresh salmon. Come on, Doris – after you've had a few glasses of champagne you won't know the difference between that and lobster."

"Oh, no?" The head waiter was approaching. He bent over Doris, coldly impersonal.

"Can I help you, madame?"

"Oh, it's nothing at all, thank you. We'll have hors d'œuvres and salmon." She watched him walk away. "Dirty little Frenchman," she said. She sat and sulked.

"Here are the drinks, anyway," said Cross. "Cheers."

"Bung-ho," said Doris gloomily. "This is a lousy joint. You'll have to do better than this. A lot better."

"Don't hurry me," said Cross. "I've all sorts of plans for the future – for you and me. How would you like a nice mink coat?"

"Do you mean it? What, mink? Coo, that'll cost you a fortune." She had brightened up at once. "I'll wear it at the shop the day I leave." She gave her dreadful little giggle, that sounded so much like 'er-er-er-er-er'. "When can we get it?"

"I'll pop into a place I know during the week. You'll look all right in mink."

"I'll say! I bet Cy wouldn't ever of got me mink." She watched the waiter pouring the champagne. "Here's to you and me," she said. "Hope it bucks you up a bit."

"Don't worry. I'll give you a good time. I know just the place you'll like in Paris. A new hotel – built just before the war – overlooking the Champs Elysées. Lots of chromium and American bars and plenty of bell boys."

She leaned over and gave his hand a playful tap with her fork. "Comfy beds?"

"Excellent beds – you'll like them."

"You're not kidding! Better than that settee in Hamley Avenue, anyway. Coo, the springs were awful."

"The salmon's not too bad, is it?"

"Could be worse," said Doris, pushing forward her glass to be filled. "Maybe you and me 'ull get along all right after all. What you need's a shove now and again. What shall we do tomorrow? Spot of dancing? Of course, I reely need a new frock—"

"We'll get you one," said Cross.

"But what about tomorrow?"

"Tomorrow?" Cross smiled. "I'll think up something really special for tomorrow. Let's drink to it."

"What sort of thing?"

"Ah! – it's a secret. I'm giving a lot of thought to it. It's something that's never happened to you before, something that'll never happen to you again, and something that you'll never tell anybody about."

Doris giggled. "It sounds rude."

"No," said Cross; "if it were you'd talk about it. It's something that'll knock you absolutely cold – something absolutely unique in your experience."

Doris spluttered. "How you talk!" she said. "You'll be the death of me!"

Of course, she was impossible! How could he ever have had a moment's doubt about it?

He was back in the flat, lying in a steaming bath, thinking. He was meeting her tomorrow at the same time. And tomorrow he must kill her. He would pick her up in the car and drive out towards the country. She would probably make trouble about that, so he would have to kill her very soon after they had started. The sooner the better. He would throttle her – that would be nice and clean. Then he'd choose a quiet bit of road and drag the body into a wood and leave it there. In a day or two, no doubt, it would be found, but there'd be nothing to connect him with it. When they started going into her activities they'd probably conclude that one of her soldier boy friends had done it. It was quite usual for floozies to finish up that way. The whole thing would soon blow over, and he'd be as safe as he'd been before the girl knocked at his door.

Sharp at seven the next evening he was waiting at the old spot. He would be glad when the job was done. He no longer felt entirely confident – he couldn't get it out of his mind that he was being pushed around by events. But he'd fight back all the way. Tonight he'd done something which he hadn't felt to be necessary before. Just before leaving the flat he'd slipped into his coat pocket the revolver which he'd carried all through Poland and Germany. You never knew, carrying a body about. Something might go wrong. If it did he'd try to shoot his way out.

He'd also taken the spanner out of the tool-box again and put it in the pocket of the car beside him. Just in case.

It was the right weather for the job. No moon and a strong wind. It would be dark and noisy.

He didn't see Doris until she was opening the car door. She slammed it behind her, angrily, and flopped into the seat. "I don't see any fun riding round in a car this weather," she said. "Let's go to your place. I don't feel so good."

"What's the matter – hangover?"

"That champagne was poison. Else it was the fish. Come on, what are we hanging about for?"

"You need a drink," said Cross.

"You're telling me."

"I'll tell you what," said Cross, "we'll run out along the by-pass and have a couple of quick ones and then we'll come back and make ourselves cosy at the flat."

"You would choose a night when I don't feel like being cosy. All right, have it your own way." Cross let in the clutch. "But I still don't see why we shouldn't go straight to the flat."

"Oh, for heaven's sake stop nattering," said Cross.

"What did you say?"

"I said shut up," said Cross savagely, turning into the by-pass and opening the throttle.

"Well, hark at him!" said Doris, leaning back against the door and trying to see his face in the light of the dashlamp. "Who do you think you're talking to, I'd like to know? Aren't you forgetting something? I thought I gave the orders in this outfit."

"That's where you're wrong," said Cross. "*I* give them."

She was suddenly frightened. "Take me back. Stop, do you hear?"

Cross lashed out viciously with the back of his hand and he felt his knuckles jar against her teeth. "I told you to be quiet."

"Ooh, you damned swine!" she screamed at him. She began to yell at the top of her voice and pound with her fists at his head. The car rocked dangerously. He braked hard and brought it to a stop so quickly that she was thrown forward against the windscreen. He could see in the driving-mirror that there was nothing on the road behind. Ahead, a car was approaching but it was a good way away. Time enough! He tried to get hold of her but she fought back wildly, screaming all the time like someone crazed and tearing at his face with her sharp fingernails. He felt the sudden pain. If he couldn't stop her screaming . . . she was strong and desperate and he was an undersized man. He would never reach her throat. She was trying to get the door open. . . . He grabbed the spanner and struck at her. Her arm broke the blow but he struck again and again, beating her down, and suddenly the screaming stopped and she was slumped on the seat, quiet. It was difficult to hit her hard enough because of the car roof. He took deliberate aim and cracked the spanner head down on her skull. That was better – that should have done the trick. He was shaking with excitement. Kneeling up on his own seat, he heaved and pushed at the body until little by little the sagging lump of flesh rolled over into the back of the car. He covered it with a rug.

Peace! – at last. He'd never hear that voice again, anyway. But it had been a near thing. He'd almost bungled it. What a vicious little cat! There were deep scores down his face and neck and he felt a trickle of blood. That would take a bit of explaining. He carefully shone his torch on to the seat beside him. There was no blood there, but there would be in the back. He would have to clean it up after he'd got rid of the body. There was no respite – things were piling up.

He sat still for a moment or too. The oncoming car had passed, and there was still nothing behind. He lowered his window and listened. There was a house close by, on the right-hand side of the road, but it was in darkness. The wind was blowing in great gusts. It looked as though Doris had screamed in vain.

He would just light a cigarette first. His hands were still shaking. Now all he had to do was to drive into the country, hide the body, and remove all traces. It shouldn't take long. A simple job. He started the car. The sooner he got going, the sooner he'd be back. He drove fast. Every now and again a gust hit the side of the car and swung it off its course. He must be careful – the smallest accident would be disastrous. He tried not to think of what lay ahead – the search in the dark for the right spot, the heaving and the carrying, the risk of being seen. He kept on telling himself it was so simple he could put it out of his mind, and yet it weighed on him. He'd be bound to get blood on himself. . . . It was like seeing a film round twice.

He remembered the road from the old days. About twenty miles farther on – perhaps a little more – he would come to the wild country around Hindhead. He had often picnicked there in his youth. Just before you reached the Devil's Punch Bowl there were a lot of tracks leading off into thick woods. The trees would be bare now, of course, but if he could push the body down among the bushes it might lie there unnoticed for quite a time. He must have a look through Doris's bag before he threw it away and make sure there was no reference to himself – no address. He would do that before he moved the body. He would have to be careful to park the car where the tyre marks wouldn't show. And not to leave any footmarks. He could tie rags round his shoes, the way prisoners had wrapped up their feet in camp in cold weather.

He had to pull up at some traffic lights at Esher, and another car stopped close alongside. He had a moment of fear lest anyone should be able to see in, but there was no real danger. The body was well tucked up. Anyway, why should anybody be interested in the contents of his car? Still he felt nervous. A few nights ago there had been a routine police check-up on all cars leaving London – something to do with the crime wave. Suppose he were stopped on this road? With an effort of will he put the thought aside. They would hardly make another check so soon. But the feel of his gun was comforting.

The Rover was running like a clock, as it always had done. Just as well, with a corpse in the back. His eyes swept the instrument board, and suddenly he broke out into a sweat.

He had forgotten to fill her up! He had meant to, and then all this worry had put the thing out of his head. That showed he was slipping. Every time he had been out before on these errands he had checked the level. This time, when it was so vital, he had forgotten. According to the gauge, he had enough juice for ten more miles at most. Enough to get him into the country, but not enough to get him back. He dared not run it too fine – he'd be sunk completely if he ran out before he'd got rid of the body.

He slowed down and considered the situation. To stop or not to stop? Surely nobody would look in the back – and if they did there was damn all to see in the dark. He was still trying to decide when he saw a petrol station with three lighted pumps on the near side of the road. There was no other car there – it wouldn't take a minute. It was a small garage. He pulled in.

A youth came out of the garage and walked round to his window. "How many, sir?"

"Five," said Cross. He took some coupons out of his wallet and felt for some silver. He could only find a half-crown and some pennies. He would have to change a pound. He could hear the petrol running into the tank and the whirr of the pump. Hell, what a time it took! Cross leaned out. The youth was just putting the cap back on the tank.

"Twelve and eight, sir." Cross handed over the coupons and the note. He would have liked to slip away now, but it would look pretty odd if he left all that change. He sat grim and silent, till he heard the lad's step again. "Seven and four change, sir."

He was just going to press the starter when there was a loud and unmistakable moan from the back of the car. Cross stiffened. The face of the youth was at the window, pale and startled.

"Someone ill, sir?" Again there was a groan and dreadful stertorous breathing. Cross sat still for a second, his mind blacked-out. The youth had his head right inside the car. "Why, mister . . .!"

Cross reached for the spanner. Then he saw someone else coming out of the lighted garage. The youth gave a shout and ducked away. Cross rammed the car into bottom, let in the clutch with a snap and roared into the road.

The shouting died, but the moans went on.

Cross licked his dry lips, changed into top and pressed the accelerator to the boards. "God," he thought, "I'm on the run!"

CHAPTER XIII

For a few moments Cross drove on without a plan. He couldn't concentrate. That blackout had been a warning. He had been taxing himself too highly – the strain was beginning to tell.

The moaning, thank heaven, had ceased. Doris, unconscious again and evidently badly concussed, was snoring loudly. She had had her revenge, all right. If only he'd made sure of her . . .! But what was the good of thinking about that now?

The hunt was up. All his schemes were in ruins. The time had gone by for blueprints and timetables and castles in Spanish America. There was no question of a fortune now. All he could hope to salvage was his life. Whether he survived or not depended on his speed, guts and ruthlessness.

At the first opportunity, with the instinct of a hunted animal, he doubled back on his tracks. He felt better after he had taken two right-hand turns and was driving back towards London. The immediate task was to throw off any close pursuit – and then to find a hiding-place, however temporary.

Those chaps at the garage would have phoned the police by now. The youth had seen more than enough to make him suspicious – and Cross had threatened him with the spanner. They would describe the car – they would know the make and would probably remember the colour. At this very moment, in all likelihood, the flying-squad was getting its instructions. In a quarter of an hour, half an hour at most, a cordon would begin to close round the district.

He had got to decide quickly what to do. He could see that the car was his greatest danger – he ought to abandon it. It was for the car, not for him, that the police would be looking. But if he abandoned it the police would certainly pick it up and identify him through the registration number. It might take them a little time – a few hours, perhaps – to knock the right people up and get at the records, but those hours could be invaluable. He could see now that he ought to have driven out into the country and hidden the car right away, but already he was back in the near-suburbs and there was no obvious safe hiding-place. He daren't risk going back.

Whether or not they found the car, they would identify him by the petrol coupon. But they might not think of that at once. In any case it would take longer.

One thing was clear: by tomorrow morning he would be 'wanted for murder'. They'd have got to work on the petrol coupon long before then. There'd be a description out, and every policeman in the country would be keeping his eyes skinned. They'd be watching at the airfields and the ports. He would be far worse off than a deserter – he would have no base, no plans, and no friends. He wouldn't be able to get any money, except by violence. He wouldn't be able to manage for long with nothing but a gun – not in England.

He was getting things sorted out a bit now. He must postpone identification as long as possible – that meant sticking to the car. By doing that he would have the night before him as a free man. Just the night – the hours of darkness. Twelve or fifteen hours to save himself – that was all.

He must get out of the country. He must get to *Truant* right away. He could hide the car there, and he could go off in the boat. It had come to the worst. There was no other hope at all. The chance was slim, but at least it was a chance.

He would be able to think about details when he got to *Truant*. He would have a breathing space there. He would tuck the car away behind the refuse destructor – nobody would be likely to come searching there in the dark.

He felt a bit better, now that he had decided what to do. But he had a long way to go. He must join the main road again. There were risks in that, but in the dark he would lose himself on these unfamiliar secondary roads. Again he swung to the right.

Surely he could cover these last miles without being stopped? The trouble was that these radio cars moved into action in a flash. A 999 call from the garage, a swift transmission of the message, and the whole mobile force would be looking for him. Right now, probably, they were on the watch. He remembered how smartly they had picked up the two men who had stolen his Vauxhall. What years ago that seemed!

The built-up areas would be the worst – people, cars, traffic lights. There was Doris . . . she might attract attention. Was it worth stopping to finish her off? Perhaps he ought to. But he drove on.

He was driving as fast as his lights and the traffic would allow – faster than was safe. Once he nearly came to grief on a bend but he got out of the front-wheel skid just in time. He was approaching Esher and slowed to avoid attracting attention. There seemed a lot of people about, too many cars to be pleasant; too many street lamps. He got held up behind a Green Line coach. He was keeping a sharp look-out to left and right. Suddenly, in the centre of the little town, he saw a police car, stationary on the near side. He had just passed the coach. As he accelerated a uniformed figure suddenly rushed out from the pavement and held up his hand. Cross changed down and roared by, switching off his lights to prevent his number being taken. He heard a long whistle and a shout, and in the driving-mirror he could see the flying-squad car shooting away from the kerb.

It was touch and go, now. They would be calling other cars – the ring was closing. And yet he hadn't far to go – if he could throw them off just for a few miles he would be safe till morning.

The traffic lights ahead were just turning red. He opened the throttle. He was doing forty, fifty, fifty-five. No need to think, now. Sixty miles an hour and the red light was rushing towards him. Well, if he was unlucky it would be a quick death. He roared to the crossing, crouching over the wheel. He caught a glimpse of a bus towering, heard a screech of brakes, the shattering of glass. Chaos behind him! Something more to add to the account. The road was broad; he was touching sixty-five. Had the police car hit the bus? No, it was still there, not half a mile behind. Its great white beam, reflected in the windscreen, dazzled him. It was hanging on, gaining. Cross pushed the accelerator to the boards; the Rover was flat out now. The police had a bigger, faster car; they would catch him. He was coming into Kingston; at least he knew the roads well. At all costs he must avoid the centre; one check, one traffic block, would end the chase. They were close on his tail – hardly a quarter of a mile in it, now. Should he stop and shoot it out? They might not have guns. It seemed the only way.

No! He knew a better way. He braked hard, skidding round a curve. Ahead, the road forked. The left fork, little used, went straight to the river in a hundred yards and turned along the bank. Just before the fork he switched off all his lights and swung to the left. If the police hesitated at the junction, he might just do it! Cross slowed the Rover and opened the car door as it approached the river. It was tricky. He balanced on the running-board, the door right back against the coachwork. Five yards from the bank he stepped off and dived for a low wall. As he fell into wet grass, he heard the great splash of the Rover hitting the water and the police car roaring up with its lights blazing.

Had they seen him? He would know in a second. He crouched

with his gun at the ready. No one came to the wall. He heard voices at the bank, sharp instructions. He had beaten them.

He dared not look. He must get away from here. The car, he knew, would be completely submerged in ten feet of muddy water. It would take them hours to get it up, to discover the registration number, to find out that he wasn't in it. Cross wriggled his way along the inside of the wall, away from the river. There was little immediate danger now – it was pitch dark and the wind was blowing harder than ever. Presently he felt it was safe to walk upright. He seemed to be in a field or large garden. After fifty yards or so, he climbed over the wall back on to the road, hidden from the river by a slight bend, and set off into Kingston at a smart pace. He was just an ordinary honest citizen once more, with the right to look anyone in the face – till morning.

Suddenly he remembered Doris. Well, that was the end of her, anyway. Though the future was about as black as it could be, Cross felt curiously elated. He had been reprieved. He had fought his way through into the clear. Just to walk along the pavement in the raw gusty air was a pleasure. It would be good to have a drink. He *would* have a drink. It might be his last one for some time. He stopped under a lamp to examine his clothes. His knees and coat were a bit wet and muddy, but they would pass in a crowd. He ran a comb through his hair, wiped his smarting sweaty face with his handkerchief, and straightened his tie. He would call in at the 'Crown' – just for a quick one.

The saloon bar was comfortably full and he had to squeeze through to the counter. He ordered a double whisky. The barmaid gave him an odd look.

"Been fighting, mister?"

"Sort of," said Cross. He emptied the glass. "Give me another, love, will you?"

"You won't 'alf cop it when your best girl sees you."

"She did it," said Cross briefly. He drained the glass again. "Good night."

That was better. Now for the next round! He might still make it. This wasn't the first time he'd been hunted – and he'd got away with it before. Right across Europe – for months, with only a gun and his wits. You could get a long way if you were always ready to shoot. People didn't expect it. And most people weren't tough – they were kindly. So if you were tough you could get the better of them.

He'd be able to get to *Truant* all right, now. He joined a bus queue, took a twopenny ticket, and got off a quarter of a mile from the boathouse. Several people on the bus had stared at his face. Still, there was no law against getting scratched.

He walked quickly down to the water's edge. There was *Truant*, a blessed white shape out in the river. He stopped at the fringe of the soft mud, where three or four dinghies had been left dry by the tide. The wind showed no sign of abating. It was north-easterly, strong and cold. He shivered, and drew his coat more closely round him. He wished he had more whisky.

It had been easy to say, "I'll get away in *Truant*." It was quite another thing to do it. He knew there was no alternative, but as he thought of what lay ahead his spirits sank. He could get her engines started without trouble. He could take her down the river. That was easy – though it wouldn't be pleasant. But what then? It would be pitch black in the Estuary, and there'd be half a gale blowing. He didn't know the buoys and lights, he knew next to nothing about tides and shoals. It was a thousand to one that he'd run her aground or founder in big seas. Either he'd be rescued, and hanged, or else he'd drown. He had no fancy to drown. Of course, he could shoot himself before either of those things happened. Come to that, he could shoot himself just as well here.

Even in this sheltered reach upriver the boat was rocking and pitching as the wind met the incoming tide. He could just imagine the sea off Southend – all hell would be loose. He had guts, but not that sort of guts. That just wasn't his line of country. He knew for a certainty that he would never make a safe passage to the Continent alone. There was only one man of his acquaintance who could do that – Geoffrey.

He lit a cigarette, shielding the lighter with his cupped hands, and inhaled deeply. If only he could take Geoffrey with him! How much surer, how much less lonely it would be! His fingers closed snugly round the revolver in his pocket. Maybe he *could* take Geoffrey with him. There were ways of making people do things .... He had learned a few in the camp. He wondered where Pamela was. It was half past eight – there was still time if he moved quickly. He would need all the luck in the world, but he was overdue for a break. At least it was worth a chance.

He knew where there was a telephone box, just beyond the boathouse. His fertile and tortuous brain was evolving a plan as he walked. It was a fantastic plan, a terrific plan, but it might work. It was no more far-fetched than his alibi had been, and that had almost worked.

Hell! – the telephone box was occupied. A tall youth was leaning comfortably against the inside wall, the receiver to his ear and a vacuous smile on his face. Every few seconds he opened his mouth wide to say something, and then shut it again. Cross walked rapidly up and down past the box, glowering. Then he went and leaned ostentatiously against the glass. These were golden moments that were dribbling away. He didn't know where the next box was, or how far away. He rapped angrily on the glass. The youth looked up, grinned amiably, and nodded. But he went on listening.

Cross pulled open the door. "Do you mind, old man? – it's urgent. My wife's having a baby." He kept the door open.

The youth said: "I'll have to ring off, Mabel. There's a chap having a baby. I mean his wife. See you at the Odeon tomorrow. Yes, the usual time." He hung up.

"Thanks," said Cross. He hadn't needed to act the part. No father-to-be had ever looked more anxious.

Now for it! Had he got twopence? Yes, thank God, he'd collected some change at the pub. He inserted the pennies with fingers that were not quite steady. Would Geoffrey be in? Would he fall for the story? Another couple of minutes would decide. He dialled Welford Avenue and waited, almost choking with suspense.

He heard the ringing tone and the click of the receiver. Someone said, "Hello." It was Mrs. Armstrong. He said, "Hello – this is Arthur."

"Good evening, Arthur." Mrs. Armstrong's tone was polite rather than cordial. At least she seemed quite normal. Evidently no alarm had been sounded yet.

Cross took a deep breath. "Geoffrey in?"

"Yes, he's in the lounge with Miss Pamela. They've just finished dinner. I'll call him – hold on."

So the gods had changed sides! Pamela was there, too. He heard Mrs. Armstrong calling, distantly, and footsteps beside the phone at the other end. "Hello there," said Geoffrey.

"Listen, Geoffrey. Listen carefully. I've got big news."

"Go ahead, I'm listening."

"I've found out who killed Uncle."

"Good lord!" There was a second of stunned silence at Geoffrey's end. "Are you certain?"

"There's no doubt at all. It's an incredible story. I've got the man here."

"You've *got* him – where the hell are you?"

"I've got him on *Truant*. I'm speaking from the box near the boathouse. I came to the boat for a bit of peace and quiet, and the dinghy had gone and there was a light on *Truant*. So I borrowed another dinghy and rowed out. The chap was in the cabin, reading a log or something. We had a bit of a scrap and I managed to sock him with a spanner. He's there now, tied up. He's quite secure, but I need your help."

"Right – I'll come. But how do you know he's not just an ordinary thief? What makes you think he did it? Who is he?"

"I don't know who he is – but he did it all right. It's all in a book he's got. It's a long story, but there's no doubt about it, Geoffrey, old man, this is going to clear the whole thing up."

"It's incredible," said Geoffrey. "Anyway, I'll ring the police and we'll be right over."

"Wait a minute," said Cross quickly. "Are you there?" For one panic moment he thought Geoffrey had rung off. "Listen, there's something else. There's been some funny business going on. At least, I think so. Something with *Truant*. This chap was mixed up in it. So was Uncle Charles."

"What do you mean, 'funny business'? I don't believe it."

"Well, I'm telling you. Do as you like, but if I were you I'd leave the police out of it until you've had a look round. There's a sort of diary, and some figures, and a lot of stuff about tides, and something about a submarine. It may make sense to you."

"It sounds a lot of nonsense. Anyway, I'll come right over. I'll have to bring Pamela. The chap hasn't got a gun or anything, has he?"

"No, he's quite safe – I trussed him up pretty tight. But make it snappy – it's a bit of a strain here alone. I'll go back now and keep an eye on him. You'll have to borrow a dinghy – there are several lying about."

"Okay," said Geoffrey. "We'll be there in fifteen minutes." He hung up.

Cross walked quickly back to the river. He had several things to do. It was essential that Geoffrey should suspect nothing until he reached the cabin. Everything must look right. If there had been a man aboard in the first place, there'd have been a dinghy already at *Truant* before Cross rowed out. With Cross aboard, there'd have to be two dinghies there. At the water's edge he made someone else's dinghy fast to *Truant*'s, and rowed them out together. Then he tied them up conspicuously on the bank side of *Truant*, so that Geoffrey would see them as he climbed aboard.

Inside the cabin Cross lit the paraffin stove and the oil lamps. He might just as well be comfortable while he waited. He drew the curtains over the ports. Then he checked over the fuel. He reckoned there was enough to take them to Holland with a fair margin. Finally he took out his revolver, cleaned it carefully, and re-loaded it.

He sat near the cabin door, waiting. *Truant* was straining at her moorings as the flowing tide streamed by, and every now and again she rocked violently as a gust of wind hit her broadside on. It was going to be a bad night.

Geoffrey had gone back into the lounge looking very worried.

Pamela said, "What's happened?"

"Something pretty odd. It was Arthur. He says he's got the murderer on *Truant*. Someone he doesn't know. Found him there by accident. And he says it looks as though the old man was mixed up with something fishy. Do you think Arthur's drunk?"

"Did he sound drunk?"

"No, he was most lucid."

"Geoffrey, it may be the end of the mystery. It *had* to be something pretty odd – you know that. Only something quite unexpected would make sense. Can I come too?"

"Might as well." He fetched her coat. "Arthur said something about a log-book and tides and a submarine. It sounds frightful. Dad would never have got mixed up in anything like that. *Never!*"

"There's probably some mistake. Anyway, we'll soon know – there's no point in worrying now. Hadn't you better tell the police?"

"Arthur says not. I suppose he thinks we might be able to cover something up, though I don't see how we could, anyway, if the chap that did it is alive. He'll spill the whole story. Of all the crazy nightmares—"

"Geoffrey, you don't think Arthur's up to some trick himself?"

Geoffrey looked grim. "If he is, God help him! I must say he sounded genuine enough. Ready?"

"Eager!"

Geoffrey laughed. "Better not worry Mrs. Armstrong until we know. I'll just tell her we'll be back later. Mrs. Armstrong!" He went through to the back sitting-room.

"She takes a poor view," he said, as he joined Pamela again. "Right, let's go."

CHAPTER XIV

As soon as Cross saw the lights of Geoffrey's Morris swing round the corner of the boathouse he went out into the cockpit. It was too dark for him to see clearly what was happening ashore, but in the lulls between the gusts of wind he could hear voices. One of them was Pamela's. So that was all right! He heard the sounds of yet another dinghy being heaved down the mud and gravel to the water's edge, and presently the creak of oars in the rowlocks.

"Is that you, Geoffrey?" he called out.

Geoffrey's voice came over the water, strong and clear.

"Yes. Everything all right with you?"

"You're just in time – I think he's coming round." Cross peered down at the water as the little boat swung alongside. He reassured himself that it contained no one but Geoffrey and Pamela. "Gosh, I'm glad you've come," he said. "It's been grim sitting here on my own, wondering if the fellow would try to start something."

"We were as quick as we could be," said Geoffrey. He clambered aboard and gave Pamela a hand. Then he turned to Cross. "Now where is this chap? Let's have a look at him."

Cross stood away from the cabin door so that Geoffrey could go inside. Pamela followed close behind. Cross stayed in the doorway, his hand in his coat pocket, clutching the butt of his gun. He was braced for a crisis. You never knew how people would take a sudden shock.

Geoffrey turned, bewildered. "I thought you said he was in the cabin?"

"He's in the forepeak," said Cross curtly. As Geoffrey and

Pamela went forward, Cross moved into the cabin and shut the door behind him.

Geoffrey had turned again, his face dark. "I say, is this your idea of a joke?" He seemed to fill the whole cabin.

"No," said Cross, "it's no joke." He produced the gun, holding it against his palm with a finger lightly on the trigger. "I suggest that both of you sit down. Over there, behind the table." He spoke quietly. This was the critical moment.

Geoffrey stared at Cross; stared at the shining bluish metal of the revolver. He said: "What the devil are you up to, Arthur? Have you gone mad? Here, give me that gun." He made a movement as though he were going to get it.

"Stand back, you fool!" Cross cried. "If you make another move I'll shoot. I mean it." He was right back against the cabin door, half crouching. He looked small, but incredibly menacing. His finger was tightening on the trigger.

Pamela, standing just behind Geoffrey, put a restraining hand on his arm. She was pale but composed. "Better sit down, darling," she said. "I couldn't bear it if you got hurt."

"Sensible girl," said Cross. "Behind the table, both of you. That's better. Now we can talk in comfort. For a moment, Geoffrey, I thought you were going to do something rash."

Geoffrey's knuckles were white. "What the hell *is* this? Suppose you explain."

"Certainly," said Cross. "But before I tell you, let me warn you again that if either of you makes a move I shall shoot. Just try to control yourselves. Now then, you want to know who killed your father, Geoffrey. Well, I did." He was quite motionless, watching Geoffrey's eyes. "And tonight I killed a woman who knew too much about it. So you see it really won't make any difference to me if I kill both of you as well."

There was complete silence in the cabin. It was like waiting for a pebble to hit the bottom of a chasm. The paraffin-stove flared yellow in a sudden draught, and then the flame turned blue again. Nothing else happened.

Then Pamela said softly: "Geoffrey, he *did* do it. I know he did."

Geoffrey was taut, dry-mouthed. He still couldn't believe it, in spite of everything. He said, "Why did you do it?"

"It's a long story," said Cross. "Come on – call me all the things you want to, get them off your chest. I don't want you to work up to a white heat later."

"You must be crazy, Arthur. You'll never get away with this."

"We shall see," said Cross. His eyes were hard and bright; his torn face was pale and the scratches stood out angrily. There was a glitter of nervous energy about him. "We're taking a trip tonight," he said. "To the Dutch coast. You're going to drop me there."

"Now I know you're crazy," said Geoffrey. "There's a gale blowing. This boat wouldn't live for an hour in the open sea."

"I've got to take that chance."

"You won't take it with me. You don't think I'm going to help you get away? You're out of your mind. You must be. It's the only explanation."

"I'm as sane as you are. Anyway, we can argue about that later. Let's get under way."

"We can't," said Geoffrey. His eyes never left Cross's face. "The water's not high enough. It'll be an hour before we can get through the half-tide lock."

"That's right," said Cross. "I remember. Well, that gives me the opportunity to do a little more talking."

"You'll be hanged for this," said Geoffrey.

"Of course I will, you damned fool, if they catch me. What do you think I'm going to all this trouble for?"

"You swine!"

"That's better," said Cross coolly. "Though you might just as well save your breath. You'll need it all before the night's out."

"We're not going anywhere."

Cross gave the gun a little flick. "Aren't you forgetting this?"

"If you think you can make me take you across the North Sea – on a night like this – at the point of a gun, you're just out of your mind. It's a harebrained scheme. I'd get my hands on you before long, and, by heaven, I'd break your neck. You might just as well give yourself up, and take your medicine."

Cross smiled his sardonic smile. "Obviously, you're going to need a little while to get to know me," he said. "I think perhaps, before we go any further, I'd better give you a little insight into my character. Then you may not feel like getting so rough. Now, about your father. I wanted his money, of course. That was a pretty good reason for killing him. I've killed plenty of people without any reason at all."

Pamela was holding tightly to Geoffrey's arm, drawing him down all the time. She said, "What about your alibi?"

"It was a fake. Pretty clever, too. It had you all taken in, didn't it? I merely changed the name of the street with a little thing I invented, and chose my witnesses carefully. I'd have got away with it, too, if it hadn't been for that woman."

"How did she find out?"

"She was in the bombed house. And I wasn't."

"I see." Pamela was fascinated by his utter detachment.

"It surprises you, doesn't it? You didn't think I was capable of it?"

"It doesn't surprise me in the least," said Pamela. "I always thought you were capable of it. I just couldn't see how you could have done it. Now I begin to understand. It was – diabolically clever. You don't mind telling us all this now?"

"It doesn't matter any more, my dear. The police are after me for killing the woman. When you're wanted for one murder, an extra two or three don't mean a thing."

"So that rigmarole you told me over the phone," said Geoffrey, "was just a pack of lies, like everything else?"

"A full pack. I see the recollection rankles. You *were* a bit of a sucker, weren't you?"

"I suppose that's how it strikes you. I'm not really used to this gangster stuff. I hadn't any reason not to believe you. Don't worry – I'm getting adjusted pretty fast."

"The sooner you know what I am, the better. Once you realize I'm a blackhearted devil, quite beyond redemption, you'll be ready to play along with me."

"Haven't you any human feelings?" said Pamela.

"None – not a spark. It's a matter of complete indifference to me whether you two are alive or dead by morning. All I'm concerned with is my own safety. The only reason I don't shoot you now is that it doesn't pay me. I need your help. If you get me safely to Holland, maybe I won't kill you – maybe I'll let you both go. It depends how you behave. The chance of life will be an incentive for you. You'll be surprised how the smallest spark of hope can keep you going. Of course, if the carrot doesn't attract you, there's always a stick. I think I can make you co-operate, all right. I was in a German camp, you know. . . ."

"You told me about it," said Geoffrey. "I remember I was fool enough to feel sorry for you."

"Yes, you were pretty soft – it was rather misplaced sympathy."

"I suppose you were lying about that, too."

"Not altogether. I was in a camp, all right, but I wasn't a prisoner. I was working with the S.S. They had a special foreign detachment. I joined it."

"You've got quite a record, haven't you?" said Geoffrey. He was glad that his father had been spared that knowledge, at least.

"I didn't fancy half a dozen years as a prisoner. Joining the S.S. seemed a much better proposition. On the whole, I still think it was. Free uniform, plenty of good food, status of a sort, companionship. I must say I had quite a good time in the camp. Mind you, I didn't like it at first. The work, I mean. You remember what I was like, Geoffrey – a fairly normal sort of chap, with all the usual inhibitions and the conventional ideas of good behaviour. To start with, I thought the things I saw and heard were horrible. They turned my stomach. I was squeamish. My conscience troubled me."

"That takes some believing," said Geoffrey.

"It wouldn't if you had any conception of what I'm talking about. The thing is that I had a conscience, but I also had a life to lose. When I was first caught I got into a pretty bad camp. That part of the story I told you was true enough. I saw how other people were being treated. It seemed very unlikely that I should survive such treatment. So I decided to save myself in the only way I could. Once you've done that it's an easy slide downhill. At first you're badly shaken by the brutality and the horror. You think you've got into the company of inhuman devils. You almost wish you were dead. You're still sorry for people. Then you think that things might be worse – after all, *you* have plenty to eat, it isn't *you* that's getting hurt. And you're not alone – you're in the business with a lot of other men, quite good fellows off duty, all taking orders and carrying them out. It's easy to shift the blame. After a while the horrors begin to lose their sharpness. The novelty goes. It's only human nature, after all. Really, it's amazing how you can get used to seeing men hanged and women raped and little kids beaten up. 'Let them scream,' you say, 'I'm all right.' There's no sense of guilt any more, because you've done it all and seen it all so often. After a while you even get to like it. We're all sadists at heart. But that stage doesn't last very long. In the end you don't even get a kick out of it. You can't think of any new ways of inflicting pain. After that, killing becomes pure routine – a chore. Just like swatting flies. I'm not exaggerating."

Pamela said: "You're so anxious to talk about it that I should say it's still very much on your mind. You know it was a hideous crime."

"You're getting the wrong angle on this," said Cross. "I'm not trying to interest you in a psychopathic case. I'm just trying to convince you that you'd better not try any tricks when we get under way. I've known people who'd take a chance even against a gun. Geoffrey here is an impulsive sort of fellow. I want to persuade him that it wouldn't be worth while. Let me tell you about my last night at Klooga – that was the name of the camp. It was the night before the Russians came. We could hear their guns, very close, and the Commandant had had orders to pack up and destroy everything before he left – every trace. That meant the prisoners, too. Do you know what we did? We made them cut down pine trees and lay them criss-cross on the ground. When there was a nice layer of wood, we made them lie down on it – neatly, in rows, like sardines in a tin – and then we shot them. Men, women and children – it was all the same to us. Then the next lot of logs went on top of the bodies, and so on. A layer of wood, a layer of flesh." He grinned. "How do you like my bedtime story?"

"You devil!" breathed Geoffrey, the veins standing out on his forehead.

"Exactly. Hold fast to that idea. Of course, the prisoners weren't all dead. There were so many of them – hundreds and hundreds – and we had to shoot them in a bit of a hurry. When the pyres were high enough we threw petrol over them and set them alight. You should have seen them burn – a most dramatic sight. Something to remember all your life. I stood with the other S.S. men around the blazing heaps of wood, and every now and again what had once been a human being would squeeze out of the edge of the pyre – the edges never burned quite so well, it must have been something to do with the draught. Anyway, these chaps would crawl out, screaming like fiends out of hell, sometimes with charred stumps of arms and legs, and they'd go twisting away into the grass, and then we'd go after them and pot them off."

Once again, as he paused, a complete silence fell in the cabin. Pamela's face was distorted with horror and loathing, but she made no sound.

"I see I have your attention. Well, that's my background story. You'll understand, Geoffrey, that killing your father seemed really a very small thing. And it wasn't just that I could use a lot of money – I desperately needed it. I thought my past might catch up on me. It was a bit sticky when I finally came round in hospital – our security chaps asked a hell of a lot of awkward questions. But I'd thought up a story. I'm rather good at making stories sound reasonable – you know that, Geoffrey, don't you? So I got through the net all right. But I knew that wasn't the end of the trouble. We hadn't been able to clean up at Klooga as thoroughly as we'd intended. A few of the prisoners didn't turn up on bonfire night – there was a bit of a flap on, as you can imagine, and we couldn't find them. They've probably talked their heads off to the Russians. There were some records, too, that didn't get destroyed. A Russian tank broke through at an awkward moment. It always seemed pretty certain that sooner or later the Russians would turn over their material to our security people, and that when that happened I should probably be for the high jump. So I had to get a lot of money quickly and go to some country that didn't bother much about war criminals. You're sure I'm not boring you?"

"Go on," said Geoffrey, "finish your piece. Just what are you leading up to?"

Cross opened the cabin door a trifle and listened. "I don't think the wind's going to be as bad as I thought," he said. "And the tide's rising nicely. Yes, as a matter of fact I am leading up to something. Just now, Geoffrey, you seemed rather reluctant about taking *Truant* to sea tonight. Well, obviously I've got to find a way of making you. Also, of seeing that you behave yourself. You may be thinking, for instance, that as we go down the river you'll have an opportunity at some moment or other to catch me off my guard – to get your fingers round my throat, which I'm sure you'd like to do. You may think that you'll be able to hail a police-launch or shout to a tug, or play tricks with the boat, or catch me off balance in a heavy sea. I've been in this game a long time – I've a fairly good idea how your mind's working just at the moment. I've got to take precautions against any of those things happening."

The confident taunting voice was maddening.

"I'll tell you what I'm going to do," Cross went on. "I'm not going to worry about you, Geoffrey, at all. I'm going to keep close to Pamela. You're in love with her, aren't you? And she's in love with you. You're both full of wonderful plans for the future. You'd just hate to see her getting hurt – much more than you'd mind getting hurt yourself. You'd do everything you could to protect her. And quite right – she's well worth it. So Pamela will be my hostage. At the first sign of any funny business by you – the first sign – I shall shoot her." He looked at Pamela with narrow eyes. "But I shan't shoot her dead. I shall do something I learned in the camp. I shall shoot her where it'll hurt her most and longest. I know this sounds like cheap melodrama. I don't particularly want to do it – but I shall have to if you make me. I do want you both to understand that I'm in deadly earnest. Now what about it?" He moved slightly, and turned the gun on Pamela.

"Don't!" Geoffrey cried, and sweat stood out on his face.

Cross grinned. "There you are, you see – it works. I've seen it happen so often. There's nothing so potent as evil. And, after all, why shouldn't it work? You'd be pretty foolish to make me put a bullet in her stomach when all you've got to do to avoid it is to carry out instructions and get me to Holland. Now, shall we get busy? First of all, Geoffrey, I'll have to ask you to tie her up. I can't risk a war on two fronts. You know where the rope is. All right, you can stand up. Get the rope from the locker. Pamela, you sit on the other berth." He waved the gun.

Geoffrey slowly got up, stooping for lack of head-room. He motioned to Pamela. "Better do as he says. We've no choice." She tumbled over to the other berth and slumped down, her dark eyes wide with fear and horror.

Geoffrey looked at her, looked at Cross, looked at the table between them. He measured the distance with his eye. The gun was pointing at Pamela. If he hurled himself across the cabin, got into the line of fire . . .

Cross said, "I shouldn't, if I were you."

"I think you're bluffing," said Geoffrey, watching the trigger-finger. "I'll tell you why. You daren't shoot her. If you did, you'd have no hostage, and then I should try to kill you. You'd have to shoot me too. Then where would you be? How would you make the passage?"

"You're not very bright, Geoffrey. I've thought it all out, you know. I can't be worse off than I am at present, without your help. I've nothing to lose if I can't get that help. If you won't co-operate, shooting Pamela won't do me any harm. I shall be sunk anyway. But you've everything to lose – both of you. You're a fool if you can't see that. I'll make you a promise – if you do land me safely on the Dutch coast, I'll undertake to let you go. And you can both live happily ever after. Isn't that worth a little inconvenience? Doesn't that make you want to get under way at once?"

"How can we trust you?"

"Use a little common sense, my dear fellow. Once I get to Holland, what do I gain by shooting you? It isn't as though you have secret knowledge which might put me in danger. The police here can hang me without your help. Still, have it your own way. We've talked enough. Are you going to tie her up or not? I'll count three, and then . . . One!"

"Stop!" cried Geoffrey. ". . . All right, you win!"

"I thought you'd be sensible. Now then, get to work. And see that you make a good job of it."

Geoffrey went into the forepeak and dragged a coil of rope from the port locker. He came back and began to tie Pamela's hands. She said, "Don't worry – I'll be all right."

Geoffrey tied her feet. "I'll think of some way out," he said in an undertone.

"If you're just whispering sweet nothings," said Cross, "they'll keep. If you're cooking something up, you know the consequences. I hope those are good nautical knots you're tying, Geoffrey. Better take two or three turns round her middle to keep her arms from moving. Tighter than that!"

"She won't be able to breathe," said Geoffrey thickly.

"Of course she will. What's a little discomfort in a good cause? You and she will be laughing about this together in a day or two. Anyway, I'll be looking after her from now on. She and I are going to be bosom companions."

Geoffrey turned on him – menacingly large, but ten feet from the gun.

"Well," said Cross mockingly, "what's on your mind now? Don't worry – I've no designs on her honour. Too much to think about. Now then, we've got to arrange ourselves. Geoffrey, you go round behind the table. Okay, hold it." His eyes swept the cabin. "Now I'll come over to Pamela. All right, Geoffrey, you can go into the cockpit. I've got the gun snugly up against her. Just the right spot. Now remember, this is my last warning. You've got the run of the boat, Geoffrey. Keep outside the cabin. If you want anything, shout. Your job is to get us to Holland. At the very first sign of trouble of any sort, the gun goes off, and you'll have the pleasure of hearing your lovely lady screaming in agony. And I mean the first sign! Don't think you can monkey with the fuel – I've checked it. If it runs out before we get to Holland, the gun goes off. Any accident, and the gun goes off. No excuses taken. Your one hope is to make a good landfall quickly. I'm desperate."

"You've made yourself quite plain," said Geoffrey. "You're smart, Arthur, aren't you? If anyone had told me that one day you'd make me rope Pamela up . . ."

"That's nothing to what we made some of the prisoners do. You must remind me to tell you about it some time."

Geoffrey gave a last look through the cabin door. "All right, Pamela?"

"It's a nightmare," she said. "I've stopped thinking."

"That's right," said Cross. "Come on, Geoffrey, let's get started."

Geoffrey switched on the navigation-lights and pressed the self-starters. The engines quickly sprang into life and he revved them gently. He made his own check of the fuel. There should be just about enough, he decided. They would use a lot getting out of the Estuary in the teeth of the gale, but they'd have the wind on the beam once they'd turned for Holland.

He snapped on the binnacle lamp while the engines were

warming up. "I'll have to lay off a course," he called out. "If I don't do it now, while we're lying quietly, it may be impossible."

Cross came to the cabin door. "How long will it take?"

"Twenty minutes, perhaps, if you move that gun of yours. How do you expect me to make calculations with you standing there trigger-happy?"

"I'm an old hand with a gun," said Cross. "You play fair, and I will. But get a move on – it's ten o'clock."

Geoffrey bent over the little chart-table beside the wheel. It was going to be difficult to concentrate anyway. First he had a look at the tide-table. High water at London Bridge would be just after midnight. They would be all right now for the half-tide lock. The wind was about force five. Outside, in the Estuary, it would be stronger. The leeway would be tremendous. They would reach the sea at about five or six in the morning. It would be almost slack water – the last of the ebb. They would have a foul tide for six hours after that – by which time, if they were going to make it at all, they should be well on their way. He examined the chart of the Estuary, though he knew its main features by heart. It had not been brought up to date – that was an extra risk. He'd have to stick closely to the deep channels – once he got off his course he'd be piled up on a bank in no time in such weather. He'd better go straight out through the dredged channel to the Nore Lightship and into the Oaze Deep. He'd change course at the Red Sand buoy, if he could find it – anyway, he'd be able to pick up the flash of the East Red Sand light. The channel south of the Girdler was too narrow – he might be set on to the Pan Sand or the Tongue. Better to go by the Shingles and through the South Edinburgh channel. Then he'd be all clear for the Kentish Knock and the open sea.

"Where do you want to make a landfall?" he called out.

"I leave it to you," said Cross. "A quiet spot – preferably with sand-dunes on the coast. No villages, no towns. If we touch down where it's inhabited, and get spotted, so much the worse for you."

Geoffrey turned up the chart of the Dutch coast. "If a miracle happens," he said, "and we don't founder or run aground or hit a mine, we ought to be off the Dutch coast in the early hours of Saturday morning. Somewhere between Flushing and the Hook. . . ."

Cross said: "I want the mainland, don't forget. None of your islands!"

"It's all islands there. What about further south? On the left bank of the Scheldt, opposite Flushing. Or further up still, near Terneuzen. Here, look at the map yourself. I don't know what the country's like." He threw a small pocket-atlas across to the cabin door.

"That was a dangerous thing to do," said Cross. "And don't think I'm not watching you. Yes, I can see where you mean. It looks quiet enough on the map."

"For all I know," said Geoffrey, "it may be built up and industrialized. Don't blame me if it is. It's your choice – it's you who'll be on the run – *if* we ever get there."

"We'll go and have a look at it, anyway," said Cross.

Geoffrey returned to his dividers and his charts. "I hope the compass is all right," he said. "It's a long while since it was swung." He worked on silently, calculating probable leeway and tidal set. It was routine, almost second nature, but it took time. Finally, he flung his pencil down. "There we are. Care to see the course?"

"You know it means nothing to me. It's your pigeon. I'm relying on your seamanship."

"And I'm relying on your promise. But I warn you again, it's a suicide trip. We've no steadying sail, and if we had we couldn't use it in this wind. She'll roll like a barrel – probably be swamped. You'll want to turn back before we reach the Nore."

Cross's reply was lost in a gust of wind. He went back into the cabin and sat down near to Pamela. It was a lot warmer inside.

Geoffrey went forrard and cast off the mooring. Then he moved quickly to the wheel. It was only a few days ago that he had been doing this for pleasure! He let in the clutch and *Truant* began to nose forward against the tide. In a short time she was doing a steady six knots downriver. It was just 10.30.

CHAPTER XV

The first few miles were covered without incident. Geoffrey had to keep a careful look-out all the time, for there were some sharp bends in the river and the banks were barely visible from midstream. Occasionally the scudding clouds gaped for a brief moment to show a patch of stars, but there was no sign of any real improvement in the weather. The glass had been falling fast. There was a hint of snow in the air. Altogether, Geoffrey thought, the weather prospects for this trip were just about as bad as they could be. He knew that nothing was more dreaded in the Thames approaches than a really black nor'easter. That, it seemed, was to be their portion. He wished he had been able to dress more warmly – his lounge suit and city overcoat were quite inadequate. Presently he remembered that there was a suit of oilskins in the locker beside him and after he had struggled into these and tied the strings securely under his chin he felt much more comfortable. At present the wheelhouse gave a good deal of protection from the wind, but its silly little electric wiper would almost certainly stop working when they started shipping big seas, and then he would have to have the glass window down and take the full force of the wind in his face.

However bad the weather became, it would be more friendly than Arthur. This whole adventure was fantastic. The more Geoffrey tried to review the situation calmly, the more hopelessly unreal it seemed. It was inconceivable that the three of them should be in the position they were in – butting down the river into a frightful winter storm with thirty hours of sheer hell ahead. And yet there they were – event had followed event in an unbreakable chain, and brought them to this. One desperate man had accomplished it all.

Still, Geoffrey felt better out here at the wheel. That awful tension in the cabin had gone from the boat. The fact was that Arthur, with his horrors and his gun, had completely dominated them while they were stationary. Now the centre of authority should gradually shift. You couldn't navigate a boat with a gun. Geoffrey would come into his own, with bad weather as his ally. Arthur was a killer, not a sailor.

There was hardly any traffic on the river. Between Richmond and Kew Geoffrey saw two or three tugs with their strings of barges, working up to Teddington on the last of the flood. The men aboard took little notice of *Truant* – all they were thinking of, no doubt, was a snug berth and a warm bed. The only other vessel on the river was a small launch towing the empty hull of a naval landing craft, probably to be converted into a houseboat upstream. Occasionally a light would gleam from the window of some house near the bank. In those houses, thought Geoffrey, people with peaceful minds were cosily chatting about the events of the day. Little did they dream . . .

He was quite sure of one thing. The promise that Arthur had given was worthless. It was most unlikely that they would be allowed to go free once they had deposited him in Holland. It was true enough, as Arthur had said, that the English police had quite enough evidence of their own to hang him. But they hadn't necessarily enough evidence to catch him. Arthur would want a fair start, a long start. Was it likely – he being what he was – that he would let two people get away alive who knew just where and when he had landed? Wasn't it much more likely that he would silence them and open *Truant*'s sea-cock before he abandoned her?

In that case Geoffrey had somehow to get hold of the gun. It was the only chance. It wouldn't be easy – Arthur was cunning and alert, and he wore the gun as other men wore clothes. But he might make a slip. It would mean watching every change in the situation – and there would be many changes. At sea something always happened that you didn't expect. There would be moments of near-contact – food would have to be passed from the cabin, and help given in sudden emergency. Arthur might get ill in a bad storm. Geoffrey decided that if there were the least chance he would take it. Arthur, in spite of his threats, would obviously be most reluctant to shoot till the very last moment. The trouble was that Geoffrey couldn't take that cool view of the situation when Pamela was being actually threatened. It might be bluff, yes, but suppose it wasn't?

Geoffrey considered the chances of help from outside. By now the police would be on Arthur's track; they would soon be searching for himself and Pamela as well. Some time in the morning, probably, they would discover that *Truant* had gone from her moorings, and the river police would be on the watch. They would be hampered by the weather – it wouldn't be possible for them to scour the Estuary in a north-easterly gale – but radio messages would be sent out. There was a good chance that *Truant* would be recognized and reported long before it got anywhere near the Dutch coast. In fact, it was a virtual certainty. The mere fact that such a small boat was out in such weather would attract attention. They might well be offered assistance. Yet the one thing above all others that Geoffrey had to fear was the approach of a police-boat or a rescue party, for that would mean the end of hope for Arthur, and he would take his spiteful revenge. It seemed clearer than ever, now, that the gun was the key to everything.

They slid under Hammersmith Bridge, making seven knots with plenty of power in hand. Geoffrey was keeping well out in the river.

He was unfamiliar with these reaches and there were no landmarks to help in the darkness. *Truant*'s navigation-lamps threw a cheerful glow of red and green on the restless water; even here, far up the river, the surface was disturbed and *Truant*'s bow was gently rising and falling as she pressed forward. She was beginning to come alive. Soon those bows would be high above his head, lifting to great waves, and he would be holding grimly to the wheel, waiting for the slide down into the trough. Then they would see what Arthur was made of.

Geoffrey wished he could see into the cabin from the wheel-house. So far it was Pamela who was having the really bad time. He suddenly became worried at the long silence inside the cabin, and gave a shout.

Cross put his head cautiously out of the door. "What's the trouble?"

"How's Pamela?"

"Good heavens, I thought we were sinking! She's all right. Not very friendly, I'm afraid. She says the ropes cut her."

"I expect they do. What's the good of keeping her trussed up like that, anyway? There'd be no risk in making her a bit more comfortable. If you drive us too hard, you know, we'll . . ." He hesitated.

"You'll *what*?" Cross sneered. "Risk a bullet in the girl's guts because she's a bit cramped?"

Geoffrey tried a different tack. "Look, Arthur, I've got a tough job ahead. How the devil can you expect me to navigate the boat with an undivided mind if I know Pamela's in a bad state? I'm worrying about her all the time."

"I dare say – still, I'm taking no chances. But I'll ease the ropes a bit if it'll make you happier."

"It certainly will. And I say – what about eating? This cold air is giving me an appetite. Can't you pass me something out?"

"I'll fix something," said Cross. "I'll see what stores we've got."

"You'd better do something about it pretty soon," said Geoffrey. "The boat won't be as quiet as this much longer. Why not make a cup of tea?"

"That's a good idea."

"And listen – get that paraffin-stove out directly she begins to pitch. We don't want a fire aboard. And see that everything's properly stowed in the cabin – you won't feel like doing it later. When are you going to take a trick at the wheel?"

"I'm not," said Cross. "That's your show."

He went back into the cabin. Pamela was sitting with her back to a bulkhead, facing the cabin door. She looked completely dispirited. Her tied hands were dropped on her lap, and her head was bent over her chest. She might have been asleep, but when Cross prodded her she looked up.

"The captain says I'm to loosen your ropes," he said. He leaned across her and eased them very slightly. She shivered. The touch of his fingers was like lice on her body, but she wanted the ropes loosened.

"Is that better?"

"A little. I'm all right."

"Cigarette?"

She shook her head. Cross lit one for himself. "We're making good progress," he said cheerfully. "I'm going to make a cup of tea now. Brighten you up."

She said nothing. She was watching him, watching everything he did. Especially she was watching the gun. He went over to the cabin door, locked it from the inside, and came back smiling. "Now we can give the trigger-finger a rest," he said. He slipped the gun into his coat pocket. She watched him go into the galley, opposite the toilet in the forepeak. Presently she smelt methylated spirits and heard the roar of a primus and the sound of lockers being opened and shut.

"This ought to be your job, really," said Cross, poking his head round the corner. "Come on, my dear, snap out of that gloom. I'm trying to be affable."

"I know," said Pamela. "It makes you more revolting than ever."

"You do hate me, don't you?"

"Hate you?" Pamela's face was expressionless. "Not *hate*. You just make me feel horribly sick. If you had two heads you'd seem human."

Cross shrugged. "Why should I care what you think?" He opened a tin of ship's biscuits and a tin of spam. She could hear the kettle beginning to boil. He went and made the tea. She watched him come back into the cabin with a steaming mug and two large biscuits with a layer of spam in between. "This'll keep the captain's strength up," he said. He set them down near the cabin door, took out his gun, and unlocked the door.

"Here's the tea, Geoffrey," he called. He put it down on the deck close to the wheelhouse. "Better come and get it, but keep away from the cabin. Sing out if you want some more." Cross backed into the cabin. This time he didn't lock the door behind him.

"Now then, beautiful, what about you? Tea? – not that you deserve it!"

"I can't drink with my hands tied," she said.

"Hold your face up, and I'll feed you."

She turned away. "I'll do without."

"Better have some. There'll be nothing more for hours."

Pamela closed her eyes. "I'm so tired," she said. "I feel so weak I can hardly move."

"You've not got much stamina for a budding doctor," said Cross. "Too much beauty, not enough brawn. Here, hold your hands out.

I'll untie them just while you drink the tea. But mind you behave yourself."

She held her hands up, watching him. Cross, still holding the gun, fiddled at the rope with fingers that seemed all thumbs. He was inexpert with knots. He had intended only to loosen the rope a bit more, but suddenly Pamela's hands were free and she gently wriggled her arms free too. Cross stepped back quickly. "You ought to be all right now," he said.

She rubbed her hands together, chafing the white marks that the rope had left on her wrists, exercising her fingers. "That's better," she said. He passed her the mug of hot sweet tea, using his left hand; then he leaned back against the table, a couple of feet from her, sipping his own.

"Good, isn't it?"

She nodded.

"Want anything to eat?"

She shook her head.

"Well, for heaven's sake stop staring at me. You give me a pain."

She drained the mug and held it out to him. "I think I'll try and sleep now," she said. He stood up to take the mug. At the same moment she rolled herself bodily off the bunk against his legs. He lost his balance in a wild effort to keep it, and sprawled on top of her. The gun slipped from his hand as he tried to save himself and went sliding along the smooth linoleum of the cabin floor.

"Geoffrey, quick!" she yelled at the top of her voice. "Quick!" She tried to hold Cross by the leg, but he shook her off and made a wild plunge for the gun. He retrieved it in a flash, turned, and gave Pamela a brutal crack across the mouth with his fist. Geoffrey was at the door. Cross pushed the revolver barrel against Pamela's body. "I'll shoot!" he screamed. "Stop, you fool, I'll shoot!"

Geoffrey stopped in his tracks, six feet away. Something jarred the boat from end to end, and the note of the engines changed. Pamela gave a little sob.

"All right," said Cross, "the fight's over. Get back to the wheel. So that's how you play fair? You'll pay for this, both of you!"

Geoffrey didn't move.

Pamela said: "I'm sorry, Geoffrey. It nearly worked."

"I know. Better not try it again, though. It's too risky. Are you all right?"

"Yes – I will be."

"Shall I go back to the wheel?"

"I think you'd better."

"I'll say he'd better," said Cross. He bent over Pamela as Geoffrey left. "As for you, you plotting little bitch, I'll lash you up so tight you won't be able to stir. So you're tired, are you – you're so weak you can hardly move?"

She lay on the floor, watching him, afraid. A drop of blood trickled from the corner of her braised mouth.

"You're a pretty sight now," said Cross. "I've a good mind to knock your teeth in." With one hand he grasped the neck of her dress, with the other the rope round her feet, and with an effort almost beyond his strength he lifted her back on to the bunk. He still held the gun. Suddenly he took the V of her dress in both hands and tore it apart. "There," he said, "at least you've something to show for your pains." He tied her up, clumsily but effectively.

He went to the cabin door again. "What's happened to the boat?" he shouted. "Why have we stopped?"

"She's stuck in the mud," Geoffrey called back. "I've tried reversing her out, but she's too firmly in. She must have gone straight for the bank."

"Surprising, isn't it? Well, you know what happens if you can't get her off."

"She'll float in a minute or two," said Geoffrey. "The tide's still rising." He revved the engines gently, waited, revved them again. Slowly *Truant* began to pull out. She was free. The whole episode had taken less than ten minutes.

"I hope this'll be a lesson to your girl friend and to you," said Cross. "It was a damned near thing – I was just going to shoot. I don't know how you imagined you could get away with it."

"Suppose the gun had gone under one of the bunks?" said Geoffrey.

"Well, just try it again, that's all," said Cross lamely. For the moment he was shaken. "Where are we?"

"That's Wandsworth Bridge just ahead."

"We're making pretty slow progress." Cross went below, scowling.

They were getting into the heart of London now. The familiar lines of great buildings were silhouetted against the glare of the city's lights. The hands of Big Ben stood at half an hour after midnight; along the bleak Embankment one or two late trams were running. The tide was near the turn; already it was slack near the banks, and very soon it would be ebbing. Geoffrey closed the throttle a bit, now that they had no longer to punch against the flood. The river, full almost to street level, was wide and choppy. The vicious wind kept scooping up the tops of the wavelets and hurling them against the glass of the windshield. *Truant* was beginning to roll and plunge, and her decks were wet and glistening.

They were still almost alone on the river. A big coastal collier overhauled them and passed in a green glare. Geoffrey couldn't believe she was going far on a night like this. There was plenty of water now – no fear of going aground again. *Truant* shot under

Blackfriars Bridge, rocking and shaking in the confused water left by the collier. These bridges were always a headache at night – the sooner they were away from them the better. London Bridge now, and then Tower Bridge – the last of them.

Just as they were passing the entrance to the London Docks, Geoffrey spotted a green light ahead, then a red and green, and then green again. There was something approaching right ahead. He put the wheel well over to port to avoid the wash, and slowed a little.

Cross stuck his head out. "Now what's happening?"

"I think it's a police-launch," said Geoffrey, straining into the darkness.

Cross stared too, suddenly on edge. He said: "Better be careful, Geoffrey. It's up to you."

"It's a chance to call your bluff," said Geoffrey.

"Why don't you?"

"I daren't."

The launch had taken a wide sweep across the river, turned, and come up almost alongside. It was the river police all right – Geoffrey couldn't see the flag but he recognized the low beamy lines. Cross stood in the doorway, strategically placed to shoot.

The launch drew level. A searchlight swept *Truant*'s side and went out, leaving the night blacker than ever. A voice came from the cockpit of the launch, magnified by loudspeaker. "Ahoy, *Truant*! Everything all right?"

"Yes, thank you," shouted Geoffrey through his megaphone.

"Where are you bound for?"

"Holehaven."

"It'll be blowing hard out there! Sooner you than me! Good night!"

"Good night!" The launch turned away.

"Nice work," said Cross, relaxing. "Good chaps, those river police – never interfere with people on their lawful occasions."

"It seems," said Geoffrey, "that the alarm has not been sounded yet."

"Not yet," said Cross. "It's a good job we got away early. Why did you say Holehaven?"

"What did you want me to say – Holland? They'd have had a party aboard with strait jackets! Holehaven's the farthest point that anyone but a complete lunatic would be bound for on a night like this. It gives good shelter from the north-east. We may have to run in there yet."

"Oh, no, we shan't," said Cross.

"You're an ignorant fool," said Geoffrey. "You don't know what's ahead of you."

"I know what's behind me." Cross gazed out at a dark pile of buildings looming up on the right bank. "Is that Greenwich?"

"Yes, that's the naval college."

"You'll have a good story to tell when you get back," said Cross.

"*If* I get back. Lord, this wind! I can hardly hear you. How's Pamela?"

"I think she's dozing. That rough-house shook her up a bit, but it was her own fault."

"I say," called Geoffrey, "what do you suppose you're going to do when you get to Holland?"

"That's my worry."

"Not altogether. What's the drill for getting you ashore?"

"It depends where we hit the coast, and what it looks like. If it's quiet, and the wind's dropped, I'll take the dinghy and row myself ashore. We'll have to decide when we get there."

"Why make for Holland? It's a hell of a long way. Why not France or Belgium? It would save us hours – we could keep inside the banks. It's a slim chance, anyway, but we'd be much more likely to make Calais than the Scheldt."

"Nothing doing," said Cross. "I want to get as far east as possible. I'll cross into Germany – just one more displaced person. That reminds me, have you got any money?"

"About five pounds."

"I'll have it. Not that it'll last long."

"You won't last long either! You've had some luck, but it can't hold. Anyway, we shall all be drowned by this time tomorrow. It's difficult enough to hold the boat to her course even here."

"I don't fancy drowning," said Cross, "but I suspect it's better than some deaths I know of. A bullet in the stomach, for instance. What time shall we reach the Estuary?"

"Just before dawn, I should say. You'll know all right when we get there. I hope you're a lousy sailor."

"I'm a pretty good sailor," said Cross. "I was always better than average in planes, anyway. So if you're planning to knock me out while I'm vomiting over the side, you can think again."

"We'll see," said Geoffrey grimly.

They had covered the long two miles of Woolwich Reach in good style, but as *Truant* turned north-east into Gallions Reach she took the full force of the wind head on. Geoffrey opened up both engines, for the gusts were hitting the hull with such violence that it was difficult to keep any way on the boat. They were still miles from the sea, but conditions were beginning to get unpleasant. The sky was completely overcast, and crystals of dry snow were settling in the corners of the windshield. As the wind met the ebb again *Truant* began to pitch and shake, her timbers groaning, her propellors racing. This was worse than the steady roll or the long pitch of the open sea; the troubled water was worrying at her, pushing her around. Geoffrey could hear something clattering about in the cabin, in spite of what he had said about stowing everything properly.

Spray was coming aboard in great flurries and freezing on the glass. It was impossible to use the windshield any more. Even without it visibility was negligible. He could see nothing at all except the fixed shore lights on the north bank, and over on the starboard bow the flash of the white light on Tripcock Point. The wind now was almost continuous. It came whistling and screaming over the Essex flats, with nothing to bar its way, and it burst upon the ear like gunfire. You could hear the beginnings of it, far away, and follow the crescendo in all its gathering strength, and then wait for the explosion round your ears, the impact of the noise and fury. It was numbing, deafening, frightening. It bruised your senses. It wore down your resistance. When the lulls came they were a blessed relief, like the brief cessation of pain in an aching tooth.

As *Truant* struggled on Geoffrey knew that they could not reach Holland – not till the storm abated. He would be utterly exhausted in such weather long before they sighted land. It was too much for the boat; too much for one man. *Truant* might survive in the Estuary, in the partial shelter of the mainland and the banks. It would be wicked enough even there. With visibility next to nothing, and a big sea running, it would be impossible to spot the buoys, to find the channels. As for the open sea, they wouldn't stand an earthly. The best thing to do was to go out to the Nore, straight up the dredged channel, and see what it felt like. Even Arthur might agree that they should seek shelter and wait awhile, once he'd had a real buffeting. His morale wouldn't be nearly so high in an hour or two.

They were safely round Tripcock Point and into Barking Reach.

Geoffrey's thoughts went back to his early sailing days. Just here he had had his first adventure. He had been bringing a little two-tonner down the river – a pocket-sized cabin boat with a two-stroke engine – and as night fell they had tied up to a cluster of barges moored just off the point. And in the early hours one of the barges had started to swing round, closing in on the two-tonner, and Geoffrey had shinned up the coal-black side of a barge named *Joe* in his pyjamas and hauled his lovely little boat just in time from between the converging monsters.

It had been fun – afterwards. Boats were always fun afterwards. He began to think of Pamela again, and of the plans he had had to sail her round the Estuary. The prospects didn't look so good now.

If only he could get the gun! He came back to that every time. If he'd been inside the cabin instead of outside when Pamela made her attempt they would have been homeward bound and safe by now.

What was needed was a sudden shock – something that would throw Arthur off his balance and allow enough time for Geoffrey to get at him. Now if the boat were suddenly run aground . . .

It was the germ of a plan. Geoffrey knew all the immense risks – somehow he must guard against them. There would be no lack of dangerous shoals, but he would want one that was steep-to at the edge, so that he could set *Truant* at the bank like a horse to a gate. That would shake Arthur all right!

It would have to be low water, of course – *Truant* didn't draw enough to ground at any other time. Next low water out beyond the Nore was in three or four hours – they wouldn't be there in time. It would have to happen twelve hours later, in the afternoon.

It must be a falling tide, too. If *Truant* struck on a rising tide and were damaged – as she could hardly help being if she grounded suddenly and at speed – she might float off and sink. And that would be the end of them all.

But if he could choose his time carefully, she might dry out on the bank and give them an hour or two's respite. She would probably break up, though, when the tide rose again. What were the chances of quick rescue? Perhaps he could attract attention first, without letting Arthur know, and run the ship aground afterwards. Could there be a rescue in such a sea? It would be incredibly hazardous.

He looked at the glass. It had risen a tenth! Not much, but it seemed like a good omen. It was the right direction. Once the wind began to moderate the sea would soon lose the worst of its fury.

He swung the boat into Half-way Reach, steering for a red light on Rainham Jetty, a mile and a half ahead. Once again he bent over the chart of the Estuary, trying to recall old familiar banks, digging down into the past for half-remembered features. Steadying himself against the wheel, he flicked over the tide-tables, noting times and places. If this wild plan of his was to succeed there must be no error in his calculations. He must choose his bank, he must choose his time, he must know just how much water there would be, and how long the bank would be dry.

Even so, it was crazy – utterly crazy. What had happened to many good ships before would happen to *Truant*. She would break up.

But *they* had gone aground accidentally. He was going to cast his ship away at the spot he chose. He looked at the chart again, and suddenly he had an inspiration.

Confidence came surging back. For the first time since their journey started he had real hope. A few moments more, and his plan was finished. He would make for the Girdler Sand, ten miles out from the Essex and Kent coasts. He would try to get there at five o'clock that afternoon – sixteen hours ahead. There was more than enough time – he would have to stooge about a bit in the Estuary, and meanwhile perhaps the wind would drop. He would go in from the north, from the Alexandra Channel, with the wind behind him. And he would pray that help came quickly.

CHAPTER XVI

All through the night *Truant* chugged down the river on the ebb tide. Pamela, having used up her reserves of energy in one heroic fling, had fallen into uneasy sleep. Cross, the gun resting lightly on his knee, sat opposite her with an almost blank mind. He was too tired to think; he dared not go to sleep. He had kept the cabin door locked since two in the morning, and given Pamela a little more freedom when she wanted it, but he knew the lock was only a slight defence and he could not relax.

Geoffrey was looking forward to daylight. Dawn might not bring any improvement in the weather, but at least it would lessen the strain at the wheel. Now that the tide was low it was more important than ever to keep well away from the banks, where great strips of putty-coloured mud were ready to grip and hold any boat that came too near. Once Geoffrey felt *Truant*'s keel touch, but the drag was only momentary and he soon swung the ship back into deep water. There was nothing to compensate for the ceaseless effort and the acute discomfort. There was still nothing at all to be seen except a few shore lights, an odd riding-light or two, and occasionally the outline of a ship against a wharf or the tall mast of a dried-out sailing-barge. There was almost nothing moving. There were some liners with steam up at Tilbury, looking as though they might be away on the next ebb. Now and again a solitary tug slipped by, and from far down the Estuary an occasional siren told of heavier traffic at sea. But that was all. It was a lonely vigil, with nothing but the nerve-racking wind for company.

Lighted buoys made it easier to keep to the channel once the boat was in the lower reaches, but there was less and less shelter from shore buildings. Broad marshes stretched away for miles on either hand. Geoffrey rounded Lower Hope Point close to the flashing red buoy, picked up the West Blyth, and turned into Sea Reach. Steering was straightforward enough now, apart from the physical effort of holding her against the wind, for the Chapman Light was winking brightly four miles ahead. There was already a faint glow in the sky beyond. Very soon *Truant* had Holehaven on her port bow. In an hour or two, thought Geoffrey, there would be hot breakfasts at the old Lobster Smack Inn. Now if he and Pamela had been alone they would have turned here and anchored off the jetty in sheltered water, and rowed over to the pub and joined the breakfast party. Life that morning could have been a pure delight.

What was the good of wishing? It wouldn't be long now before they were at sea. *Truant* was beginning to pitch violently in the steep waves, and repeatedly Geoffrey had to brace himself against the sudden motion. He would be black and blue by the time this trip ended. The whole boat was enveloped in salt spray and his oilskins were dripping. Every now and again, as *Truant* burrowed, the crest of a wave broke over the cabin top and icy water shot into the wheelhouse through the open windshield. Geoffrey's feet felt like blocks of stone and his hands were numb.

The boat pirouetted past the East Blyth, and Geoffrey strained to catch a glimpse of the next buoy. A big wave lifted *Truant*'s bows, and as she fell into the trough the next one hit her with an impact that shook the ship. It was difficult to keep her head-to-sea, with the darkness hiding the waves and the wind all the time trying to swing her broadside on. But there was no immediate danger – the engines were pulsing strongly and there was plenty of power in reserve. It was the sort of struggle that, in other circumstances, Geoffrey would have loved. Merely to be out here, in so small a boat and in such weather, could be counted an achievement. As long as she didn't start taking the seas green, she should be all right. He started the engine bilge pump, hoping to keep her dry below.

As dawn turned to daylight, familiar landmarks came one after another into view. Back there on the port quarter was Canvey Point, where he had once spent three glorious days among the saltings, the shingle and the green crabs, fitting out a sailing-boat. Farther to the right he could just make out the row of neat villas on the front at Westcliff, and faintly on the port bow the long thin streak of Southend Pier. There was a sliver of pale blue sky in the east, wide enough to let through the first yellow rays of the sun. The barometer was still rising, very slowly. It looked as though they were going to have a fine day after all, with a moderating wind. At the rate the clouds were moving they would soon blow away. Visibility would improve – that would be a mercy. As Geoffrey gazed around he suddenly felt immensely exhilarated. He forgot Arthur with his gun and his mean looks. The sea was incredibly beautiful – a wildly tossing waste of pale green water with white horses cresting every wave and the young sun turning the spray into clusters of diamonds. It was a splendid world and Geoffrey had it all to himself. Far out towards the Nore there was a wisp of dark smoke on the horizon, but no ship was in sight.

He watched the gulls being blown about the sky like sheets of paper. He watched the water creaming away from *Truant*'s bow in a lovely curve. He watched the green and white wake. The ship was riding well. There was motion, of course, motion in all directions, rising and falling, diving and twisting, lurching and recovering. But the ship was buoyant and rose to the water magnificently. It would be different once they left the shelter of the land.

Soon after daylight, as a gust was beginning to gather itself for the next onslaught, Geoffrey heard a key scraping in the lock of the cabin door and Cross emerged. He looked far from happy; his wispy hair was matted, his face was sickly. There were dark circles round his eyes. He looked as though he could have been flicked overboard with a finger's end. But he still had the gun. As he stepped out, sniffing the wind, *Truant* buried her nose and took some green water over her foredeck. It swirled over the cabin top and fell foaming into the cockpit.

Cross, suddenly soaked through, clung to the cabin door with one hand, swaying. "Where are we?" he asked. "How are we doing?"

"Fine," said Geoffrey. "Bracing, isn't it? This is only the beginning, of course. Is breakfast ready?"

"It's too rough to get the stove going. I'll sling out some more spam – if you want it."

"Of course I want it. Do you think I run on air? I'm starving. How's Pamela?"

"She's all right so far." Cross gazed round at the tossing sea. "Do you really think it's going to get worse?"

"Much worse," said Geoffrey cheerfully. "Any moment now we shall hit the open sea. We're sheltered here by the Maplins. Out there you'll be able to feel solid water breaking over the ship. Feel like turning back?"

"No," said Cross.

"Then hurry up with the breakfast. Why man, you're not even a good steward! We could have had hot tea if you'd tumbled out a bit earlier."

"You don't imagine I've been sleeping?" said Cross. He went below, leaving the door open.

Geoffrey glanced at his watch and slowed the engines. He had to keep plenty of way on the boat to breast the seas and prevent her broaching to, but he didn't want to get too far too quickly. They had hours to waste. He was steering by compass for the Red Sand

Tower, seven or eight miles ahead. He would see the Nore later on, of course, but he found it impossible to pick up the ordinary buoys any more. They were hidden in the plunging seas. If his allowance for wind and tide was anything like correct he could do without the buoys.

The seas were getting steeper every moment. Why the hell didn't Arthur come out with that food while they could still stand on their feet? If Arthur passed out, of course, their troubles would be over; but he couldn't leave the wheel to see how Arthur was doing. The danger from Arthur seemed to be fading as the danger from the sea increased. Geoffrey knew how quickly disaster could come – how a single breaking sea could overwhelm a small boat, stop its engines, leave it a waterlogged hulk to settle and sink. He was watching every wave.

The morning was as bright as its promise, but the sunshine was deceptive. The wind was still blowing out of the north-east, dry and cold, with unabated violence. At one moment a big sea and a heavy gust hit *Truant*'s port bow together, and she heeled until the lee coamings were awash. But she recovered. Geoffrey gave silent thanks for the big lead keel and the load of ballast laid amidships as he throttled up and brought her head round again.

Suddenly he had a pang of doubt. There was a wall of green water ahead – a mountain bearing down on them. Its crest was curling. He turned the boat into it, wrestling with the wheel, muscles taut for the shock. Anything might happen now! *Truant* lifted bravely – it was like going up in an elevator – but not quickly enough. The ship staggered – the top of the wave broke shatteringly over the cabin. Geoffrey held on to the wheel – there was nothing he could do now. He was going down and under – he was conscious of immense pressure, of water everywhere. It seemed that the ship was being smashed to pieces. His arms were almost wrenched from his body. He was gasping and choking. Then he was out again in the sunlight. The cockpit was a swirling mass of foam. The whole of the wheelhouse had gone – wood and glass and metal. A piece of glass had ripped his cheek and blood dripped on to his oilskins. But *Truant* was still afloat, and miraculously the engines were still running.

Cross was at the cabin door again. He looked scared. It was the first time Geoffrey had seen him look scared. "There's a foot of water in the cabin," he said.

"What the hell do you expect?" Geoffrey shouted. "The pump'll clear it. Where's my breakfast?"

"Do you really want it?"

"Of course I want it, you fool!"

Cross dived below and in a moment staggered out again with a couple of spam sandwiches.

"Hand them to me," said Geoffrey hopefully. "I can't leave the wheel." He had one eye on the sea, one on Arthur.

"Not likely," said Cross. "Here, catch!" He threw the food across. "You must think I'm pretty green."

"You certainly look it," said Geoffrey. "Has Pamela eaten?"

"She doesn't want anything. My God, look at that sea!"

It was bigger than the last. Cross almost fell into the cabin. Geoffrey throttled up the engines and *Truant* climbed diagonally up the side of the great green mass. Then he turned her head into it, and crouched behind the cabin bulkhead as the boat lifted. He was certain that he had been swept overboard, but when the sea had passed he found he was still holding the wheel. He got the ship back on her course and looked around. He saw that the dinghy had been swept away. The chocks that had held it on the cabin roof were still there, but the ropes had snapped like string. It had disappeared, and there was no possibility of recovering it.

Geoffrey called out, "Arthur!"

Cross peered out. "Well?"

"The dinghy's carried away. That last sea. It looks as though you'll have to swim ashore if you ever sight land again."

Cross looked blankly at the bare cabin top. Then he looked at Geoffrey.

"I didn't do it, you know," said Geoffrey. "Intervention of Providence. It shows they're going to get you!"

Cross swore and went below.

Truant ploughed on through the tumbling waters. Often her screws were out of the sea altogether, racing noisily. Geoffrey was wondering how many more such seas he could take. They must get some shelter. With the wind forward of the beam, and a foul tide, *Truant* was making only about four knots, with a bit to spare. But they were coming up steadily to the Red Sand Tower, and it seemed to Geoffrey that it was almost time to put the first part of his plan into operation. He began to sheer away to the south of the East Spile buoy. The water shoaled here, but there was plenty for *Truant* and the tide was still flowing. If he could work round to the south of the Red Sand it would give him a bit of a lee. In the shallower water the sea was more confused than ever but the waves were not so high. It would be very wet, but less dangerous. Choosing his moment, he opened the engine cover and strained with both hands to break the joint of the fuel-pipe which fed the port engine. He wriggled it backwards and forwards violently, and suddenly something gave. There was a rush of oil; he switched off both engines and gave a shout. He staggered across the cockpit to the fuel-tanks and closed the feed-tap.

Cross appeared. "Now what the hell's happened?"

"The fuel-pipe's fractured. I'll have to try to anchor while I fix it." *Truant* was wallowing helplessly and drifting fast. Geoffrey climbed on to the cabin top and worked his way forward along the port rail to the windlass. The ship was beam on to the seas – there wasn't a moment to lose. He let go the anchor and paid out forty fathoms of chain. It was a heavy chain for the size of the boat, and should hold. He clung to the windlass, watching the boat's head swing round. That was better – wind and tide were both coming in from the same quarter and *Truant* should ride safely.

He scrambled back into the cockpit and took a quick cast with the lead. He made it nearly four fathoms – and judging by the lead line she wasn't dragging. She oughtn't to drag with that scope of chain out. It would be hellishly uncomfortable and difficult to work, and they'd ship a lot of water. But things might be worse – the sun was shining, and the gusts seemed less severe. He banged on the cabin door. "I'm coming in," he shouted.

"What for?"

"You don't think I can mend the pipe out here?" He opened the door.

"All right," said Cross. "But be careful!" Geoffrey went in – his first spell below for eleven hours. The air was warm and close. Suddenly he felt completely exhausted. His shoulders ached as though he had been on the rack.

"I suppose you haven't staged this, have you?" said Cross from the other end of the cabin. "It won't get you anywhere if you have. I'm keeping the gun dry, and whether I go to hell your way or mine, I shall use it before I go." His eye was a little wild, he looked a sodden scarecrow, but still his hand was steady and his nerve unbroken.

"You won't need the gun if I don't get this pipe soldered," said Geoffrey. "How's it going, Pamela?"

She gave him a wan smile. "I suppose it'll end some time. It's all right while I'm lying down. You must be worn out."

"Don't you believe it – it's meat and drink to me," said Geoffrey, but his enthusiasm sounded forced. "Got a bad head?"

"Pretty bad. I'm not sure I like boats after all."

"Cheer up!" said Geoffrey. "The glass is rising. Five minutes on *terra firma* and you'll have forgotten you were ever ill. Arthur, can I make some tea? I'm all in. So is she."

"Who the hell cares what she feels like? And we've no time to spare. They may be out looking for us in an hour or two. I want to get off the end of that anchor chain. Come on, get cracking on the pipe."

Geoffrey sat down on the bunk opposite Pamela. He had four hours to kill. He said: "I can't go on without something. It's up to you, Arthur. If the wind drops we'll be lying in the Scheldt before morning. I think your luck's going to be in. But I'm not a perpetual-motion machine. If you want the job done and the ship navigated, you've got to give me a break."

"Okay," said Cross. He sat down beside Pamela. "Go round behind the table and stay in the forepeak. I'll give you fifteen minutes for a snack. But keep your distance, and if you lurch, lurch your way! This trigger's getting pretty hot."

Geoffrey edged his way over to the galley and got to work on the stove. It was swung in gimbals, so that it remained horizontal however much the boat rolled and pitched.

"The teapot's broken," Geoffrey said accusingly.

"It's a wonder the whole cabin isn't wrecked," said Cross. "It was that last sea that did it."

"I'll use a jug," said Geoffrey.

Cross was fidgeting. "The sooner you're out of there, the better I'll be pleased," he said. "For heaven's sake, what are you cooking?"

"Only a couple of tins of soup," said Geoffrey brightly. "It'll be quite good with spam broken into it. Like some?"

"No! Hurry up."

Geoffrey made the tea and sweetened it with condensed milk. With *Truant* plunging and rolling and snubbing at her anchor chain, every movement was difficult, but he could afford to be patient. There was a lot of water on the floor of the galley and in the cabin, slopping to and fro with every change in the angle of the boat. Now that the engines were stopped the pump wasn't working.

Geoffrey poked his head into the cabin. "Don't mind if I spend a penny, do you?"

"Go ahead," said Cross irritably, "but hurry." Presently he heard Geoffrey at the galley again.

Geoffrey said: "It's going to be difficult carrying these things out. Tea, Pamela?"

"No, thanks, Geoffrey. I don't want a thing. Really."

"Arthur?"

"No! You can stay and have your snack there. And make a good meal while you're at it – it'll have to last a long time."

"I don't think much of the working conditions on this ship," Geoffrey grumbled, his mouth full of stew. "This is good, Arthur – you ought to try it. Meat soup – nice and fatty."

"I said no, blast you!"

"I thought you said you were a good sailor?"

"I'm still on my feet, you'll be sorry to notice. I tell you I'm not hungry. Anyway, your time's up."

"It's funny," said Geoffrey, "how no one is really in charge of this boat. Most unseamanlike. Half the time you do as I say; half the time I do as you say."

"That's right," said Cross.

"No wonder we're in a mess." Geoffrey finished the stew. "Well, that's a lot better. Now I want some tools. They're in the locker under your feet, Arthur. The ones I want are in a canvas roll."

"Get back behind the table," said Cross, "and I'll throw them over to you."

"I'll just take a look outside," said Geoffrey. Pamela's eyes were closed; the barrel of the gun was right against her. Even a lunge at close quarters would be dangerous. He went round the table and into the cockpit.

He took another sounding, and made sure the anchor was holding. Then he looked round the horizon. There were many more tell-tale wisps of black smoke on the skyline, but the only ship in view was a large tramp, thrashing up the Oaze Deep on the other side of the sandbank. She might have spotted *Truant*, but if she had she gave no sign. Anyway, the day was still young. Interference at this stage might be fatal.

Geoffrey went back into the cabin and settled down to a spell of tinkering. He had certainly made a mess of the pipe. He held it out for Cross to inspect. Cross merely grunted.

"If you heat the soldering-iron," said Geoffrey, "it'll save me the trouble of crawling round that table again. I've left the stove on."

"Heat it yourself," said Cross.

Geoffrey shrugged and worked his way back to the stove. It looked as though Pamela had dozed off again. The strain and the motion had been too much for her. Anyway, that was the best thing she could do. Cross, too, seemed sunk in lethargy, but Geoffrey had no hope that he would sleep. Geoffrey had only to make the slightest sudden movement and the hand stiffened on the gun. He went into the forepeak and thoughtfully turned the soldering-iron in the blue flame.

"Isn't that trigger-finger of yours getting a bit cramped?" he called out.

"No," said Cross. "As a matter of fact, I'm being particularly careful just now. If you're thinking of doing anything with that soldering-iron, I shouldn't."

"You'll break before I do," said Geoffrey. "How long do you think you can keep awake and alert in this sea without food and rest? You might just as well give in."

"And be hanged? Not likely. While there's life there's hope. You said yourself just now that we'd be in Holland tomorrow. I've been in tighter spots than this, Geoffrey. The war was splendid training for Civvy Street, wasn't it?"

"It's made you rotten through and through."

"It hasn't made me forget how to enjoy life."

"Enjoying yourself now?"

"I'm buying the future. The price is a bit high, but it'll be worth it. I never give in."

"You sound like Hitler," said Geoffrey. "Come to think of it, you're rather like him. Bad types!" He worked on slowly, methodically. He cleaned the broken joint with petrol and scraped it with a file. He covered it with fluxite and applied the solder. He waited while it hardened. Then he went outside to fix it. He was away a full ten minutes, till Cross gave him an angry shout.

"Just finishing," he called. Another five minutes passed, and then he came back into the cabin. "The damn thing's come unstuck," he said. "I knocked it when the ship lurched. Now I'll have to do it again. Ever tried soldering?"

"Yes. And I never had to do it twice."

"I don't suppose you ever had to do it with a sea like this running."

"You talk too much. Why do you talk? We've nothing to talk about. Finish the job and let's get away. We could be making good progress now."

"Don't you believe it. You haven't seen the worst of it yet by any means."

"The wind's dropping."

"Yes, but the seas won't go down much before tonight." Geoffrey applied the soldering-iron for the second time. "There, I think that should do."

"Did we lose much fuel?" asked Cross suddenly.

"Not much. There's plenty left for the trip. And for the trip back!"

Cross was poker-faced.

As though to remind them that the weather couldn't be ignored, a sea suddenly slapped over the cockpit and foamed into the cabin.

"I'd better pump her out," said Geoffrey. "Or would you like to? That's an idea. You pump her out and I'll sit by Pamela. No? All right, have it your own way."

Geoffrey went and seated himself on the bottom rung of the companion just outside the cabin door, and went to work on the rotary. He pumped spasmodically for fifteen minutes. "Any better?" he called out.

"Yes, it's gone down a few inches."

"I'll give it a bit more. The engines will soon dry her out when I get them going." He pumped slowly, gazing round the horizon. The wind was only a zephyr now compared with what it had been, and the sun was beginning to feel warm. It was really quite pleasant sitting there. Geoffrey looked at his watch. "Good job I'm not working on piece-rates," he thought.

"It's almost dry now," Cross called. "Let's get going."

Geoffrey went in and collected the mended pipe. "Why don't you take a turn on deck, Arthur?" he said. "It would do you good – blow the cobwebs away."

"You always did have a childish sense of humour," said Cross.

"God, this is a hell of a trip! It would give me real pleasure to put a bullet in you."

"I don't feel exactly friendly towards you," said Geoffrey. "Don't let my idle chatter mislead you."

He went and put the pipe back where it belonged. It was a good repair; the joint was as strong as ever. He turned the fuel on and soon the engines were running again.

He put his head into the cabin. "I'm just going to heave up the anchor," he said.

"About time, too. Do you know we've been here well over two hours?"

"So we have," said Geoffrey. "Anyway, it's been quite a cosy spot, don't you think?" He went forward to the windlass again and began to turn the handle. It was hard work – the seas were still piling in from the east, the tide was running fast, and *Truant* was heavy. As he strained on the handle, he wondered if it would be possible for him to smash the skylight and get at Arthur through the opening. Then he saw it was a crazy thought and dismissed it. There wouldn't be time – it was the old story.

The anchor was aweigh. Geoffrey heaved it aboard and stowed it securely. Clinging to the rail, he made his way back to the cockpit. There was still an hour to kill. He set the engines at half speed. Away to the south he could see a tall beacon rising from the water. He studied the chart. Yes, it was the Middle Beacon – a good seamark. With the tide almost full there would be plenty of water everywhere. He would stooge around the beacon for an hour or so.

He felt much better for his meal and the rest. Pamela, fast asleep, was off his mind. He filled his pipe – the first since Richmond – and puffed gratefully. *Truant* was running before the wind now, and the motion was much easier. Geoffrey watched the waves coming up astern, and admired the way the little ship lifted and let them go hissing and foaming under her transom.

Outside in the main channels it would still be hell. But conditions were improving every hour, and Geoffrey was hopeful. He wouldn't have changed places with Arthur, gun or no gun.

"The little rat!" he thought.

All the same, the man had guts.

CHAPTER XVII

For nearly an hour Geoffrey kept *Truant* on a circular course around the Middle Beacon. During that time Cross came up once and took a quick look round.

"We don't seem to be making much progress," he said suspiciously. "That land over there looks almost the same as it did when we stopped."

Geoffrey glanced over his right shoulder towards Sheppey. "It's further," he said confidently. "Much further. Distances at sea are very deceptive. We've covered three or four miles in the last hour."

Cross still seemed sceptical, but he was not really in a position to argue. He would have liked to stay on deck and watch the coastline for a while, but his head was getting very bad and it made him dizzy to watch the steep seas rolling up and the boat at all angles to the horizon. He went below again.

Geoffrey looked at his watch. It was after one o'clock, and the tide was ebbing fast. In about three hours, he calculated, there would be only three feet of water over the Girdler, and by five o'clock the sands would be uncovered. If he arrived about four, conditions would be just right. The Girdler was only ten sea miles away, so there was plenty of time, even allowing for the slow progress that *Truant* would make with such a sea running. But he decided that it was time to make a move.

Soon they were running over their earlier anchorage, south of the Red Sand. There was still plenty of water everywhere for *Truant*'s five-foot draught, but Geoffrey was anxious to keep closely to his course and he watched the compass needle carefully. Everything, absolutely everything, would depend on his reaching the right spot at the right moment.

As they ploughed north-eastwards into deeper water, they were hit once more by heavy seas. Geoffrey had been right not to expect an easy passage, wind or no wind. The motion of the boat was so violent and the horizon so unsteady that it was still impossible to be sure of spotting the buoys, or of identifying them once they were spotted. He missed the East Red Sand buoy altogether, but the Shivering Sand Tower was a good seamark, and as he approached it he was able to check his course.

All afternoon the engines chugged away steadily under his feet. *Truant* took several small seas, but the pump soon cleared the cabin and cockpit. There was quite a lot of shipping about now, but most of it was away to the north in the Oaze Deep and the Knob Channel. Not a sound came from the cabin. It was almost as though Geoffrey had the boat to himself.

At half past three he suddenly spotted a buoy right under his starboard bow, deep in a trough, and recognized the black and white horizontal stripes of the West Girdler. Two miles away to the east he fancied he could just make out the upperworks of the Girdler lightship, marking the other end of the triangular shoal. It was the northern apex that he was making for. Presently he could see the cone on the top of the Girdler beacon as well. There were plenty of seamarks and he knew exactly where he was.

He had a little time to spare, and decided to turn northwards to the vicinity of the Knob buoy and work back across the Alexandra Channel to the Girdler, due south on to the highest part of the sandbank. Away to starboard he could see a black speck and a wisp of smoke – a steamer coming up into the Estuary against the ebb. Geoffrey crossed its course well ahead of it, looking for the Knob buoy and keeping a close eye on the time. But he failed to spot the buoy and swung the ship's head round for the Girdler again. The steamer was coming up fast. It was a small cargo-boat and it was in a hurry. This was his opportunity, Geoffrey decided, to attract attention. He kept *Truant* steadily ahead across the steamer's course. As he strained ahead, steering for the distant Girdler lightship, he saw something else which he had been eagerly seeking – the key to all his plan. Sticking up out of the still-covered sandbank was the black hulk of an old wreck.

Truant and the steamer were now on converging courses. The tramp had not yet seen the small boat – and in any case it would expect Geoffrey to keep clear. Geoffrey kept going hopefully. They must see him soon. It would be too bad to get run down at this stage. Suddenly there came a tattoo of warning blasts from the steamer's siren – they'd seen him. Geoffrey expected that the noise would bring Cross out of the cabin again, but there was no sign of movement.

The oncoming ship was bearing down on *Truant* at eight or nine knots, throwing up a great bow wave against the ebb. Geoffrey had plenty of power in hand, in case at the last moment he had to take evasive action. The siren went again, angrily, and he could see someone gesticulating on the bridge. Suddenly, as the rusty bows of the steamer seemed to hover threateningly over *Truant*, Geoffrey heard the bell ringing on the bridge and saw the vessel alter course. It swept past *Truant*'s stern only twenty yards away. The captain – if it was he – was shaking a fist. The steamer's siren blew three blasts – two shorts and a long. It was the international code signal for, "You are standing into danger."

"How right you are!" Geoffrey said softly to himself. He waved. He hoped they would report the incident, and his position. No doubt they would watch him as long as they could.

Now *Truant* would get the steamer's wash. It was a bad moment as the bow wave set up a cross sea and bore down on *Truant*'s stern in a furious agitation of creamy water. For half a minute the boat plunged and twisted, while Geoffrey clung to the wheel desperately. Once again water was swirling into the cockpit and the cabin. Slowly it subsided, and *Truant* seemed to rise out of the water and shake herself.

As the crisis passed Geoffrey became aware of a new sound. There was heavy surf breaking on the Girdler right ahead – Geoffrey could already make out the line of white foam. This was something far more deadly than white horses! He could see great waves breaking round the wreck.

The time had come for action. Geoffrey switched off the engine pump and shouted at the top of his voice, "Arthur! – I want you."

In a few seconds Cross appeared. He looked in bad shape. His face was a dirty yellow colour, like old parchment. But he still had the gun. He leaned over the gunwale, vomited, and pulled himself up again by the door frame. "What the hell was all that?" he said.

"A big ship – nearly hit us. We got its wash. How's Pamela?"

"She's passed out."

"Do you still want to go to Holland?"

"Yes," said Cross, through his teeth.

"Then you'd better pump," said Geoffrey. "The engine pump has packed up and we're shipping too much water."

Cross grasped the rotary with his left hand and began to work it backwards and forwards without much strength, keeping his eye fixed on Geoffrey all the time. The thunder of the surf was very close now – the wreck was a quarter of a mile away, straight ahead. Geoffrey gave both engines full throttle. *Truant* plunged forward, hitting the seas so hard that it felt as though the hull would crack wide open. Geoffrey watched the white line, the terrifying breakers, and braced himself against the wheel. He put up a silent prayer, and waited. Cross had stopped pumping as the engines roared and was staring ahead. He was shouting – he was moving. Any moment now! – it was a matter of seconds.

Then *Truant* struck. She was doing a crazy ten knots, and her bows hit the steep-to edge of the sandbank as though it had been a wall. The impact was horrible – Geoffrey was conscious of rending wood and of the short mast carrying away as he took the shock with his shoulder against the wheel. Then he hurled himself towards the cabin door through knee-deep foam. The crash had thrown Cross clean through the opening. Geoffrey dived in after him, careless now of the gun. It was a desperate all-or-nothing. He saw a shoulder and grabbed it, snatched at a handful of wet hair and hung on. He took a blow in the face and hardly felt it. He didn't know whether they were fighting on the floor or the ceiling. Everything was chaos, noise, water. The gun came round and Geoffrey gripped the wrist that held it – a thin feeble wrist. A wave surged into the cabin, and for a few moments they were waist deep. As it receded they fell against the table and smashed it, lurched into the forepeak and out again. It was impossible to hold anything with all this water, all this violent fantastic motion. Cross was fighting like a madman, twisting and slipping. Suddenly, as the boat steadied for a second, Geoffrey saw a blotchy face in front of him and hit it with all his strength. Cross fell down into the water, and Geoffrey's hands were at his throat. Another wave poured in. Geoffrey could hear nothing now, could see nothing, could think of nothing. His fingers were going to take payment for the incredible agony of the last twelve hours. He pressed the yellow face down, down into the foot of water between the berths.

A torrent of green sea swept them both forward to the forepeak, but he held on, pressing down. Cross's legs were thrashing, but feebly now. Suddenly the kicking stopped.

Cross was dead.

CHAPTER XVIII

As he staggered to his feet Geoffrey saw that Pamela was still unconscious. Arthur had roped her to the bunk. For the moment there was nothing he could do except avoid being knocked senseless himself. *Truant*, he knew, was being pounded to bits. Every breaker that came roaring in lifted her six feet off the ground, and as it passed dropped her with a shattering jar on the iron-hard sand. The engines had stopped, swamped at last. She had become the plaything of the sea. One moment her bows were high in the air, and the water was draining down into the cockpit and over the side; the next her stern was lifted and the whole North Sea seemed to be pouring in again. Each wave drove her farther in towards the wreck. There was an almost continuous rending of wood. Lockers burst open and showered their contents into the frothy bilge. The lamps had smashed to bits and glass was flying. The lead ballast was battering its way through the hull. Geoffrey slumped on the soaking berth at Pamela's feet, wedged himself with his legs against the berth opposite, and waited.

Time had never passed more slowly. He was too exhausted to think. He had been 'beaten up' by the sea. For the first time, he felt ill himself. He sat with his head in his hands, trying to keep the noise out of his ears. Surely this couldn't last much longer? The tide was going down fast – three inches every five minutes. Three feet an hour. It would be all right once the seas stopped breaking over the boat.

He was barely conscious himself – it was all he could do not to fall into the slopping bilge. He must hold on – it couldn't last for ever. Soon they would be on dry land again. The boat would be still. It would be wonderful. Already the motion was less. God, he was tired!

He must have dozed, for the next thing he was aware of was that the pounding had almost stopped. The breakers were receding, and *Truant* was beginning to settle on the bank. Soon he was able to stagger out into the cockpit and look round.

The fresh air cleared his head, and what he saw cheered him. No ship could have been more expertly thrown away. Twenty yards ahead the old wreck was high and dry. It looked like the fore part of a coasting steamer – the rest had probably been washed into deep water after the ship's back had broken. The bows stood twelve feet or so out of the sand, dark green with slime. Around the wreck a streak of grey-brown sand was already showing. *Truant* was almost motionless now, though foam still surged around. Her bows had come to rest high on the bank, and the water would drain out of the cabin and the cockpit as the tide fell.

Geoffrey went back into the cabin. Even the comparative quietness was like heaven. Pamela had not moved. Geoffrey suddenly remembered that there should be some brandy in the first-aid box, which was locked in a small cupboard above the galley. Carefully he made his way through the debris to the forepeak. The box had burst open and scattered its contents, but the little brandy-flask was intact. Geoffrey took a swig, and then set to work to revive Pamela. Now that the motion had ceased she was likely to come round quickly. He forced a few drops of brandy between her lips, chafed her hands, and gently slapped her cheeks. She opened her eyes and looked at Geoffrey. A little colour was coming back into her face. She gazed round the cabin, and suddenly she began to struggle up.

"Take it easy," said Geoffrey. "We've got all the time in the world. Here, have a drop more brandy."

She took a gulp from the flask, spluttered, and sat up on the bunk.

"Geoffrey," she said. "Oh, Geoffrey!" She was holding tight to his arm. "Where are we? Where is *he*?"

"He's dead," said Geoffrey. "Don't worry about him any more."

Pamela began to tremble violently, and suddenly broke into an uncontrollable fit of sobbing. He held her tight, protecting her, soothing her as though she had been a child. Gradually she became calmer, but he still held her close to him until she was quite quiet. Presently she took a deep breath and brushed the wet hair back from her face.

"I'm better now," she said. "I'm sorry I did that. Oh, dear, I must look an awful sight." She still clutched his arm. "Geoffrey, I didn't want to live any more. Really, I didn't. That *awful* man – and the sea. Where is he?"

Geoffrey pointed to the cabin floor, still under inches of water. She stared down at the drenched shoulder, the half-submerged head.

"What happened?"

"I ran the boat aground and caught him off guard. He got drowned."

"Yes, I see," said Pamela.

"He had the gun right to the end. There was no other way."

"Of course not," said Pamela. "Anyway, he was lucky. He deserved so much more than that. Did you get hurt, Geoffrey? You look terrible."

"You don't look so hot yourself," said Geoffrey. "Not a bit glamorous."

"I'm sorry I was so little use. I shall always be ashamed of myself."

"Nonsense – you did the best thing possible. Once you'd passed out, I had nothing more to worry about. Look, I'm going to put Arthur over on the other bunk and cover him up. You needn't look if you don't want to."

"I'm perfectly all right now," said Pamela, a shade indignantly. She watched him heave the body out of the water. "He looks dead enough," she said.

Geoffrey put a wet rug over the body.

"Now we can forget him," said Geoffrey. "I'm going to try to make some tea. How do you feel – hungry?"

"Ravenous. But oughtn't we to be doing something? What's the position?"

"There's plenty of time. I'll tell you later. First, let's see about the tea."

"We're both awfully wet," said Pamela, as Geoffrey went forward to the galley.

"Couldn't be wetter," Geoffrey called cheerfully. "There's not much we can do about it, though. We'll have to keep moving as much as possible."

"It's sea water," said Pamela. "I don't suppose we shall come to much harm." She heard the primus beginning to roar.

"We're all right," said Geoffrey, popping his head round the corner. "The meths bottle hasn't broken." He saw that Pamela had found her handbag and was making up her face. He laughed. "Now I know you're all right," he said. He went on cooking.

In ten minutes they were sitting side by side on the berth, with half a saucepan of soup each and a pile of biscuits between them.

"Just as well to make a good meal," said Geoffrey. "We may be here all night."

"Here in the boat?"

"No, not in the boat," said Geoffrey. "As a matter of fact, I've got another boat outside. Don't get excited – it doesn't float. Look!" He pointed through the porthole.

Pamela took a look. "It doesn't look very comfortable," she said. "Or very big."

"I'd better give you a situation report," said Geoffrey. "The position is that *Truant* is firmly held on a sandbank, and she's already begun to break up. There's a fair stretch of dry sand outside, and the tide's still going out. The wind has dropped, it's a good bit warmer, and it'll be dark in less than a couple of hours. By that time the tide will be in again. The sea's moderating, but it'll still be pretty fierce. If help hasn't reached us by then, we shall be perched up on the wreck of the *Hesperus*, or whatever that old hulk is called."

"Shan't we get washed off?"

"Well," said Geoffrey cautiously, "we'll have to lash ourselves on, of course."

"You don't mean I've got to be tied up again!"

Geoffrey grinned. "It'll feel quite different when I do it. As a matter of fact, I hope it won't be necessary."

Pamela looked out again at the wreck, without any increase of enthusiasm. "What are the chances of help coming?"

"Pretty good," said Geoffrey. "They're bound to be out after us by now, and I'm sure we'll have been reported by a ship that nearly ran us down. Let's get cracking. The main thing is to take everything we need. Why don't you go and have a run round on the sand?"

The cabin floor was dry now and they went out into the cockpit. The line of surf, still pounding hard, was fifty yards away. The sun was sinking in a clear sky and some of the chill had gone off the air.

"It's lovely," said Pamela. "Who'd have thought it could suddenly be like this?"

"I know. A desert island – all to ourselves!"

Pamela suddenly shivered. "It's a bit like that awful story you told me," she said. "About the Goodwins – remember? The men who were alive, but were as good as dead. How will they take us off?"

"They'll find a way," said Geoffrey. "We've planned things better. The sea's going down. Look, I'll throw you some things and you can carry them up to the *Hesperus*. It'll keep you warm."

He dived into the cabin and returned in a moment with his arms full. "They're sleeping-bags," he said. "Waterproof and dry. We're going to bed together tonight."

"I couldn't care less," said Pamela. "Shall I take them?"

"Yes, but don't dump them in a puddle. Then come back for some more."

By the time Pamela had returned Geoffrey had collected some more things in the cockpit. There was Arthur's torch, and the brandy-flask; some biscuits, and two coils of stout rope.

"We'll take these along now," he said, "and have a final look round afterwards. How does the *Hesperus* look at close quarters?"

"It's frightfully sea-weedy, and there are a lot of crabs. Nasty little green ones."

"As long as there's something we can hang on to," said Geoffrey, "that's all that matters." As they reached the hulk he walked round and inspected it. It was the fore part of a ship all right, though the name had long since been obliterated. All the plates were entirely covered in thick matted weed. The hard wood of the old deck still spanned the boat – a steep and slippery slope rising out of the sand. Geoffrey's eye was caught by two slimy iron bollards, up in the bows. After several attempts he managed to lassoo them and with the help of the rope he scrambled up.

"It's not so bad up here," he called. "Bit of an angle, but we'll manage. These bollards will do us fine." He made the rope fast and slid quickly down. "We're going to be all right, my love – I hope! But we won't go up until we have to. Let's go back to *Truant*. I've got a few things to do inside – you go and amuse yourself."

Back in the cabin he got quickly to work. Normally it would have broken his heart to sacrifice the boat, but nothing could prevent her becoming a total loss. He had noticed one or two gaping holes in the hull. From one of the stern lockers, now without its lid, he dragged a five-gallon drum of paraffin and splashed the contents all over the inside of the cabin. Then he knocked the tap off the fuel-tank with a hammer and let the thick diesel oil drain into the cockpit and form a deep pool there.

He would need something dry to start the blaze. He thought rapidly, and remembered the first-aid box. There had been a big roll of gauze – that should burn all right. He climbed out of the boat, lighted the gauze, and flung it into the cabin. Then he stood back.

Pamela joined him. She said, "You're not burning the boat?"

"It's no good to us," said Geoffrey. "This is going to be quite a spectacle."

He had left the portholes open, and a gentle breeze fanned the flame. In a few minutes the fire had got hold and a great pillar of flame shot high into the air, topped with black smoke. The roar and crackle was audible above the thunder of the breakers.

"If we live to be a hundred," said Geoffrey, holding Pamela's arm, "we shall never see anything quite like this again."

It was true. The sun was just dipping below the horizon, leaving a streak of pink and green across the sky. Against the pale sunset the pillar of fire looked rich and red. It was turning all the sand red, and their faces glowed red in its light. Around was utter desolation. The gulls were screaming on a higher note, scared by the fire. Beyond the burning boat the breakers were coming in again, full of menace, eating up the narrowing island of sand.

Geoffrey, watching the crackling torch, said, "Well, they ought to see that, anyway."

Pamela suddenly laughed, a little hysterically. "I thought you were just being dramatic," she said. "Giving him a funeral pyre!"

"What – *him*?" Geoffrey shook his head. "I was thinking only of us. Every ship for ten miles round will see *Truant* burning."

They stood fascinated. The burning oil was sizzling, the burning cabin top was falling in in a shower of sparks. Water was beginning to hiss around the red-hot hull and steam was mixing with the smoke. It was getting darker.

"We'd better keep moving," said Geoffrey reluctantly. "I wish there'd been some dry clothes for you." He looked down at her. "That dress will never be the same again. It's all torn."

Pamela had pinned it. She said, "It got torn when I tried to get the gun."

Geoffrey put his arm round her and they walked up to the wreck.

The tide was coming in fast now. The waves were breaking over all that was left of *Truant* and shooting up the sandbank, almost to the foot of the wreck.

Geoffrey said: "It looks as though we'd better get aloft. Up you go! Take it very gently – hang on to the rope all the time. We don't want any broken legs." He threw up the sleeping-bags and climbed up after her, dragging the rest of the rope.

"Okay," he said, "now see if you can get into your bag. It'll keep your tummy warm, anyway. I'd better make you fast – it's so easy to slip." He put a rope round her, under her arms like a lifebuoy, took a few turns round the slippery bollards, passed it through a rusty ring in the deck and then made it fast to the broken end of a thick wooden rib.

"You'd have made a good spider," said Pamela. "Aren't you going to tie yourself too?"

"I can hang on to you for a while," Geoffrey said. "I'm still hoping someone will come before we get wet again. Cosy?"

"Not really."

"Wet, cold and miserable?"

"Not miserable."

"Lean back against me. I'll tell you when my leg goes to sleep." He put an arm round her. "I'm not miserable, either. Can I kiss you?"

"I don't feel in the least romantic."

"Neither do I, but I think it's called for." He put his face against her damp hair. "Will you marry me when we get ashore?"

"After I've had a good sleep," said Pamela. "I'm so tired I could almost sleep here."

"You can if you like. I'll wake you."

It was dark now. The sandbank was almost covered, and foam was reaching the edge of the wreck. *Truant* had disappeared in the water and the darkness. Away to the south-east, on the other side of the shoal, Geoffrey could just catch the flash of the Girdler lightship. Three white flashes every fifteen seconds. He watched, and suddenly he saw another light wink. It was white, too, but a little lower down. It flicked on and off once or twice, and suddenly Geoffrey stirred.

"They're signalling," he cried excitedly, almost sliding down the deck. He groped for his torch and waved it. The Aldis lamp was talking now. Geoffrey could read it like a book. He watched tensely, slowly spelling out the words aloud.

"HOLD ... ON ... RESCUE ... TUG ... COMING," he read. He

waved the torch again to show that he had got the message and held Pamela a little tighter.

"It's wonderful," she said softly. "You're really quite clever, Geoffrey."

"It's too cold to purr," he said. "You're not so dumb yourself."

Pamela looked down at the water. "I hope they hurry. It's like one of those old-fashioned films, where the villain tied the heroine to a stake at low water and you watched her till it was up to her neck, and then you had to come back next week to see how she'd managed."

"The hero always fixed things," said Geoffrey. "Look!"

Away to the west – and not far away – a rocket suddenly went up from the sea and a shower of white stars scattered in the sky.

Geoffrey flicked on the torch and waved it in the direction of the ship. "There's something coming down the channel," he said. "I can see its starboard light." He kept on waving the torch.

It seemed aeons of time before the green light came abreast of them. The tug was standing as close in as it dared, beyond the breakers, and above the noise of the surf Geoffrey heard the anchor chain rattling through the hawse pipe. He knew they were taking risks, but a small boat would never have lived in this sea. Suddenly a searchlight broke the blackness, and the wreck was held in a brilliant beam. They both waved.

"You're in the limelight for once in your life, anyway, my love," Geoffrey said.

A loudspeaker blared above the noise of the sea. "We're going to try and get a line to you," someone shouted. "Can you hear?"

Geoffrey waved in acknowledgment. It was going to be tricky. He saw a rocket leave the ship and watched the parabola until the end of the line fell into the sea, well short of the wreck. The second attempt was better. The rocket fell level with the wreck, but the line was still hopelessly out of reach.

Geoffrey was tense with anxiety. The target was terribly small. "We'll try again," said the voice. "Ready?"

The rocket came sizzling over and dropped behind them. Geoffrey could see the line in the white glare of the searchlight – it had got caught up round the wreck, and a bit of it was washing about in the foam at the foot of the sloping deck. He slid down to the tumbling water with the help of the rope. It couldn't be very deep yet – three feet at most, except for the waves. He waited, watching the greedy sea. Suddenly he dropped down, still clinging to the rope. The water was waist deep, clutching at him, trying to drag him away from the wreck. He grabbed the line and pulled himself up, hand over hand, by the rope. It had not been too bad after all.

Pamela said, "Oh, darling!"

Geoffrey hauled in the line and made fast the heavy rope that followed, once more thanking heaven for the bollards. He pulled the breeches buoy in. "Ready, Pamela? It's much safer than it looks – the last word in comfort at sea! Put your legs through the canvas. That's right – now your arms over the buoy." He made her secure. "Don't worry if you get a ducking – it's quite usual. Happy journey!"

"Be careful, Geoffrey," she called. "Be very careful."

"I'll be with you in five minutes," Geoffrey shouted. "You can pour me a drink."

He watched her progress over the surf, watched her drawn to safety. In a few minutes he had pulled the buoy back again to the wreck. He made himself secure and gave the signal. The tug, he decided, had arrived none too soon. Seas were beginning to surge up the sloping deck.

Once, as they pulled him across, the rope dipped and a breaker snatched at his legs. But there was no danger, and soon eager hands were stretching out to help him aboard the tug.

Almost the first thing he saw as he stepped on deck was the anxious face of Inspector James!

It was an hour later. They were all sitting in the cosy saloon of the tug – Pamela and Geoffrey, the Inspector, and the red-faced tug-master. The two survivors had been provided with dry clothes and hot blankets, and they were comfortably full of warm food and ship's rum. Pamela's head was nestling unashamedly in the crook of Geoffrey's right arm. The Inspector, looking very benign, was puffing contentedly at his pipe.

". . . And so," Geoffrey was saying, "that is really the whole of the story."

"It'll look fine in the Sunday papers," said the tugmaster.

James said: "We'll have to have a proper statement tomorrow, but there's no hurry. It's been a wicked case, but everything is very tidy now."

"I'm not quite clear," said Geoffrey drowsily, "how you happened to be on the spot yourself, Inspector. I didn't know you liked the sea."

"It was my case, wasn't it?" said James. "I was worried about you, Mr. Hollison – you and your young lady. We took the best advice we could once we discovered you were heading for the Estuary, and when it was decided a tug would be best I had a car run me down to Gravesend. I was pretty sure Cross had a gun – he was a real killer, and no mistake. I thought he'd use it. When I saw you two up there on the boat, alone and safe, it was one of the happiest moments of my life."

"It's nice of you to say so, Inspector. You must come to our wedding."

"I'd very much like to," said the Inspector. His eyes twinkled. "I take it you'll be spending your honeymoon afloat!"

The tugmaster was smiling too. "If you ask me," he said, "they'll be like the old sea captain when he retires – you know the story, Inspector? He sets off walking inland with an oar over his shoulder, and when somebody says, 'What's that you're carrying, mister?' he knows he can settle down and build a house there. Eh, Mr. Hollison?"

There was no reply. The survivors were both fast asleep.

THE END